SHOTGUN

These Violent Times

Shotgun: The Dr. John Bishop Saga
by C. COURTNEY JOYNER

Shotgun

Shotgun: The Bleeding Ground

These Violent Times: A Shotgun Western

SHOTGUN

THESE VIOLENT TIMES

C. COURTNEY JOYNER

PINNACLE BOOKS
Kensington Publishing Corp.
www.kensingtonbooks.com

PINNACLE BOOKS are published by

Kensington Publishing Corp.
119 West 40th Street
New York, NY 10018

All Kensington titles, imprints, and distributed lines are available at special quantity discounts for bulk purchases for sales promotions, premiums, fund-raising, educational, or institutional use. Special book excerpts or customized printings can also be created to fit specific needs. For details, write or phone the office of the Kensington sales manager: Kensington Publishing Corp., 119 West 40th Street, New York, NY 10018, attn: Sales Department; phone 1-800-221-2647.

PINNACLE BOOKS and the Pinnacle logo are Reg. U.S. Pat. & TM Off.

ISBN-13: 978-0-7860-4174-9
ISBN-10: 0-7860-4174-9

First printing: July 2018

10 9 8 7 6 5 4 3 2 1

Printed in the United States of America

First electronic edition: July 2018

ISBN-13: 978-0-7860-4175-6
ISBN-10: 0-7860-4175-7

CHAPTER ONE

"'Eye' Witnessed the Slaughter"

At first, the two mounted men kept some distance from their quarry, staying tight in the charcoal-gray moon-shadows that fell like jagged patches from the tall sequoias. But then the ground became uneven with erosion caused by frequent gully washers, and the rest of the trek was handled without much skill. In the past, when they were out waylaying travelers instead of tracking, they'd managed skittish horses through narrow cuts in the Colorado woods. This time, though, they couldn't keep the appaloosas steady or quiet. There were predators in the dark, in the cool air . . . and up ahead, even though that killer was not looking for the two men. As the animals fought against their bits, the hands of the riders repeatedly went for their sidearms, their ungloved fingers falling fearfully on worn, dry leather in anticipation of some kind of fast draw.

Pop, pop, pop, they'd cut him down, just as they had in their minds and in talking about it. One shooting high, the other low. Had to hit something.

The lead man would anxiously peer into the darkness ahead, the rear rider from side to side; then they'd each look up into the pitch surrounding the trees left and right. When nothing happened they would toss whispers to each other, laughing through their teeth, then shut up. They were playing it like excited kids, not like the killers they were.

After a long moment of silence and calm, one of them idiot-cackled, "Two in the chest, two in the head. Right?"

"And a third if it's needed."

"It won't be. He stays safe."

"That's how it'll be then," the other agreed. "You 'n' me will be . . . what did they call the old magicians? The ones who turned lead into gold?"

"Al . . ." the head rider said tentatively, searching for the word.

"Al?" the one behind said. "His goddamn name was Al?"

They chuckled very, very quietly and briefly as an owl hooted, startling them.

A blind man could have shot the slender, idiot pair from their saddles. A sighted man could have done considerably better. This man—this man could have erased them entirely.

John Bishop rode as if the two men weren't there, as

if they hadn't been following him for hours. Stubbled chin pressed to the top button of his slicker, collar turned against a fresh drizzle brought in on the wind, an empty left sleeve pinned across his chest, Bishop didn't break his horse into a run to lose the two riders in pursuit, and he wasn't going to double-back and waste time on them. There was no point. He could hear their nervous laughter; they did everything stupid, careless, but whistle. Plus he was too tired and sore from covering so many miles in so few days. Besides, their careless chatter, clomping hoof-falls, and unwashed scent had already branded them amateurs. Even exhausted, he didn't have to struggle to figure out where they were going and what they'd try next. He didn't even have to think hard to figure out how they came to be here.

Misty dampness fell on him when the last of the trees was behind him. It started to rain, then rain hard. He had two consolations. First, only the living could be discomfited by rain; second, the pair behind him would hate it way more than he did, since their horses would really fight them now, every uncertain, muddy step of the way. Coming from the woods, he picked up the south road into the town of Good Fortune, as the up-mountain waters from the storm came in a wave of deep black, rushing to his horse's knees, splashing up to its belly. Bishop got to the road's center, graded a little higher, but with its edges falling away into mud, washing to the bottom of the hill.

The man's dark Fish Brand slicker glistened now and then in the cloudy moonlight as he angled down a slope, one hand tight on the reins, horse moving straight through the wash, then picking up speed toward the Good Fortune Church of Redemption. Running ahead of churned water and broken tree limbs, he reached and rounded the church, and continued to the back of the Hospitality House and its open stalls for overnighters. Even in the dark, he knew his way. He smelled the pig slop to the north, the two public outhouses to the south, built by and for the church. Just a short walk ahead and he reached the large open door of the stable.

The troughs plunked loudly, full from the rain, and a lantern hung from a shoulder-high hook just inside. He could see halfway into the structure, but heard all the way. He waited a moment, expressionless. The packed dirt floors were swept clean of hay, and Bishop's was the only horse. He dropped from the saddle, the rain trailing off his garment, then sent a spray of water flying from his hat after snapping it against his hip.

He leaned toward the stable's lamp and lowered the wick, darkening the stalls, before wiping his eyes with the side of his one hand to see beyond the pigs and the hotel to the distant woods. To make out any movement along the tree line. Shapes that might be the men. But the only thing moving was the wind-carried rain, drenching muddy streets and pouring from the stable's tin roof.

Leaning against the closed door on the other side, a man said, "Seems like you rode dee-rectly into the eye of the storm, Doctor."

"You ever breathe through your nose?"

"Eh?"

"Seems like you still wheeze like one of Mott's hogs," Bishop said.

The man came forward with heavy steps. "My lungs is my lungs. And you, you bring *two* storms."

Bishop one-armed the saddle from his horse, wiped it down. "Always the soul of a poet, who'd sell out his grandma for a dollar."

Joseph Daniel Avery was a transplant who used the extortive skills he had learned as a New York City policeman to build a career in the West. The story of how he came to leave was one the fattish man loved to tell, and tell often. There were two police departments in 1857, when he was a shavetail just in. The Metropolitan and the Municipal. There were jurisdictional squabbles and the Municipals lost. Avery was one of them, and they did not give up power without a fight. It was 800 to 300, the odds in favor of Avery's side—and they lost. They were beaten and ousted and unable to work. So Avery came west, using the talents he had picked up in nearly two years: working with reporters, working with gangs, working with smugglers, working with prostitutes, all the while patrolling with a cheerfully rosy face and asking the Irish women on his beat how their flower boxes grew.

"You do me a wrong," Avery said, fingers pressed to his red waistcoat. "Wouldn't do it for under five dollars."

Bishop finished bedding his horse. "And we talked about usin' 'Doc,' versus 'Doctor.' You recall?"

"Forgive me, I can't help admiring a man of education," Avery said. "But I'll be careful about using titles. Even for a surgeon."

Avery grabbed the railroad lantern, turned it on high. It shined dully off his bald head, the flesh scratched here and there with old scars from blunt instruments. Hooked over his right wrist was an umbrella, which he let slide to his fingers. It was a bright red frilly thing forgotten by a working girl. A smirking grin still lived in the saloon owner's round face, despite the punishment he had taken in his forty-odd years.

Finished with the saddle, Bishop turned toward the back door as though he had no intention of waiting. Avery quick-stepped to catch up.

"You, sir, have been in the *Gazette* again," the beefy man said.

"What of it?"

"Nothin'," Avery said. "Nothin' at all."

With a grunt, Bishop yanked loose the ties securing a carpetbag to his saddle, hefted it to his shoulder as they walked. His eyes moved left and right—a habit in any new place. "Get yourself a stable boy? Never seen the place this clean."

"I did it just for you. Now, it's drink time."

"You're making me feel special," Bishop said warily. "I don't like that."

Avery laughed, his velvet-coated belly shaking, as they stepped into the rain and navigated the side of the hotel. He kept the red umbrella over them both. "Maybe it's the weather. We've been getting soaked on-and-off—mostly on—for a week, but I approve. Smells fresh, don't you agree?"

"Fresher."

"Makes me happy," Avery said, talking loudly over the patter. "You know why? It makes everything look silver. That's a right thing for a silver boomtown, even a dead one. But, my friend, I feel we're on the eve of resurrection."

Bishop let the "my friend" pass without contradiction. "A poetic soul won't stop double pneumonia."

"I'll nurse myself with rum and cocaine," Avery

said. Almost added "Doctor," but stopped short. "As for you, I believe you're immortal. At least, that's what the penny dreadfuls say."

Bishop did not comment on that either. Cheap literature, sensational thrills. Consumed by readers in filthy cities or on remote spreads who never experienced actual, bleeding horror. The kind that played through your memory as slow as a cloud crossing the sky, one cloud after another cloud after ano—

"You're not sporting your double-barrel special," Avery went on.

Bishop heard but his mind was back on one particular day, a day he could never leave. Or which would not leave him, he wasn't sure. He once asked about the difference. Asked a Chinese, an old man on a cattle drive Bishop encountered. The skinny wisp of a man knew the language but didn't talk much. Didn't even ask about his arm. Wasn't like Avery here, which told Bishop the Chinese cook probably had something to say. Getting himself a plate of fried corn and warm bread, Bishop asked the man where he had worked before this.

"Trains," the Chinese had replied.

"Cooking?"

The man had nodded.

"Like it?" Bishop had asked.

The Chinese looked at him before turning back to the chuck wagon. "It is gone. If you stay fixed in a moment, the world passes you by."

And that, in a phrase, in a quiet sentence thrown off as casually as Bishop had brushed rainwater from his cheek, was his own life since that day. Since that day in the Colorado foothills where he had settled with his wife and little boy, tending to settlers trying to build the West. A quiet day, a quiet existence, until—

"Are you okay?" Avery asked, showing uncustomary concern. Another hint.

"Fine."

"I said—you're not sporting your double-barrel special," Avery went on.

It was easier to answer than to not bother. The Chinese fella also told him something else, unsolicited, when Bishop returned the plate.

"It takes more energy to do the right thing at the wrong time," he had said. And that was truer than any truth Bishop had ever heard. It fit with the other piece. A moment passes, you're still in it, the events and people that created it—gone.

"Fools see it, they're encouraged to try," Bishop answered Avery to end the discussion. For now. "I just want a little hot coffee, a lotta sleep."

"I can accommodate," the other man said, his eyes searching his companion. "But your rig's tucked into that horrendous carpetbag, yes?"

"You so eager to see it?"

Bishop took the man's next move as a "no." Avery shivered all over, not from the rain. He was like a jelly, this man, this opportunist, shaking in some spots after others had stopped.

"Still selling guns to the Comanche?" Bishop asked.

"I try to supply whatever my local customers demand," he said. "You should understand."

"How do you figure?"

"The North sold to the South during the war. Guns. Food. Medical supplies." Avery slapped his vest proudly. "I am a man of enlightenment. We are all Americans."

"You get that from your reading?" Bishop asked.

"The dreadfuls?" Avery snickered. "No, sir. The Constitution." They'd made their way to the front porch of the Hospitality House and Avery opened a tall, slatted door to the saloon with a grand gesture. "But . . . I do so admire those others. Enter, and bear witness to my latest effort."

Bishop cleared the door. Stopped. His dark eyes grew. Not brighter, just larger. "What in hell do you call this?"

"A tribute," Avery said proudly, hanging the lantern on a peg by the door, then collapsing the umbrella. Water rained on his muddy boots, flecking the wood floor. "I'm truly gratified that it took your breath away."

Avery walked to the bar, lay the lady's umbrella beside a Colt .44-.40 carbine, loaded. He placed a carved-silver strainer over an absinthe glass, added a sugar cube. It was a delicate operation for the fat-fingered man, who alternately watched Bishop drop the carpetbag on a chair, move through the saloon, and shake his head with an expression that had shaded from surprise to "Sweet Mother of Jesus," leaning toward disapproval.

Most of the place was as Bishop remembered: polished oak bar with a large French mirror behind it, long-ago cracked, and a scattering of poker tables filling up the empty spaces; all worn-out felt and phony gilt like most places he'd been to outside of a big city.

But now, corner to corner and floor to ceiling, pages from newspapers, *Harper's Weekly*, *The Police Gazette*, special editions of *Deadwood Dick*, were pasted to the walls, smothering them. Hundreds of overlapping photographs, sketches, editorials, and headlines:

Doctor/Killer and His Double-Barreled Law

The Mysterious Bishop Heals, Then Slaughters

CONFESSIONS OF DOCTOR DEATH

BLOOD LOVERS:
The One-Armed Avenger of Colorado
And the Cheyenne Who Kills With Him

DEAD MAN RIDING

¡Me Llaman Escopeta!

Avery poured the absinthe, melting the sugar, then took a cobalt-blue bottle from his vest pocket. "So how does it feel, being a living legend?"

Bishop said, "Not exactly what I'd call it." He wiped his eyes with his palm heel. "I'm content just being 'living.'"

"Amen to that."

Bishop squinted his tired eyes. He was trying to take in a *Police Gazette* cover, showing him standing before a stalled locomotive, shotgun rig aimed, the engineer with hands raised in fear, the fireman on his knees, praying.

"Jesus—"

"Is that an observation or a description of the savior there-depicted?" Avery smirked.

"Don't add blasphemy to your sins," Bishop cautioned, ignoring the fact that he was the one who took the Lord's name in vain. He had been justified. Avery was just a slob.

The overweight bartender added a few careful tears of laudanum to Bishop's absinthe, then prepared his own. "What would you prefer for my establishment?"

"Prefer?"

"Yeah, on the wall? Some burlesquer sprawled on a couch? A cancan line with all the goods in ruffles and shadow forcing drunks to squint?"

"I really don't know," Bishop said. "Or care." He looked around, noticed a bullet hole near to the wall. Someone had fired on the way to falling backward, already hit. He looked to where the shot would have originated. There was a dry, brown smudge on the floor.

Avery snorted. "You're just too modest. Wasn't it Doc Holliday who claimed, 'I've had credit for more killings than I ever dreamt of'? Those imaginings are who you are now."

He thought, then, of other wisdom. Not the Chinaman. The Cheyenne. One in particular, a friend of his named White Fox. *Aenohe Nestoohe*—Howling Hawk. Bishop actually was two people, she had said. His man-self and his winged-self. When he assumed the stance, by the campfire, no one doubted that he was soaring on the night winds. There was a tragic irony in the fact that Avery might be right. That every man was two men. The real and the shadow.

Avery held out the two glasses. Bishop shook his head once. Avery set one down, raised one. "To the penny-dreadful creation, risen from the grave, and standing before me! *Salut!*"

Bishop was now at the other end of the bar, grabbing a dusty bottle of Rip Van Winkle, holding the neck like he was strangling it. His other self was. His self that the Chinaman warned about. His memory skidded back, like it was on ice, right to the day . . . the moment the men invaded Bishop's home and demanded to know where he hid the gold he stole with his brother, Devlin. Bishop had no idea.

"The last time I saw my brother was the day before he was hung," the medic and former lieutenant had protested. "He wrote a letter of regret to our dead parents, and that was it!"

He said it calmly, then loudly. It didn't matter. The men were tone deaf. The leader of the gang, Major "Bloody" Beaudine, had been Dev's cell mate and didn't believe that. He didn't believe that John Bishop had nothing to do with the robbery. The wife and son of Dr. John Bishop died that day. He lost an arm that day. His soul, too, died that day. But not his body. A beautiful Cheyenne named White Fox found him and brought him to her blacksmith husband. She nursed him to health, and her husband, who had a curious sense of inventiveness, made a special shotgun rig that fitted where his left arm used to be. He designed a strap across the shoulder to fire it. And then—

"Risen from the grave," Bishop said thoughtfully.

"That's right," Avery said, still holding the glass. "The two of us."

"How long have we known each other, Avery?"

"From my rebirth to now," Avery said, raising his glass even higher to toast the deed as well as the man. "When my mine caved in—our town's last mine—you performed surgery right in this very room. Traveled fifty miles to get *both* your hands bloody. Saved my life. Why?"

"Just makin' sure you remember real history, is all."

"Like you do?" Avery questioned. He was always

probing. Bishop was always reticent. "Oh, I know our history."

Bishop shook the memories from his head by taking a long, hard pull from the bottle. Shook it back with a loud, hissing "*Ahhhh.*"

"But I'm not recalling you as a bourbon drinker." Avery chuckled at this, finally easy-sipping his green.

"Got an itching for Chinaman corn, and this is as close as I can get."

Avery seemed puzzled but let it go. His eyes drifted from Bishop to another time. His expression grew reflective. "You saved me, you saved some miners, but you and me and them couldn't save this town."

"I'm a medic, not a miracle worker."

"But I was supposed to be," Avery said. It was a moment of rare honesty. "Do *you* recall that I'm the mayor?"

"The bullshit sheriff too," Bishop added, mock-saluting him with the bottle.

"Not bullshit," Avery protested vaguely.

"You grabbed the reins of as many official horses as you could get to control as many avenues of profit as you could handle," Bishop replied. That was partly the scotch.

"It was not for me," Avery said.

Bishop gave him a look.

"Well, not all," Avery admitted. "I wanted to do what I could do to save all of this. I am it, it is me; without each other we are nothing."

"The real man and the shadow man," Bishop snorted.

"Shadow?" Avery flipped a lapel, revealing a tarnished star with bent corners. He tapped it with the side of his thumbnail. "Not shadow. Silver. Maybe all that's left in Good Fortune. Since the silver played out, we've only twenty people living here. Twenty people. Mild case of influenza could kill this town. Good Fortune's a near-corpse, and I'm the one combing its hair before the funeral. We're famous for two things: being the worst silver strike in the state, and you riding through every year."

Bishop had a second swallow of bourbon in his throat. "You really do that badge proud."

Avery said, "You know, I feel I do. I'm what you'd call the soul of what's left. The heart. I just keep beating."

"And welcoming every new arrival," Bishop observed.

"Damn right, sir. Your exploits have always meant visits by newspapermen, curiosity seekers—"

"Bounty hunters?"

Avery made a face. "I look at them as guests. They all pay to stay, question me about our long and close friendship, take in my artistic tribute to you." He swept a hand across the clippings behind him. It was the gesture of a carny barker. This man had more shadow selves than the Hydra had snapping heads. "It's my civic duty to keep this enterprise going any way I can."

Bishop looked to Avery. More scotch spoke. "You really think I'm going to let this paper tombstone stand?"

"Why shouldn't you?"

"Because it's not a biography. It's not a tribute. It's an obituary without the last line, you vulture."

Avery raised his hands in mock self-defense. "That's your view. But if I may make an observation?"

Bishop waited.

"Your reaction's blinding you to something greater," Avery said. "Those magazine inventions you despise could be a stroke of fortune."

"For?"

"Us both."

"That mine collapse damaged your head."

"Hear me." Avery's voice lifted as he downed the last bit of liquid sugar. "Say you're here, minding your business, just wanting your precious sleep, when one of those squirrels happens by and foolishly tries to collect a reward on you."

Bishop understood. "So this becomes a place where I gunned a man down."

"I'd put up a *glorious* monument." Avery was now sipping the absinthe Bishop had refused.

"You already have," Bishop said with a sweep of his dark eyes.

"No, no. I said 'glorious.' Real. Bigger. Better."

"And even bigger and better if I was the one got gunned down?"

Avery's mouth twisted. "No. Different, then. Solemner."

Bishop put the bottle down and then his one hand was against Avery's windpipe, fingers digging in like he was a dinner rabbit caught in a snare.

"I didn't survive a war and a massacre and all hell's else being stupid," Bishop snarled. "I still have two eyes. Waving that lantern and umbrella out there. Who'd you tell I'd be here?"

Avery gagged and Bishop relaxed his grip, but he didn't release the man. He lowered his hand, tightly grabbed the lapel over the badge, and pulled him forward, hard.

"Who?" Bishop demanded.

"What I've said—told—doesn't matter," the mayor-sheriff-bartender gasped, quivering again like a deep dish of aspic.

"Matters to me."

Both of Avery's hands were hanging off Bishop's one, pulling hard, as he got out: "Every damn move you make's written about."

He twisted to one side, Bishop's fingers still tight into his flesh, and reached under the bar for a folded newspaper. He slapped it in front of Bishop, trying to get him to look. To let go.

Bishop didn't yield. "The two coffee boilers who were lumpin' after me? Them?"

Avery shrugged. Bishop's hand went back to his throat.

"Who paid you to set this up? And how much?"

"They didn't *have* to pay me!" he managed in a croaked whisper. "No one did! Weeks ago, they knew you'd be here. The papers wrote all about it!"

Avery's face was starting to purple when Bishop let go, fingers leaving moon-shaped marks on the fat man's throat. Stumbling back, slipping on a wet spot from the umbrella, Avery landed against the cash register and frog-gulped for air, holding on to the bar, trying to calm.

"Drink some water," Bishop told him.

Avery slumped forward across the bar, on his elbows, his dignity spilled out like an upended bottle. "Is that . . . medical advice, *Doctor*?"

Bishop didn't take the bait. That was an old life, like the Chinaman had implied. Right now, though, Bishop didn't mind being reminded. He wasn't in a mood to forgive Beaudine or Avery or the two green rips who had been tailing him. If he had been rigged, he would have shot the paper museum in front of him all to blazes.

The absinthe and laudanum warmed Avery in waves, as he rubbed feeling back into his triple chins. He spoke his next words softly, carefully, as though he were testing a fist-loosened tooth.

"Everybody wants to know about that gun," Avery said. "What kind of a twisted soul would wear such a thing? Are you more gun than human being, or is it the other way 'round?"

"And what do you tell them?"

Avery smiled thinly. "I say, 'Thankfully, I have no idea how it feels to be a one-armed man.' But henceforth I will add, 'I now know what it is to be choked by one.'"

What a scum. Even that he would turn into legend, into money. Bishop remembered the first time he had encountered that manure. Bishop and White Fox had been out on the trail, glued by mutual need and attraction they tried to fight. She had left the drunken blacksmith but wasn't needy. That was part of the draw. There was a mountain snowstorm, a hellish fight with Sergeant Bates and his renegades. Bates, a now-blind officer who blamed the medic for the loss of his sight. Bishop and White Fox battled the renegades, the rig-making corpses and history and news. The yellow press gave Bishop a new name, "Shotgun," which he hated more than "Doctor" but in a different way. It was a devil to the dead angel he was. But Bishop really wasn't either. He read every scrap of the trash that turned his tragedy and resurrection into money. A penny. Another penny. Thousands of them. Tens of thousands. Men got rich. Bishop got a reputation.

Now he got a wall.

Bishop resisted the urge to fling the bottle. He turned to Avery. "Keep massaging your neck."

"That's, uh . . . fitting advice. Fingers fixin' damage done by fingers."

"Don't think, Avery. Doesn't suit you."

There was a thick, tense moment of silence, like a fever wanting to break, as Avery collected himself. He inflated his hoggish chest. "Look, I'm just saying, you've got enemies, and then you've got the simply curious."

"Same goddamn thing." Bishop's dark eyes were now drink-assisted slits. "I'm askin' once more, how much did this bunch pay to target me?"

"And I say again, it's not me laying you out for some kind of an ambush. If I was, I wouldn't tell you anything."

"You didn't," Bishop reminded him. "I know what's comin'." Bishop picked up his carpetbag and put it on the bar with, "Last time. How much?"

Avery rolled his head, getting more feeling, though his eyes remained fixed on his guest. It was his first and only show of something that approached fortitude. "Look. Every fall you make this trip. Same month, same days. I can set my watch by your actions, and so can anyone else who can read, or knows someone who does."

"Did they pay you in gold?"

Avery's shoulders slumped as that little flourish of courage evaporated. There was no sense continuing the lie. "Silver."

"They knew the specie of the whore," Bishop remarked, rubbing his fingers together to indicate coins.

"So, then. The whore asks—you want to top the offer?"

"Nope," Bishop said. "Just want to make a different one." He unhooked the carpetbag latches, revealing the stock and custom triggers of the double-barrel tucked inside.

"Oh my." Avery peered into the bag. "So, the penny dreadfuls are accurate after all."

"Here's a suspicion I haven't told anyone," Bishop said.

Avery leaned forward eagerly.

"I think the man who made this got the idea from the dreadfuls," Bishop said. He placed a hand in the satchel. "Here's what I want, Avery. I want you to get those boys to ride off."

"You think they'll listen to me?"

"To the carbine under the bar," Bishop said.

Avery shook his head. "Let me tell you something. Something from experience. Scared men come looking for a legend, they been drinking. They been drinking, they don't hear. They don't see too good either. They will shoot me to prove they got nerve."

"Your problem," Bishop noted.

"Maybe I get one, the other still comes up. You still got the same problem."

The former medic considered this. "Maybe you open the umbrella. They laugh themselves to the floor. Then you shoot."

"Be reasonable, sir," Avery implored.

Bishop closed the bag and turned toward the door.

Avery looked around the recent arrival. "The storm's worse. You're not thinkin' of going out there. Consider your horse."

"That's not what I'm considerin'," Bishop replied. "I'm on my own business, nothing to do with you, and less with anyone else. All those Jim-Bobs have to do is—nothing."

"Friend . . . sir . . . you know that. I know that," Avery added agreeably. "But the nobodies always seek the somebodies, like moths to a lantern. All I can do is—well, hang the lantern where it does the most good. Make them flutter a little harder to get to it. 'Cause flutter they will."

Bishop seemed to consider that. It was a new, reflective expression, and Avery waited, like a boy eyeing the jar of huckleberry suckers, hoping he got one because his father just spent ten dollars on feed.

Bishop had spent too many years moving. The Civil War. The war with the renegades, with Beaudine, with the men who tried to steal John Chisum's cattle ranch—nothing but bloody flesh created instead of healed. That was not the life he had sought. It was the one that had been thrust on him. Lucid from drink, he let himself hear what his own soul was saying. *Enough.*

"I'm not spending the year being chased," Bishop said. It was more to himself than to Avery. To the other man he said, "You try to convince them."

Avery deflated visibly. "And if they arrive, and if their desire for confrontation is greater than their common sense?"

"Then try again," Bishop said. "Christ, I don't have much patience anymore. Especially tonight. All I want is a little peace." He lifted his carpetbag with, "Treat them to the good whiskey . . . make them understand every action has its cost."

Avery said, "I'll put forth your message. But I am not optimistic."

"Put it forth with some of that big 'heart' of yours, Mr. Mayor. You'll be doin' everyone a favor. Them mostly, but me too."

Avery watched Bishop take the stairs, then said, "You'll want the old room at the end of the hall. Sixteen steps from the landing, so you'll hear anyone before they reach the door."

"You got it all worked out," Bishop said.

"Whether you believe it or not, I'm on your side," Avery said.

Bishop didn't believe that any more than Avery himself seemed to.

The sleep-it-off room was narrow and crowded with emptiness. It was wrapped around a chimney giving heat that was a dry fog against the skin. Bishop sat hard on the edge of an old bunk, taking the double-barreled rig and special, high-grain shells from the carpetbag, laying them out beside him. The room was barren of drunken miners reeking of unwashed skin and clothes, snoring from the corners, or barking for a fight, and the only sound was the storm shaking the room's one crown-glass window in its sill.

Bishop loaded the rig, swiveled it shut. Locked.

He kicked the carpetbag along the floor to another bunk, then half-hid it, making sure one end stuck out from under the bed, so as to be in the light from the hall when the door opened. Just enough to be seen. Bag positioned, and cradling the rig, he fell back on the bed, its slats cracking, almost giving way, as he sank into its straw mattress like soft mud.

This was the best vantage point of the room, and it felt good.

Bishop dropped his head into the filthy pillow, edges spitting feathers, dust clouding up and with it the stink of every drunk who'd ever used it, but he didn't care. The pillow promised sleep. Maybe for once, more than ten minutes' worth. He shut his eyes in the deep darkness, listened to the rain slamming on the creaking roof, heard a rattle in a drainpipe that sounded a little like a man hanging. He hoped that exhaustion would keep him from remembering, but it never did.

This time the image that returned, like winter, was one of Beaudine's men. Bishop had remembered the man as being jaundiced, who had gone to see the only other physician for a hundred miles. Bishop couldn't remember the man's name—either man—but the doc said he'd treated the outlaw for malaria and told Bishop and White Fox where to find him. They found him. They hunted the outlaw, and when he drew, Bishop inaugurated his new rig. His tired body jerked as his sinew remembered that first release. Powerful, sending lightning through the jaundiced man's bones from skull to heel. Fast. So fast. Before dying from a gaping, blood-pumping wound where his guts used to be, the outlaw told Bishop that Beaudine and his men were still searching for the stolen gold, which they thought had been hidden in a played-out mine in the far mountains.

Encroaching sleep was not enough to keep Beaudine's monstrous face from his mind. Christ, what would? What *could*? And Bishop's defiant heart began to race and his good arm began to throb and his lips drew back involuntarily from his teeth, forming a snarl like some mountain cat—

The voices came from downstairs: Avery's and three others.

Bishop was alert and rolled onto his arm, peered toward the door. In the next fluid movement he adjusted the shotgun to lay flush against his leg. He pulled a Cheyenne blanket, colors worn out, around his shoulders, then angled to one side, exposing his left arm amputated to the elbow, and listened to the voices. That loud burst of a bad joke, laughter, and panicked silence. Just like in the woods. His nostrils didn't flare but they surely smelled death.

Then, there was a crack.

Not a shot, but the sound of bone snap-pounded by metal, probably a gun barrel. Followed by something heavy falling, smashing through wood, hitting the floor. It was easy for Bishop to picture Avery, a turtle on its back, another gash in his bald head, this one with blood washing from it, but still talking his nonsense until the edge of a gun came down again. A gun for sure . . . Bishop knew that thud of metal-on-flesh-on-bone.

Bishop pressed the barrels of the rig flush against the side of the bunk, steady across his knees and hidden by the lower folds of the Cheyenne blanket. Fabric that was so familiar to his touch, comforting under other circumstances. Now, his ally. He heard every footfall on the stairs, then the six feet reaching the landing, then outside the door.

Words whispered: "Remember what fat boy told us to look for."

"When he was cryin'."

A little bit of nervous laughter and then the door

squeaked on its hinges, one of the three men pushing it with the death-end of a tarnished-silver Colt. This first man shouldered the side of the door frame, staying back, making himself a harder target in case Bishop let loose.

But all that was heard from the room was the steady breathing of sleep, and the storm shaking the window glass . . . a noise like the distant crying of a lost foal.

The creeper-along in front pushed the door completely open. The three men walked in, two pushing the one in front along. The first stumbled, caught himself, and they looked to each other for next moves. Fighting not to speak. Then, more steps, and eyeing what they could see of Bishop in the lamplight: curled on the bed asleep, hair streaked gray, his half-arm resting on the blanket, involuntarily twitching from the elbow joint.

The lead man nudged his partners, pointing his gun at the carpetbag that was tempting from just under the bunk. One grabbed the handle, pulling it to the middle of the floor.

Bishop stirred, but only to sink deeper into the straw mattress. The stuffing was old and cooperated by failing to crinkle.

"Looks old," one whispered.

"Take the rig," the other hissed, "then take him."

The one in front set his pistol on his knee, then freed the carpetbag's leather straps, opening it slowly, without sound. He reached in, pulling out a tangle of gun-oiled rags, and Bishop's infamous beaver-skin bandolier. He held the skin up as a trophy, mouthing a war whoop, as his partner twisted loose a long, wooden box that had been jammed into the bag tight, bulging its sides.

Expertly carpentered, with a detailed painting of the double-barrel against a setting sun, it was a perfect, miniature coffin for the gun rig. One of the assassins snickered. Excited. Not able to stop, he bit down on his hand. His buddy turned the coffin over, trying to pry open one of its perfectly fitted sides.

Bishop hadn't moved. Only watched.

The intruder's fingers pressed the painted sun, springing the lid and loosing the large rattler coiled inside, its jaws split wide open. Striking. Once. Tearing flesh. Whipping back and striking again, fangs completely through the careless man's cheek.

Searing pain.

The victim fell back, panicking, for the knife in his belt. Trying to grab it. Rolling onto the floor, the snake's full, thick body out of the coffin. One of the partners grabbed the rattler's tail, pulling it straight, as the bit man tore the blade from his belt. He brought the knife down, quick slash, stabbing into the snake. Slicing skin and muscle. But not killing. Halfway through, just behind the reptile's hood. Stuck.

The animal thrashed as the jammed knife was yanked free, brought down again, the poison from the rattler's fangs that pierced the writhing man's face pouring into his mouth, over his tongue, and down his throat.

He jabbed the knife one last time. Sawing. Cutting off the head, the body still writhingly alive, then spinning around, slamming into empty bunks. Fighting to pull the head from his cheek, fangs staying deep.

Still fighting, slashing blind, catching his partner's throat with the knife tip.

Hitting the jugular.

Blood fountained, jetting red across the walls, as the partner panicked. Stumbling and wild-firing his pistol, while holding his throat. Blasting into the floor, the door, then exploding the snake and the head of the first man. Then, these two clowns from a Wild West show collapsed into a pile, bleeding into each other, before the echo of the gunshots faded.

It was all finished in a few dying heartbeats.

The third interloper, youngest, sporting a rough-patched raincoat and a cowlick, stood back. Mouth open. Eyes locked, not blinking, as Bishop sat up, the rig still hidden just below the bunk frame.

"Good God Almighty."

Bishop said, "You weren't with them."

"Huh?"

"In the trees. You were somewhere else."

"Here," the boy muttered. "Here."

"Watching for the parasol," Bishop said.

The young man, the youngest of the men, didn't know what to say. He just stood there dumbly, probably pissing himself because the water Bishop heard running wasn't from the rain.

"Take a breath, son."

"Not sure I can." The last intruder's voice cracked.

"What's your name?" Bishop asked.

"Edward. And Vance and Tommy—that'd be my two cousins dead there."

"Everything gone crazy, that's how it is sometimes."

"I know about *head*-crazy," Edward said defensively.

"This—they wasn't—they had a plan they was sure of." That last was spoken more to the corpses.

"They were wrong," Bishop said coolly. "But son, you don't have to be. Go on. Go on home."

"They had that plan—" He spoke directly to his dead cousins now.

Bishop said, "They were jackasses, and jackasses get themselves killed. You wanna be a jackass too?"

Jim-Bob was trying to find his thoughts, eyes fixed on the stripes of his cousins' blood, sprayed across their pants and shirt, which was all he could see in the dim light through the open door. Then, he met Bishop with, "Hell Christ, you ain't even got that special gun we all read about."

"It'd be another mistake for you to believe that."

"Another mistake," Edward muttered, disbelieving. He was thinking about backing from the room when he said, "I didn't even draw."

"You knew better. Keep knowing better."

The confused young man freed the pistol from his belt loop, with hands shaking and sweat pouring.

"You're not knowing better," Bishop warned.

The boy snickered unhappily. "See, I got nothing ahead for me, why I came on this jaunt."

"That's not true," Bishop said. "You got one of two things ahead of you. Life . . . or death. And after that, two things ahead of you. Heaven . . . or hell."

The boy shook his head defiantly, as though trying to convince himself otherwise.

Bishop was now sitting with his legs over the side of the bed, right hand on the rig's still-hidden triggers. "Use your sense, boy. All you have to do is walk." He raised the shotgun, letting it poke from beneath the

Cheyenne blanket, the flickering lamp catching the double barrels, showing up the polished steel like two small cannons.

The last intruder's restless eyes stopped. "How about that. There it is."

"Turn around, go back down those stairs," Bishop said. "I'd welcome it, you riding out of here."

"No, see, that won't work." Edward shook his head before wiping his eyes on his tattered sleeve. He had the old Colt pistol, tarnished and nicked, angled to the floor as if he were too weak to aim it straight. "I can't go back from where we broke out. Can't do that."

Bishop said, "Jail's better than what could happen here."

"It sure as hell wasn't no jail," Edward said, then steadied himself with the back of a chair, standing a little taller. "But maybe, right now, I'll get you. You so sure . . . you could be wrong."

"Not likely at all."

"Well, so you say. And goin' ahead'd be worth some money, and it'll revenge my cousins. If I don't shoot, I'm dead anyway for not dyin' with them. But at least I'll be famous for dyin' in this room."

Bishop said, "Jesus, son, that's not worth anything."

Edward was staring directly at Bishop, his face still washing in fevered sweat, but his mouth now twisting into a near-toothless smile. Defiant.

"That? That is worth *everything*!"

The pistol was firing Edward's manic words, the slug from a shaking hand punching a hole in the wall behind Bishop's head. Bishop ducked but didn't shoot. He knew he had all the advantage, was holding back, judging the boy's aim, his nerves. The wet in his eyes.

"Last chance," Bishop said. "You don't get another."

Edward yelled something guttural and opened up again at the same moment the blast from the shotgun slammed into his middle, spiraling him back through the corner window, screaming him to the ground, in the rain, blood, and shards of razor-edged glass.

The lamps threw off streaks of purple and orange that collided as Avery moved. He'd been skull-cracked before, but nothing like this; a hot pain searing between his temples and behind his eyes, as if he'd been shot with a molten needle.

He pushed himself from the floor, rolling from his barreled stomach, to lie against the bar, and reach for a whiskey towel to mop the blood streaming from the back of his head.

"I heard that double-barrel!" Avery called out. He had to yell since the blast shut his ears for a moment and the echo still rang through the structure. The big man grabbed the laudanum in a hand partly asleep from his having fallen on it, then he lurched around the poker tables until he reached the bottom of the steps. "I take it you survived in fine style, John, and they did not!"

Bishop's voice came back, "Find out for yourself."

"Well, I am very relieved," Avery said to Bishop, then to himself, draining the cobalt bottle, "and it's good for business."

* * *

Bishop's right arm went through the leather harness, pulled it up to his shoulder, then tightened the silver chain from the shotgun, across his back, to his right wrist where it was secured by a tight leather cuff.

The device drew itself into shape, conforming to his muscles, as he moved, pulling the amputee cup and gun stock to his left elbow, over the corrupted skin, sliding back to the joint, then locking it there. The silver chain hooked to the triggers, snapped tight, and was again taut across his back.

Bishop moved his left arm away from his side, swinging the double-barrel around, the weapon always adjusting, responding as an extension of his body. New brass fittings allowed it to swivel to either side, gyroscoping, then locking into position. Easy as making a fist.

His mind was no longer on the distant past but the recent past. He gave quick thought that if the young man had seen the double-barrel properly, not something hidden in a blanket, he would have ridden off, instead of trying. Maybe. But it happened the way it happened.

Bishop shifted his powerful shoulders, getting used to the rig's weight again, compensating, as Avery's bulk filled the doorway and shadowed the room. Cradling a bundle of yellowing penny dreadfuls with Bishop on the cover, copies he had immediate need for, the fat man was unsteady on his feet, leaned heavily for the wall, almost toppling over. He couldn't afford to hurt now. There was work to be done.

He took a lace handkerchief from his breast pocket, daubed his head, and pointed to the rig. "Well, some improvements surely have been made."

Bishop buttoned his shirt over the gun, adjusting the sleeve. "A little time out of the rain, that would've been fine. But this, you bastard—this is your doing."

Avery winced in pain, his massive chest heaving. "They were fools three times over. I tried to turn them 'round, back into the storm, but their zeal overtook them."

"Bullshit. How much of their silver you have on you?"

"Why do you have a problem with trustin' me, old—"

"Shut up!"

Avery dropped the bundle, the magazines scattering at his feet. "Dammit, the money is not the point. It's your history. That's what brought them up the stairs."

"I'd lay odds you wish I was the one bleeding on your floor."

"That isn't true. It also isn't fair."

"How much would *my* blood be worth—there?" He nodded to the magazines.

Avery limped to the window, handkerchief pressed to his wound, looked down at the young corpse lying among pork barrels—broken wood and bones—his chest blasted in half. "That isn't bleeding, my friend. That's the stuff of legend. You outdid anything the dreadfuls could've imagined."

"I don't live behind a desk in New York or London."

"Nor I." Avery turned from the window, rain still blowing in. "Now I've got three graves—well, one—to dig, and a window to fix. Oh, as acting sheriff of Good Fortune, I find that the killing was in self-defense. Investigated and excused."

"Not by me," Bishop said.

"You never did know how to accept a gift," Avery

said, still with the lace to his head. "I won't dare ask about that new ammunition."

Bishop finally said, "From my last war."

Avery's eyes dropped to the magazines. "Billy the Kid and Pat Garrett."

Bishop didn't bother answering. Which was an answer.

"So . . . so . . . a little more of the legend proven true," Avery said admiringly.

"Brother, you *talk* too much."

"No, I think too much! I'm naturally curious!"

Bishop shook his head. He draped the bandolier around his left arm by the shoulder, tied it off. Avery made a move to help. Bishop backed him off with a look before quick-fitting a dozen shells into the skin's specially cut pockets.

"I'd no intention of ever using these again."

"Which is why you carry so many," Avery said. "You can read all about how powerful they are in these pages. Also, weren't some of your shells called Dragon's Breath, dispensing fiery death? See? You just can't help being colorful, John."

Bishop said, "You should lie down before you collapse."

"Now *you're* wishing *I* didn't recover."

Avery knelt, dipping the edges of the dreadfuls in the pooling blood, the red seeping up into the rough pulp pages. Staining Bishop's face on the covers. "I wonder how much these'll fetch, soaked in the blood of your enemies?"

Bishop stood over Avery. "You're a soulless bastard."

"Said the killer to the merchant."

The onetime soldier had to fight the urge to kick the man, not only because he was outspoken but because there was some truth to that. Maybe that was why he bothered to associate with Avery at all. The man had no real conscience, but he did have some boundaries.

"Tell me something," Bishop said quietly. "Did you ever even fire that derringer you carry? The one in your waistcoat pocket? Or the carbine?"

"Never. Not in the bar, not behind the badge. Usually, just showing up with that silver license to use it is enough."

Bishop wondered what that kind of a conscience felt like. Not having taken a life but having stepped aside to let them be taken. Avery probably felt like a human being when he woke up in the morning. Bishop could barely remember what it felt like not to have fangs.

Avery waggled a finger. "Careful you don't get more of their blood on your boots." He glanced up briefly from his labors, as though he were waiting on griddlecakes to tan. "Do you know your eyes go completely black when you anger? Not the first time tonight you've had the impulse to kill me."

Lightly touching his head wound again, pain-wincing, Avery continued, "Your history follows you, and we all get caught up in it. So, if there's a way to offset the cost of your damages, after all these years, don't you think me entitled?"

He grinned, using his three chins and ignoring the shotgun barrels shifting toward him; the gun moving as Bishop moved. "Actually, I doubt you'll ever be able to take off that rig again. And before you boil over, you should see this latest, this possibly greatest interpretation of your life."

"Why?"

Avery offered Bishop some blood-soaked pages,

still wet across his name. "Because it's your reputation, Doctor. Not mine."

From *The National Police Gazette*, October 5, 1883:

"Eye" Witnessed the Slaughter

by VIRGIL DEMETRIUS CHANEY

I have seen the hero, and the dastardly monster. Doctor John Bishop's saga has been well documented in these pages and others, as a man who suffered a tremendous loss in his life, with the death of wife and child, and yet persevered to become a figure of righteous vengeance in Colorado, and Wyoming, and points farther West. And now, Dr. Bishop is a dastardly symbol of bloody slaughter, an instrument of violence and death.

This reporter, at risk of my own life, eye-witnessed Bishop's famed use of the shotgun he carries as furious replacement for his left arm, when riding for The Chisum Cattle Company and on August 15, 1882, he and other of Chisum's men faced down with masked marauders, in a terrible gunfight that left dozens dead and dying. Bishop himself was shot, but even as he bled, he used his skills to doctor the wounded. I have also seen the ruins of a prison, used by these marauders, turned to rubble and ash by John Bishop, as he brought deadly justice to the life of his outlaw brother.

Killing many, all for the purpose of law and order.

This now begs the question of the price of frontier justice. How can we rally around this man, brandishing a specialized weapon that perverts his own flesh and blood limbs, who has killed without warning, and without provocation, of suspected law-breakers, and sadly, the innocent alike.

The war is behind us, the railroad uniting us, while more and more brave men are charged with protecting our lives and properties. Where does this renegade John Bishop, this "Shotgun," as he has been monikered, fit into our modern, and growing, society?

This Eye Witness, who has seen too much of his slaughter and mayhem, including members of my own family who died alongside young troopers guarding a government gold shipment, declares that John Bishop does not fit into the New West.

And to that, I am personally offering a bounty of $10,000 to any reader who assists in Bishop's capture, or assassination, by sheriff, territorial marshal, any recognized deputy, or private individual acting in self-defense. All information obtained will be strictly confidential, until Bishop's capture or demise, and then will be the subject of articles/books penned with skill by this author.

CHAPTER TWO
The Demon

The blood spatters were jagged brown stars across the little girl's face, their dried edges broken by streaks of tears. Her tiny arms, dotted with a hundred more brownish little spots, locked around White Fox's neck, holding on for dear life.

"*Hávêsévemâhta'sóoma!*" said the fragile little voice. A tangle of Cheyenne and sobs, meaning "The Demon!"

Beside the fire, White Fox held the child, obscenely caked with dried blood and muddy leaves. The older woman felt the hysteria roll through her tiny body; arms and legs thrashing wild, fighting something invisible. Trying to kill it.

Screaming about the Demon.

The constable known as Firecrow watched White Fox from the other side of the tepee, shifting a bowie knife between his large, flat palms, making a judgment. He then spoke, but in the older Suhtai language of the Northern tribe. "She was burrowed-up in a hollow log on the edge of the Platte River. I thought she was a fawn, got herself stuck. Pulled her out by the ankles. She clawed me until I knotted her wrists together, lashed her to my horse. She never stopped crying 'Demon, Demon,' the whole ride."

White Fox responded in Suhtai; like ancient poetry to her. "You saved her life."

"Her wits?"

White Fox nodded. She was sure she would recover. Children were malleable.

"An orphan?"

"So it appears," the man replied. "She is not from here."

"No," White Fox agreed. She did not recognize her or the fishbone necklace she wore; that design was not of her people. There had been a fire to the north the week before. Many Comanche were displaced, she had heard. Perhaps she was one.

Constable kept turning the knife. "You understood all that I'm saying, these words of the elders?"

"All of it." White Fox thought for a moment. "For now I will call her Little Hen, because of the way her hair sticks up."

"You cannot avoid issues by talking around them."

"You cannot solve them by talking at them," she replied.

White Fox brought the girl's dampened face to her shoulder, a tight embrace, quieting her until finally, the only sound was the crackle of the hot stones in the cook fire. She took a cloth from a water bowl, squeezed the run-off through her fist, then pressed it against the child's face, letting her feel the cool.

"Fear is hot, allow the cold to help you," White Fox told her.

The young one tried to do her part. She swallowed the cries, the sniffling. It struggled to come back and the older woman held her more tightly. There was a quiet majesty to the latter. A sense of life lived, challenges met and survived. Of appreciation for both the trials and setbacks that gave her strength. She would say that her strength came from many sources. From the earth and sky. From the painted stallion she rode. From her tribe. But mostly it came from her spiritual connection to the man whose life she had saved, and who had in turn saved her own. John Bishop.

Unlike Bishop, White Fox was not a haunted soul. She existed in the moment, and right now the moment was this girl. "She's terrified," the beautiful Cheyenne woman said.

"Of the Demon," Firecrow said. "What cut her?"

"Squeezing into the log, I would expect."

"True or not, the Demon *was* there, she says. I have to know what she means, who she means, to do something about it."

"To kill someone."

"Or some *thing*. Animal or man, it makes no difference, as long as it helps the child. Prevents further injury."

"These could be bear scratches," White Fox said. "Children approach baby bears unwitting."

"Then why did she not call it a bear?"

White Fox's voice was now flat, even, honoring the old language. "Because a frightened child is not always a rational child."

"But I am," Firecrow said. "It's my duty to protect, not to prove or disprove fables."

He was referring to the story of the fish she had told the girl, and of the bear that had frightened them both. The fish could not harm the bigger animal so they let the river shield them in its current where the bear could not stand.

"There is always a place where a bear—or demon—cannot go," White Fox had said. "But first we must know what it is."

White Fox wrapped the girl in a blanket, aware of Firecrow's eyes on her, fixed and deep-set in a face carved from oak, of the knife still turning in his hands.

She wiped more blood from the girl's face, smearing away the stars, careful not to pull any damaged skin. But there was none. She rinsed the cloth, pinking the water, wiped the girl's arms and around her shoulders.

White Fox said, "I'm finding no wounds."

"Then, how?"

Firecrow had moved to the back of the tepee's curve, where scarred battle shields hung above stacks of blankets, and medicine jars. He poked at a shield with his knife, sending it sideways on its leather hanger.

White Fox was still running her fingers through the girl's hair, checking for wounds, and decided, "Those spots are mine."

"This blood here." He indicated a shield that had caught his attention. "Also yours?"

"Some of it. Mostly others'."

He shifted his attention to a harness that was made for the neck of a horse, one slot for a large hunting knife, another for a heavy tomahawk. The edge of the hatchet, poking from above the strap that held it, was new. Kept in good repair. Ready.

"You were once a warrior, as I was." He went on sharply, "Now I am a keeper of the peace."

White Fox washed more blood away. "That's a Sioux braid hanging from your belt."

"From the Black Hills War," Firecrow said, pulling at the braid that hung beside a short-blade throwing ax. "Just a boy when I took it, and this was my choice of weapon, the blade perfectly edged with leather and water. Thin and strong. I hadn't got to know my enemies yet, but it would still be my choice today."

White Fox asked, "Better than a gun?"

"Better?" Firecrow said. "Yes. With a gun you become reliant on the weapon, not on your skill, not on your purpose. A lazy man becomes fearful, cautions. Such a man becomes a victim. There should be effort in taking a life."

White Fox slipped a hand behind some clay jars by her bed, sliding a battle club hidden there within reach, keeping the handle down, and said, "More effort should go into protecting them."

Firecrow examined poultice sacks hanging from a support pole. Smelling them, balancing one on the edge of the knife blade. Approving, in the old language, of the "true medicine."

White Fox gave a cautious nod. "Medicine is anything that heals." She kissed the girl on her warm forehead. "Anything."

"Then death is a medicine?" Firecrow asked.

"Death does not heal. It is something else, beyond healing or affliction."

Firecrow was not happy with that answer. He was not happy with anything. "I used to ride patrols, now I ride patrol and bury the dead. Over a hundred this month. All fever, no war. And no healing."

From outside, a drum started to beat. Steady, then breaking into rhythms, into words.

Firecrow said, "War drums . . . but they are sending the warning of fever in the camp."

"I hear it," White Fox replied. "Always the same now. The fear of a spreading fire."

"A righteous fear, of a fire that will never go out."

"We will find a cure," White Fox insisted.

"That is why I brought the child to you," Firecrow answered. "The Demon. Maybe it is in her mind as disease is in her blood."

He was standing over a wooden case, with leather pockets for bottled medicine, and a drawer for surgical knives. He pushed at it with a moccasin, tipping it back, but not over, seeing the army medical insignia gold-painted on its side.

Firecrow measured his Suhtai words, chopping them as he spoke. "New medicine. White medicine. I can think of one thousand reasons to reject it."

"I can think of one reason not to." She regarded the girl.

"And if the Demon is in her?"

White Fox tightened her grip on the club, her body shielding the child. "Then it will be driven out."

The two stared at one another as Firecrow said, "You got this from that army doctor, the one who all the tales arc told about. Almost legends."

"There is dishonor in that?" she challenged.

"In that, no. You rode with him for how long?" The way Firecrow said "rode" suggested something more intimate.

Before White Fox could reply, the little girl screamed again, same words erupting.

Firecrow regarded the bowie, the blade angled to

catch White Fox's reflection. She watched his eyes. The blade, with her hand on the battle club. The drumming was fading, moving off.

"Fever," he said, sheathing the knife. "The baby's mind and spirit, corrupted. She will not live a week."

"She is not corrupted," White Fox insisted.

Firecrow said, "You really shouldn't be here at all . . . you should be pushing on to the reservation."

"Use your authority to push me, then?"

Firecrow measured his words again, emphasizing the old language. "If I had intended to harm or force you, I would have—"

"Tried," she added. "I have to be alone with her now. Leave."

"Very well. I have said what I came to say. For now."

Firecrow stepped through the fire to the hide-opening, and said, as though it were an insult not a commendation, "*Má'heóná'e*"—Medicine woman—before slipping out.

White Fox exhaled and let go of the club, taking one of the medicine jars and pouring root tea, then dropping quinine tablets in to break the girl's temperature. White Fox let it stir, old and new medicine mixing, keeping a hand on the girl, then sitting her up to drink.

"The Demon," the girl repeated.

White Fox said, "He's gone, he's gone."

The warning drums were as quiet as a pulse, the girl drinking, the tea soothing, taking control, and then White Fox placed both hands on her face, cradling her jaw. Gently, but letting her feel the grip.

"The blood," White Fox said softly. "Whose is it?"

The little girl looked directly at White Fox. About to scream, but then, "It came from the sky."

"You mean—as the rain?"

The girl sat stiffly, her eyes wide, her mouth the opposite.

"Tell me. You don't have to be afraid."

White Fox relaxed her hold and eased back. The girl's body reacted as if she were being pulled from the log again, out of any and all protection. Her eyes rolled back, and she cried: "A rain of blood! That came with the Demon as he rode. Blood from the sky, and flame shooting from his arms!"

White Fox held the girl tighter, keeping her safe. "It cannot be a demon, it must be a man. Tell me."

"No!" the girl continued screaming, weeping, as if speaking the spoken words once again made the spirit real. Finally she said, "*Hávêsévemâhta'sóoma.* The Demon who is half-man, and half-gun."

CHAPTER THREE
Last Rites

"Watch the bloodstains, Homer."

Avery spoke in tones that invoked a wholly inappropriate yet apt reverence.

"I'm watching," the older man said.

"They were spilled by John Bishop and they are precious indeed."

"I heard you the first four times," Homer Lancaster grumped.

Homer sighed as he dipped a paintbrush, finishing the circle of yellow around the blood spatters across the floor, some from the dead man and some from the rattler. He'd already marked the bullet holes in the ceiling and walls, and painted a circle to surround the blood spray on the door, so everyone could see. At least the open window kept the paint fumes from making him dizzy. A man like Homer who worked for a man like Avery had to be grateful for the little things.

Homer rose slowly, shuffled to a bunk, knees creaking, as Avery lifted a heavy sign, struggling to position it beside the shattered window in the corner of the room. A red bandanna wrapped his bald head, hiding his bandage.

It was a piece of old plank, with SHOTGUN BISHOP'S LATEST VICTIMS MET THEIR MAKER ON THIS VERY SPOT scrawled across it. Avery teetered, hips rolling, as he held the thing against the wall. Homer watched, then yawned.

"Lord save me, I've got a real hunger going," Homer said. "And, I ain't been paid."

Avery coughed, fat arms straining to hold the sign in place. "When word of what happened here spreads, you'll be papering these walls with hundred-dollar bills."

"Your walls," Homer noted.

"From which I will pull them like leaves, and bestow them on all who serve."

"God's manna," Homer said. "I got stuck with a suitcase of that Confederate scrip' one time," he warned as he dropped the brush in the paint can, pulled at his beard, considering. "And what d'you think Bishop's gonna do when he finds out about all this phony take-on?"

"There's nothing phony," Avery said defensively. "The men *did* die here. By his hand. Or . . . well, one hand. Just nail this damn thing, would you?"

Homer put some bent nails between his teeth, holding them as he took up his hammer. "You know I had to pull these out of a pew, one of the ones to the back of the church."

"God won't mind. In fact, He would commend you. 'Thou Shalt Raise Up Your Fellow Man.' This puts those brads to better use. Bring people back to Good Fortune, fill the church and the saloon, and we'll build anything we need to accommodate the crowds. God will be very pleased. Satan sent these men on a vile mission and was stymied."

Homer drove nails into the old plank. "How many times you get cracked in the skull?"

"Fewer than you. Better ideas? I'll consider them."

"A full church," Homer said thoughtfully as he hammered another. "I could go back to preaching again."

"Indeed," Avery agreed. "And I'll be right there among the faithful to receive your message . . . and to thank the Good Lord for His bounty."

The planking split along the knots, the nails going through the rot hidden inside the sign, to more rot in the old window frame, and Homer said, "Sure hope your scheme works, Mr. Mayor. This place could use all the help it can beg."

Avery took a step, judging the handiwork, saying, "These killings mean our begging days are truly over."

"You still ain't said what Bishop might do, he sees all this."

"John expects no better, so he won't be surprised at my exploitation," Avery said, then couldn't help his grin. "Or, he might kill me—"

Homer spit. "I'll put up *that* sign."

"—and you," Avery added.

Homer hammered faster.

Avery was looking down to the street, through the last pieces of broken glass in the window frame, and said solemnly, "But I'm guessing he's already made his plans, and they do not include me or you or Good Fortune."

Avery's hand rested on Homer's shoulder, his weight bending the old man as he followed his own look, down and out to the street. He absently touched his head, feeling the wound through the bandanna.

"Where's your gun?"

Homer didn't have to think. "Jacket pocket, downstairs."

"Get it."

"That surely ain't Bishop ridin' in."

"Just get your gun."

"Your carbine too?"

"No," Avery said. "Not how we're playing it."

"This is turning into quite a day," Homer said, shaking his head, his beady eyes growing wider. "I can probably still throw a mean hammer, if I have to."

Avery said, "I remember it well. Your wife."

Homer slipped the hammer through his belt loop. "That was an accident. My sister-in-law was on purpose."

Avery was still at the broken window. "Make this 'on purpose.' Now get the damn gun."

Avery blinked, then shook his head to clear any pain, any streaks of light, as he watched the four horses pulling the hearse around the old general store, skidding across the slop of Main Street, then angling for the hotel, where he stood.

Seen through the evening wet, the horses were a vision of ghost-riders; blazing white, with black stars marking their foreheads, all four moving as one animal. The driver, massive chest and arms, cracked a bullwhip, keeping the team hard-running, the hearse's wheels cutting ruts in the Good Fortune mud.

A once-elegant coach, black-lacquered and trimmed in silver and carved glass, the hearse's roof and sides had been extended with bolted iron plates, turning it into a rolling fortress.

Standing on the hotel porch, Avery waved to the driver and passenger as they got closer, keeping his other hand in the pocket with the straight razor and derringer.

The passenger, sporting a new homburg and with a crisp leather satchel across his knees, returned the wave, as the driver braked to a stop directly in front of Hospitality House. Wheels locked and mud churning, the horses pulled back, legs chopping the air, then settled.

"Am I addressing the law or the landlord?"

Avery displayed his lapel badge to the passenger. "As it happens, sir, both."

The man in the homburg tipped his brim with two manicured fingertips, then stepped down with, "Excellent; then this should be an efficient transaction."

Avery held in his belly, resisted the impulse to slouch. He wanted to make an impression.

The man's Germanic accent, manner, beard, and suit were all precisely cut to fit, and he stepped from the hearse to the porch without any mud clinging to cuffs or shoes, as if it wouldn't dare. He kept the leather satchel to his chest as he spoke. "I am Weiber-Krauss, a doctor, and you've had a recent death, I understand."

"You understand correctly," Avery said, nodding slightly.

"And you, sir, are . . . ?"

"Sheriff-Mayor Avery," he said, using the compound title he preferred.

The newcomer seemed to respond favorably to the title, or to the formality. Something.

"I am pleased to meet a man of such achievement," Weiber-Krauss said. "I'm here for the deceased, as you can see from the transportation."

"By whose authority, since I do have the badge?" Avery asked.

"I respect your position"—Weiber-Krauss held up the satchel—"and you'll see that I'm fully sanctioned."

"I see that you have things," Avery countered.

"There are documents in my grip. I am not fool enough to try and pass counterfeit skills—or counterfeit credentials—on a man of experience." A nod of the head in Avery's direction seemed to emphasize the respect he had demonstrated before.

"Good to know." Avery had seen the doctor's bag from the window, and the transportation of course. He had assumed why the man had come. But he wasn't quite ready to cooperate, yet. "Where do you hail from, Doctor?"

"A treatment facility, not far from here. But if you mean my origins, a village outside of Berlin."

"Berlin—the across-the-ocean Berlin?"

"The selfsame. My family is a very old one."

"I guess everyone's is, no, Doctor?" Avery suggested.

"Point to you," Weiber-Krauss said stiffly.

Avery's brow crinkled. "You know any German concern interested in raising horses?"

"Not my field," the man replied, indicating the satchel.

"No, of course," Avery said. "Tell me, how in the world did you find yourself in Good Fortune?"

"Ah, how does anyone?"

"Silver?" Avery hazarded.

"I was looking into the purchase of a mine with an eye to revitalizing it. And perhaps the local economy."

Avery gave Weiber-Krauss his laugh, with, "So you know our story."

"I've heard."

"Have you been in this country a long time?"

"Yes" the newcomer said, adding, "and it's still common practice to ask what side a man was on during the conflicts so you know how to react to him." Weiber-Krauss paused, adjusting gold-framed bifocals. "I was with the Fifth German Rifles, under Colonel von Annenberg. We hailed from New York."

The driver, coiling the whip, leaned down from his bench, his accent betraying the low Austrian mountains. "That means Union."

Avery said, "I'm well aware, thank you."

"You are welcome," the driver said. "What about you?" the man inquired.

Avery didn't think it was any of that man's business, but the question was floated just the same. He looked up at the driver, leaning even closer, his body draped over most of the hearse's roof, and said back to him, "I abstained."

The driver huffed. "A sheriff—afraid?"

"No, that means the sheriff, who was not then sheriff, abstained," Avery said. "Age and physical limitations."

Avery wasn't liking or trusting this crankier European goon. His right thumb was hooked behind a button of his vest, allowing his index finger to dangle into his pocket. It was on the trigger of the pocket derringer, and he was figuring his aim from the jacket pocket, roughly between the driver's eyes. The little guns weren't that precise, but precise enough to hit the target or an eye.

"I ask you to forgive my driver's manner," Weiber-Krauss said. "Smith is not a social animal."

"He is if you leave off the 'social,'" Avery suggested. "And . . . Smith?" he hooted. "An unusual name in these parts. Except in hotel ledgers and on the lips of a certain kind of woman."

Smith scowled down but Weiber-Krauss chortled.

"You have humor, sir, but you'd find the family name of my driver quite unpronounceable. Smith, which is actually Schmidt, is a moniker. Awarded by myself when I discovered him in a European carnival. Selected, on the spot, because each of his fists has the weight of a blacksmith's anvil."

Avery just now noticed them, and Weiber-Krauss was not incorrect.

Smith had dropped like a full bucket in the wall, transferring from the hearse to the porch. The here-and-there rotted planks bent under his weight. He was shorter by several inches than Avery but more densely packed with muscle. He took his place behind Weiber-Krauss, the coiled bullwhip in hand. His eyes were clearly taking target practice.

Avery's three-chin smile froze. "All of this is very impressive."

Weiber-Krauss smiled solicitously. "So, we know each other a little, and now you can let go of the gun?" His eyes dropped briefly to the vest pocket.

Avery remained absolutely still. He wondered if everyone west of the Appalachians knew about the little derringer.

"What about all this hoopla of your being 'fully sanctioned'?" Avery asked.

"An interesting way to put it," Weiber-Krauss said as he lit a meerschaum pipe taken from his satchel. "The correct question is, 'What about the dead?' They—all three of them—were my patients."

"I see."

"There are eager kin. I hope you will show me to them, now?"

"With pleasure," Avery said. "They are ripening."

The horses of the would-be killers were still in stalls with the bodies of the would-be killers laid out on the stable's workbench, saddles neatly stacked beside like a row of grave markers. Wrapped in blood-spotted sheets, lengths of cord were tied around the middles and throats of the bodies, lashing the coverings tight. The youngest also had a burlap sack pulled over his head, for dignity's sake, his patched raincoat buttoned, and arms angel-folded across his chest.

Avery commented on the vignette. "The youngest got a little too close, needed a little extra help keeping his parts together."

"Of all the ways they imagined their plan would work, ending here certainly wasn't one of them," Weiber-Krauss said. "Very foolish, and didn't listen to any reason from me."

Avery said, "You knew they were riding in?"

"As I think you did, yes? Weren't you complicit?"

Avery didn't answer. Bishop scared him even when he wasn't there.

Pipe in his teeth, Weiber-Krauss slipped on a pair of linen gloves, nodded to Smith, who tore open the raincoat, his thick, knotted hands like bear claws, revealing the shotgun wounds that split the youngest cousin's chest. There was a gun, still in his hand. He was impressed the mayor-sheriff had not cracked the stiffened fingers to remove it.

Weiber-Krauss tilted the body to its side, examining the bruising around the broken hip and back. "How much did you clean this boy?"

"Well, not much was needed," Avery said almost jubilantly. "Most of him was on the outside. We mopped that up."

"I see," Weiber-Krauss said, still examining the wound.

Avery said, "We wrapped him like a Christmas present, and brought him in here to join his compatriots. We figured someone would come."

"Why?"

"They said they had folk."

Weiber-Krauss looked at all three victims, then rose. "These wounds are crawling with insects, and there are pieces of broken glass."

"Again, Doctor, we got him up off the ground."

"After a fall from how high? And backwards?" Weiber-Krauss flicked pellets of high-grade shot from a chest wound, held them between his fingers.

"Yes," Avery said. This here's courtesy of Dr. John Bishop. At least, what he's become. I'm sure we'll be reading of this soon enough, yes?"

"Not by choice," Weiber-Krauss said.

"I wasn't present, thank God, but he took care of business, partly in defense of myself," Avery said. "As you claim, these three had it in their minds to challenge Dr. Bishop, and collect a bounty from some private party. I had the authority, and ruled the killing justified."

"I would expect nothing less," Weiber-Krauss said. "These three should never have tried; their thinking was clouded by war trauma. The youngster was an outright simpleton."

"He was offered a chance to leave, didn't take it," Avery said. "I heard it all."

"Which helped you reach your legal finding," Weiber-Krauss said, as Smith stepped around the side of the corpses, running the bullwhip through his hands, shedding the braids of the horse sweat.

"That's right," Avery answered, watching the driver.

"Don't be alarmed. That's his habit," Weiber-Krauss said, lifting the wrapped head of another aging corpse, feeling the rigor mortis in his neck. "Ah, Bishop. I was in residence at the State Hospital in Pueblo. Before that, I served beside Doctor Bishop during the conflict, and knew, *admired* him, quite well."

"Did you?" Avery said. "Did you ever tell your story?"

Weiber-Krauss waved a hand. "I am by nature a private man," he said.

"You worked beside him . . . but you're not a surgeon," Avery clarified.

"Mental disorders became my specialty, as I saw what plagued so many returning home." He smiled.

"But I am well familiar with the instruments of the medical doctor."

"You are also a man of achievement." Avery returned the compliment in a voice more sincere than when Weiber-Krauss had said it. As he spoke, Avery moved closer to the back wall of the stable, to the shadows, out of Smith's reach. Then he said, "John's been in my circle for years, so I'm sure you and I would have some interesting experiences to swap."

"We will have to see about that." Weiber-Krauss snapped open the satchel, fixed his eyes on Avery. "Are my full credentials necessary?"

Avery was busy looking at Smith, the whip stretched between his fists, and said, "Oh no, you've established yourself perfectly. You'll see these three are properly taken care of?"

Weiber-Krauss said, "That depends on those who have right and title to their remains. I personally would not pack them in ice and put them on a display in a pine box as was done with Jesse James; however . . . there is opportunity to charge the curious to gawk at crosses over empty graves, as their mother does."

Avery smiled. "I am not one to deny a fellow citizen a moneymaking proposition."

Weiber-Krauss smiled devilishly. "You're an interesting personality, Mr. Avery. As with your god, I think you see everything in terms of business. Certainly you dickered your friendship with Dr. Bishop, and now, these dead. Smith and I could retreat to some territorial office to investigate the events, but I prefer no issues, no conflicts."

"You're about to make some kind of proposal."

"You have a good sense of things," Weiber-Krauss complimented him.

"One has to, in my businesses."

"To begin with, I have no trouble with paying you, first, a fair sum," Weiber-Krauss said. "You moved my patients here, instead of leaving them crumpled on some floor, and that earns something."

"Just being humane." He wanted to say it would have been more efficient to feed them to Mr. Moto's pigs down a way, but he continued to play the part.

Weiber-Krauss adjusted his glasses again. "Tell me, did you get much of their blood on your skin?"

"Well, there surely was a great deal of it everywhere, and still is," Avery said. "Upstairs, if you'd care to see."

"Not necessary. And—before we continue with our business—would you tell that old man to come out from behind the far stall. I need no instruments to hear him breathing and chewing tobacco."

Avery winced and called out, "Homer!"

Homer spit as he rose. He emerged from a stall, lowering the tarnished Colt he'd been aiming toward Weiber-Krauss and Smith. He closed the door behind him, was about to say something to Avery, when the bullwhip snapped across his face, splitting his eye. Slicing off the lid. He squealed horribly, lurched forward then back as if he were on rockers, blood washing the undraped eye. *Crack*, and the other eye was seared. Homer dropped the pistol, kicking it blind, while trying for the hammer on his belt. *Crack*. Another strike lay open his face, like the edge of a hot knife. Blood landed on hay, wall, and overhead beams, carried by the end of the whip.

Avery had turned at the first explosion of the whip.

His puzzled expression froze that way. A moment later, his lower jaw fell as though unhinged.

A scalpel was in the side of his neck, buried to the handle. Weiber-Krauss stood by the open satchel, another scalpel ready, watching Avery gurgle, struggling forward on elephant-thick legs. The sheriff-mayor was trying to say something. Anything. But his knees gave out. Before he collapsed, the derringer discharged, blowing through his pocket and hitting his other hand.

Smith waited for Avery's stomach to hit the floor, then charged, fists cocked, to pummel him. Coal-heavy blows. Cracking the side of his face. Again. Splintering his collarbone. Smith's smile showed few teeth and wide gums, as he leveled punch after punch, the impact pumping blood around the scalpel, the red spurting into the air and across the tack hanging on the walls.

Weiber-Krauss allowed another punch, and then, "Enough! He still has to breathe and bleed. Don't forget your orders."

Smith rose like a titan, stood, fists still balled, chest heaving, as Homer moaned. He was on his back, hands reaching up and out. Trying to roll.

Weiber-Krauss shot the old man once in the mouth with a German pin-fire revolver, returned the gun to his satchel. The bullet had punched through, thudded into packed earth behind his head, and Homer had fallen supernaturally still. Then Weiber-Krauss cleaned his glasses with a monogrammed handkerchief, saying, "The three corpses first, then the other one. Then the one who is still alive. Can you manage?"

A push of his clubbed foot, and Smith rolled Avery over with, "Just stupid fat and gristle. Nothing to me."

"Get to it. We'll return to the Lady Freemont for cleaning, then move on."

Smith shook his head in refusal, stepping over Avery's wide belly, moving for the horses in the stalls, and repeating: "*Die pferde. Die pferde.*"

"Yes, yes, fine. Free their horses, then do your job with these others!"

Smith ignored the critical tone of Weiber-Krauss's voice, looked down to Homer, who was staring up through lidless eyes. "I should feel bad for him. He is me. Doing his job."

"He'd lived too long, and God knew it," Weiber-Krauss said, retrieving the scalpel from Avery's gullet. The man was breathing in his own blood, gurgling, red bubbles at the incision. Weiber-Krauss cleaned the wound with his handkerchief and trough water, then bandaged it, and the injured hand. When he was finished, he rose and shouted after Smith. "Hurry up with your precious horses, we have many miles to travel yet. And Mr. Cavanaugh has a ride, yet, with this other man."

Bishop had ridden hours; finding this spot, a place where the cottonwoods had grown tall and close, their branches tangling, creating a thick fan of yellow leaves between them that hung like a thatched roof over a small patch of tall, dry grass.

The quiet here, complete. At least on the outside.

The killing of the three men did not trouble him. They had brought this on themselves. Helped by Avery, but they were the ones who put one foot before the other to climb those stairs.

The older ghosts—they were the ones who gave

him no peace. Beaudine and his killers, but they were only part of it. When Bishop and White Fox found the killers in a mine, they did not realize it was a trap. Beaudine set off charges that brought the dilapidated mine down on them. Bishop and White Fox made their way to the bottom of the mine, where it was flooded, swam through a breached wall into the icy river. Half-dead, they were rescued by a mountain man and nursed by him and a chief of the Crow. Good men, humanity at its finest. Just as Beaudine and his type were humanity at its worst.

No, not quite its worst. There was Dev—

The deepest pain of all was Bishop's brother, who was not hanged. Someone else died in his place, put in the noose by a greedy warden who cherished money over life. Someone else's life, anyway. Devlin was evil. He was behind everything. Behind Beaudine. Behind all the pain. Behind a power grab unprecedented in the history of the republic.

Something in Bishop's brain shut down when he revisited that anguish. It was like a railroad switch that pushed the train of thought to another track. If not for that, a man could go mad with rage and grief and lose all control . . .

Bishop dozed, sitting up against his saddle, blanket to his shoulders, the shotgun rig lying alongside. He was trying for some true sleep, to put Hospitality House far behind, to finally be swallowed by the exhaustion he'd been fighting. There were a few moments of something between dreams and waking, but the bloody images of everything Devlin wrought played behind his lids, wouldn't leave him alone.

Shutting his eyes tighter only seemed to lock them in, trapping him. Bishop twisted, reacting, and the rig responded with his body, turning with him. He felt it, and woke.

"Oh give me peace," he said to the night.

But the night or God or whoever was listening wasn't going to help. Avery would. There was a bottle from the bar in his saddlebag, and he found it, taking a long pull. It settled his brain, let his body feel instead. He lay back again. The after-rain-ground was cool, and he felt that through the blanket while letting the whiskey do its work, as he closed his eyes again.

Then snapped them open.

Something was moving, crackling leaves under foot. The rig responded, almost before his body did, as he sat up, looking into the trees; the blue-black of the thick woods, broken only by the vague light of clouded stars.

He moved again, the rig swinging around, his shoulders tightening, the barrels aiming toward the sound of something approaching in the dark, half-hidden by the branches. Men, keeping low, with weapons drawn, stepping quickly, then stopping and taking position. They were silhouettes against the woods. Darker patches of dark. Moving, with their guns outlined by bits of light from the sky.

Bishop rolled away from the saddle and came up shooting. Taking down one, then turning, still hunched to his knees, at the one charging him, firing a pistol. Gun-flames showed up the place like flashes of lightning, slashes of hot light, as Bishop took a slug in his left arm, still bringing the barrel up, almost to the killer's chin. The trigger chains pulled, and the killer's face disintegrated, the body spinning off its feet and dropping as dead weight.

Bishop sprung to his feet, pain tearing his one arm but still loading the rig, snapping the weapon shut, and turning to kill two more. The blasts took them both off their feet and back onto the soft grass, where they landed side by side, their blood spreading, even as they still moved, and screamed.

Bishop threw himself awake.

Sat up next to a low fire he'd built, hearing the movement through the trees. Leaves crunching. Something breaking a branch in half. Turning, to see the flash of the white tail. A slash of color, darting among the cottonwoods, and ducking beneath the branches, and then stopping.

He relaxed. The smile came next, easy and natural.

The doe fixed on Bishop, and he could see her white and brown against the dark outline of the trees. She was tall at the shoulder, with a long, white neck and wide head, all showing her to be full grown. She stared at Bishop with perfectly polished eyes, the orange from the fire reflected there, and her ears twitching back with curiosity.

A beautiful kill.

Bishop was nowadays hungry, but he wasn't going to shoot. His stomach wasn't going to stop gnawing, but he knew all she wanted was to go home, just as he did. Lost creature to lost creature, he would let that happen. Resting against his right arm, the trigger lines slacked and the rig shifted, aiming down and away.

The doe bolted with effortless beauty, and Bishop shut his eyes, now seeing the deer behind his lids instead, as if she were standing guard over his peace, batting back the nightmares. A damn silly thought.

But it helped, and he let it stay, as he tried again for some sleep.

"Too close, the wheels will sink into the ground."

Exasperated, Smith got down from the driver's seat, insisting to Weiber-Krauss, "I can lift it out."

Weiber-Krauss indicated for him to go ahead. The driver unlocked the back of the hearse, the door swinging open, then moving the iron plates aside, as if breaking into a tomb. He pulled the body of the youngest man out by his belt, tossing him over his shoulders like a mail sack, one of his dead arms falling loose.

"My dear Smith—watch your methods," Weiber-Krauss said. "I don't want you hurting yourself."

"You always act like I'm not strong enough."

Weiber-Krauss's tone was of a parent reminding a child about undone chores: "No, it isn't strength, it's strategy. Bishop's victim must be placed so that it's discovered, and serves its purpose, by whatever is left inside seeping out."

"*Ja,* I've done it before," he said. Then added, "And you mean, what you put inside seeping out too."

"It's all of a piece," the German replied.

Weiber-Krauss followed Smith to the edge of the river, where he put the dead man into the wet grass, his body tilting over, as he cut the twine lacing his arms together and pulled away the rags of the bloody sheet. Weiber-Krauss pulled at the raincoat, and Smith yanked it free; the young man's body lurched over, the shotgun wounds now fully exposed. Weiber-Krauss held the boy's head back, getting close to his chest, and the wound, then nodded. Smith shouldered the corpse up and over, into the water. That would be enough to refresh the blood, cause it to run.

They stood, sun now breaking, watching the body turn with the currents; the river washed over the wounds, blood from the chest showing renewed life and stringing out as dangling red ribbons, then dissolving. Weiber-Krauss nodded his approval as the rigidly dead head and shoulders sank, then put a hand on one of Smith's shoulders for congratulations.

"Very well done. This river feeds wells for a hundred miles along the banks, the water then traveling, spreading out." Weiber-Krauss reached for his words, "Like the disease it now carries. And the shotgun wound? This is so evidently Bishop's killing. His fault, so there's the perfection in the planning. You should be proud of what we've accomplished."

"You always make the speech, the folderol."

Weiber-Krauss shook his head. "You hear so much but understand so little," he said with an edge of contempt.

Smith ignored the rebuke, distracted as Avery moaned from the hearse. He was crammed between two corpses, trying to move. His neck was freshly bandaged, and hands tied with a scrap of leather from his own stable. At the wrist, so as not to reopen the self-inflicted wound.

"The fat one," Smith said. "*I understand* that we have to act."

"There's much to do to prepare him, and the

others are strictly for chum—*kumpel*—but we'll find use for them," Weiber-Krauss said. "Now then. Let's get you fed, get you paid."

Smith coiled his bullwhip. "Do it the other way around."

Weiber-Krauss closed his eyes in assent. Smith wasn't learned but unlike the avaricious Avery, he wasn't entirely stupid.

CHAPTER FOUR
In Dark Memory

Summer midnight, and Bishop could tell when he'd crossed from that last piece of open grazing land to his own place. The heavy grass was painted with dabs of yellow wildflowers, creating a welcome-way that could be seen in the moon's scatters. Stalks of flowers marked the natural path to the blooming apple tree and the tombstone beneath it.

Bishop rode deliberately, eyes down, but following the path from the falling-down rubble of his old well, to where the smokehouse used to be, and then, the tree he'd planted on his first anniversary. The tall bay was already eating an apple from the ground before Bishop had climbed down and stood before his wife's carved name. He let his arm drop, touched the familiar lines and curves. A name, more permanent than flesh. Memories, ephemeral, also more enduring than the person who made them. How did the world make any sense? A man could not know everything, but Bishop wished he had read more philosophy, literature, understood psychology like some men he had met.

The stone was white marble that he'd promised to turn into an outdoor table, but in six months had only beveled the edges, which Amaryllis claimed to love but wondered if it would be ready for her birthday. The cutter had done a good job finishing, carving her name and their son's like her own handwriting, even the date of their deaths.

Bishop took in what he needed to see: the stone, the trees, and the charred ruins of their house. An empty door frame to a destroyed bedroom. Chimney and fireplace, with an iron kettle still hanging. Deader than his brother to him.

He started from his reverie as a finger of hot orange whipped past him, followed by another. There was no sound, just flecks of fire.

Additional sparks blew over his shoulder from behind; Bishop turned, locking the rig on a rider approaching on a scrub pony. He was a dark figure, sporting a flat-brimmed lawman's hat and holding a torch before him, spitting cinders. Bishop rolled his shoulders, setting the trigger lines.

The rider got closer, smiled without showing any teeth, and said, "First time that special's ever been pointed at me," then took off his hat.

Bishop did not change his stance.

"It ain't a good feeling, I'll tell ya," the rider said. "If you don't recall me, maybe you'll recall my hip. You built half of it."

Bishop lowered the rig. "Miles Duffin."

"Doctor Bishop," Duffin said, swinging from his pony, holding the torch, wind beating its flame.

He shook Bishop's left hand. "It's been a fair few years since Paradise, and I don't recall properly thanking you for making sure I could walk out of there."

"You were the law," Bishop said. "Good law. You earned it."

"Not that anybody knew it."

"You did me a hell of a favor," Bishop said in earnest. "That's thanks enough for any doctoring."

Duffin was closer now, and his pumpkin face, with dimples and forever-mussed hair, reminded Bishop that he'd always looked like a ten-year-old who'd strapped on Daddy's gun belt to play sheriff.

Duffin shook the round head as though he couldn't believe life himself. "A shavetail and near-cripple, but I overcame, and am now, if you can believe it, a marshal. Working out of Fort Collins."

"Not a social call," Bishop said knowingly. He eyed the restraint cuffs dangling from the marshal's wide belt.

"Your name came up in a dispatch, and I asked to be the one to find you. And here we are."

"Simple as that. Hunting me down?"

Duffin smiled like an embarrassed schoolboy. "No, no. I was hoping for a true reunion, maybe a meal someplace."

"Oh, a *meal*," Bishop snorted. "Not chow, not grub—"

"You're a famous fellow, Doc," Duffin said with a crooked grin. "*You* earned a good steak. At the fort, they can't believe you operated on my hip." He added as an afterthought, "I don't have a warrant or anything."

"I suppose you got a reason though?"

Duffin nodded.

The double-barrel was down by Bishop's side again, the trigger lines slack, but he didn't like where the conversation was going. This could be about what happened in Avery's place, but the sheriff-mayor had already cleared him. Even the commanding officer at the fort would have reached the same conclusion. Bishop could feel the muscles in his back, and down his neck, tighten, the rig shifting, as if the mechanics were reacting to his instincts before he could.

"I apologize for doing this on your wife's birthday, but that's how come I knew you'd be here," Duffin said, shifting from foot to foot, favoring the leg Bishop had not operated on. "I read you always made this trip on this day, and I surely understand."

Bishop, who hadn't taken a step from the tombstone, said, "Cold as hell out here, Miles. I'm cold and you're dancing."

"Yeah, let's finish up here." Duffin held out the torch. "You mind?"

Bishop took the torch in his left, as Duffin pulled a rolled document from his saddlebag, unfurled, and presented it to catch the firelight. Dog-eared with torn edges, it was covered with purple-inked drawings, diagrams, and specifications.

"Doctor, this drawing yours? I'd hate to be in error."

Bishop looked it over. "You're not."

Duffin shook his head. "Well, I can't make it out, not a bit. What's all this for?"

"It describes a kind of mask and outfit to wear in areas that've been mass-infected," Bishop told him. "Yellow fever, any kind of pox."

"Well, I guess a doctor's no good if he's sicker than

the patient," Duffin said, still boyish. "It looks like some kind of diver's suit. Ever build one?"

"Presented the plans to my commanding officer; he rejected them without looking," Bishop said. "When I settled in practice, I played with the idea, but that's all. Where did you get these, Miles? It's been years."

Duffin rolled the plans. "If I saw that riding toward me, I don't know if I'd believe my eyes. If I was a kid, I'd be scared to death. Probably soil my britches."

"I'm still confused," Bishop said after a moment. "You accusing me of something?"

Duffin took a stance before Bishop, now favoring his rebuilt hip, his attitude changed in the torchlight, speaking and holding himself like a veteran lawman, not to be challenged. He regarded Bishop for a moment, with eyes that seemed to have suddenly aged, suddenly seen more.

"I'm doing my job," he said, "and seeking your professional opinion, if you choose to give it."

Bishop nodded.

The rig stayed angled downward, but Duffin glanced over his shoulder at the double-barrel before flipping open a saddlebag, with, "I have this here."

Duffin reached in and held up what looked like the small globe to an oil lamp, with a fluted neck curving into a bulb-shaped base. The base was shattered, and a tag declaring the globe OFFICIAL PROPERTY OF MARSHAL DUFFIN hung from its side.

"Looks like a grenade, but made out of a special glass," Duffin said. "Our doc at the fort, he's not as good as you, melted some of it down, said it had wax mixed in."

Bishop planted the torch in the ground beside the

gravestone, took the tube, examined it in the firelight. "There are traces along the bottom."

"That's maybe so it wouldn't break until it was thrown," Duffin said. "I mean, if you had a bunch in a sack or something you wouldn't want them knocking around and cracking."

Bishop held out the broken globe. "Looks like a Harden Fire Extinguish grenade."

"Almost, but something different inside. Smash it against a tree, shoot at it, open it up. That one was cleaned out real well, but there was blood in the bulb, and our doc said it was crawling with smallpox."

Bishop had a feeling it was something like that. "And?"

"It's being used to attack the tribes."

Bishop crushed the tube. "Go to hell. You really believe I'd have something to do with this?"

"Oh I'm sure not," Duffin said. "But you're not the only one who invents whatchamacallits. There's a lot more of these things, Doc, and you know the man that made 'em."

White Fox didn't hold back her painted mare as it ran full-out along the cut trail, to the mountain's base. The pine trees were a constant, steady wall on either side, and she angled her body below branches, ducking and holding tight, as the painted galloped . . . tight to the trees, hooves barely touching ground. Muscled speed.

Even as the sun had dropped, she kept the painted moving. Staying low to its back and neck, her legs braced around its middle, racing through the dark.

The painted leaped a small ravine, landed hard

but kept running, without breaking stride. White Fox, battle shield across her shoulders, made sure that Bishop's medical kit was still lashed behind her saddle. The kit slipped in its ropes, and she could hear the rattle of empty medicine bottles and scalpels jangling inside, blades colliding with amber and cobalt glass.

White Fox slowed the painted as the ground dropped off toward the edge of a muddy stream. They followed the dipping hill to the water, the field kit tilting to one side and its lid hanging open. Scalpels scattered to the ground.

The painted drank and cooled down, as White Fox pulled the battle clubs from her saddlebags and hung them on her belt, careful with the gun-metal blades, before pulling the knotted ropes tight around the medical kit, securing it.

As the horse rested a moment, White Fox's delicate finger traced Bishop's name and army medical seal painted on the lid. Gold flake chipped off at her touch, small pieces falling away. The flake stayed on White Fox's fingertips, the lettering on the insignia now all but gone, leaving only a smudge of lines and slashes where John Bishop's name and rank had been.

She thought back, the memory vivid—

"So, do you think John Bishop's '*Hávêsévemâh-ta'sóoma*'?"

It was the week before when Miles Duffin had asked White Fox the question, impressing her with his pronunciation. He'd crouched beside her in the tepee, warmed by the low fire, as White Fox and a Cheyenne widow, who called herself Wooden Leg, tended to the little girl, who was now lying on the only bed, wrapped in the only blanket.

Duffin pressed, but with his always-smile. "Do you think so?"

"What about *your* thinking?" White Fox said. "You must believe this, or you wouldn't be here. I have not seen you in—"

Duffin picked up, "Three summers?"

"Don't say it that way, you sound like a fool," White Fox said, not even looking at Duffin. "*I* was going to say three years, by your calendar."

Rebuked to momentary silence, Duffin watched as the child's fever compresses were changed. Wooden Leg peeled off the dried, stained pieces of cloth from the girl's body, dropping them into bowls of water that were thin-cracked along the sides and repaired with painted mud. The rest of the tepee was also damaged. Support poles snapped, the bison hide covering the slit like an open throat. Battle shields and clubs were torn from the walls, and in a heap under smashed medicine jars and shredded poultice sacks. Littered scraps. The ruins of a life, though the lives refused to be ruined.

White Fox soaked some cleaner linen strips, then laid them across the girl's head and upper arms, to absorb the fever-heat.

Duffin said, "Three years, that's how long you've been here, working your medicine?"

"That is how you see it?"

"I don't understand—?"

"Do you know anything?" White Fox interrupted. "I haven't been here three years because they keep moving us. Men like you. Or worse," White Fox said. "There was a constable here."

"Firecrow," Duffin said. "I know him. Angry. That's why I figured you'd want to deal with me."

"We don't 'deal' with anyone," White Fox said. "Policies and those who execute them change like the seasons. All that matters to me in the world right now is this child."

"I understand," Duffin said, hoping she believed him. He meant it. The marshal put a hand under the girl's jaw, feeling her temperature. "What's her name?"

White Fox did not answer, not immediately. Wooden Leg, face an ageless mask, and framed by black and steel-gray braids to her waist, finally spoke, using sign language. She brought her hands together, fingers forming a bird's wings and tail, before making a swooping motion.

The fire threw the hand shadows around them.

"Her name is 'Migisi.' The Eagle," White Fox said. "Wooden Leg knew the child. Her parents, dead in a raid. She doesn't trust you."

"I understand that too," Duffin said.

White Fox said "Migisi" down around the little girl's ears, letting her hear it over and over, and then the girl said her name back. In a quiet, almost-gone whisper.

Wooden Leg mixed tea with the last bit of quinine from Bishop's medical kit. White Fox lifted the tea to Migisi's mouth. "I haven't seen John Bishop since your town, Paradise."

Duffin nodded. "A lot of dead left behind."

"Migisi, open your eyes," White Fox said to the girl, taking hold of her hand. To Duffin, "That was the last of Bishop's medicine. We've been attacked by those in fear. What they couldn't steal was destroyed. Many of them are dead too. They run. Collapse from fever. Even kill each other."

"All this brought by the attacks, this demon, or whatever the heck you want to call it," Duffin said.

"Listen, there's more to the fort dispatch than I can tell you, but you're going to have to come with me, one way or the other."

Wooden Leg covered her mouth with her hand, two fingers pointing outward.

She had called him a liar. Duffin knew the sign.

"No, ma'am," he said. "White Fox is coming. I'm not playing a game."

White Fox looked to him, his hand absently moving near his gun, and Duffin was now exactly what she imagined: a "man of the law" who'd slaughter them without taking a second breath.

"You are the messenger of the ignorant," White Fox said as she stroked the side of the girl's face. "'*Hávêsévemâhta'sóoma*' is the child's word for what she saw," White Fox said. "I learned your language from the poetry of Mr. Edgar Poe. If he were writing of this demon, it would have told about more than a being. It would have been about the fever. About you being here. It would have been the spirit of everything wrong."

"White Fox, I don't understand what you're talking about," Duffin admitted. "Look, I'll see you get medicine from the fort. I'll help you in any way I can. But you *will* be with me when I ride out to Bishop's place."

Migisi didn't thrash or scream under the caress of White Fox, but held her hands as tight as she could until White Fox had to separate from her grip. Wooden Leg took the girl's hands, then covered them with her own before nodding to White Fox. Giving her permission to go.

White Fox said to Duffin, "I will come, messenger, but on my own. Not as a prisoner. You see that you keep your word about medicine. As for Doctor Bishop, I will make my own mind up. Do you agree?"

Duffin's mouth registered dissatisfaction. But that was pride talking. He knew he could trust White Fox.

He removed his hand from his holster and agreed with a single nod.

There was not a moment of the meeting that White Fox had forgotten. She put it from her mind as she brought the painted down from the back side of the trail, slowing her pace, still undecided about John Bishop. But ready to confront Duffin about the medicines from the fort and getting them back to the Cheyenne camp.

She was riding over a path she'd known for years, one that she'd run bloody-barefoot, escaping her drunken husband. Now she was on the painted, coming up on the old Bishop place with a different purpose, making her way through a split in a broken fence, stepping over the fallen rails. Then stopping. Cold. The painted snorted.

White Fox sat up straight, stretching against the saddle, sharp eyes watching figures at a distance, moving behind the burned remains of the farmhouse's chimney and fireplace.

They didn't speak, and the deep shadows made it impossible to tell their age or anything else about them. They were just there. Three in black, with guns, staying low and crouched, backs to the charred stone. Not looking at each other. All appeared to have two arms.

White Fox threw a leg from the painted, dropping into the tall grass, making no sound, and pulling the battle shield from across her shoulders. She moved down the grade, stopping behind a deep gathering of Apache plumes that formed a tangled wall of shrubbery.

The three hadn't made a move. But beyond them, searching the darkness, White Fox could see Bishop and Duffin by the tombstone, torch planted, as Bishop dropped the glass bulb in front of him, then smashed it with his heel.

"Go to hell. You really believe I'd have something to do with this?"

"Oh I'm sure not," Duffin said. "But you're not the only one who invents whatchamacallits. There's a lot more of these things, Doc, and you know the man that made 'em."

"I know you, too, Marshal," Bishop shot back. "Does that make me a lawman?"

"Ain't the point, and it ain't all," Duffin said. "There's a man cut in half with your shotgun. Found in the river and filled with this disease, accordin' to our medic. I just want to hear your side of how it all happened."

"What man are you talking about? What river?"

"You in a shooting at the Good Fortune Hospitality House?"

"I was a target," Bishop said. "Target shot back."

Their voices were distant across the open landscape, their words echoing to nothing after they spoke, lost in the miles of silence. Seemingly alone. At least, to them.

White Fox had unhooked the tomahawk from the harness on her saddle, her eyes never leaving the back of the house. She felt the short-bladed weapon's weight, how the handle laid in her palm, getting used to it again, while still only looking dead ahead. One of the figures moved around the side of the house, the other two taking positions behind burned timbers with guns raised. Staying to the dark, blending into shadows, and still silent.

White Fox angled her body forward, targeting.

She saw Duffin step to Bishop, his silver Colt out from its holster, but still low. Bishop's rig snapped into place also, just as one of the figures at the side of the house lifted a Winchester, slow-chambering the bullet with his hands covering the hammer action to mask the sound.

White Fox recognized the trick from his movements, but Bishop and Duffin were locked on each other and didn't hear or sense the figure's presence.

The battle shield was now mounted at White Fox's elbow, and she held the tomahawk out from her side, the handle aligned straight along her arm, fingers tight. Ready to release.

Winchester stepped from his cover, rifle at his shoulder.

White Fox hurled the tomahawk, the handle spinning, blade slicing the air before cleaving his head from behind—a pumpkin falling apart in a red geyser. Dead fingers spasm-shot the Winchester into the fireplace stones. A muzzle flash, then ricochet, as the shots reported back. Gunfire, reaction, and gunfire echo. All happening within heartbeats.

Simultaneous action, as—

White Fox ran for the painted.

Bishop turned at the blast from the Winchester, rig up, barrels leveled, as two shadows moved from the side of the house, shooting. Bullets striking the headstone, screaming against the white marble. Sparks. Bishop dropped to a knee, firing the first barrel, then the second. Slugs still streaming around him. Roar of power from the rig, and both thrown off their feet by the buckshot. Landing doubled-over bloody into the grass, as—

White Fox swung the horse around, charged from the hill, riding hard for the corpse of the first gunman. She leaned out of the saddle, her body angled to the ground. She grabbed the war club from his skull, bringing it up bloody, then galloped for the old well.

Bullets tore at Duffin, fired from the dark. The marshal took cover by the apple tree and returned fire. Shooting at movement. At shadows. White Fox leaped in front of him. He followed her motion, grabbing the torch and throwing it toward the well. Shedding fire as it arced, throwing off orange, showing up the figures and lighting the ground beneath them.

White Fox and the painted, the torch's fire spreading out as wings behind them, leaped over the old well, landing on the other side of the rubble. Smashing with the club end of the tomahawk. Once, then twice. Two more guns charged from the dark, even as the torch landed behind them, setting the grass on fire.

Small flames. Growing. Showing their silhouettes.

Bishop moved on them, shooting. Both barrels. Reloading as the silhouettes were hurled backward. Puppets with cut strings, hitting the ground as flailing arms and legs.

One was still trying to shoot, bringing up a pistol. Firing up at White Fox on the painted. Dying aim. White Fox reared back, bringing the horse down on the outlaw. Hooves into chest. Bones splitting. He screamed, but with no voice. An open mouth, and muscles moving in his throat. Silence, as he slashed at the painted with a long knife, the horse jumping back, and the outlaw rolling from beneath. Standing, a Buntline special out of his long coat.

White Fox smashed him with the shield, then brought the war-blade down, his blood spitting back. But he didn't react. Only grabbed for her, pulling her wild from the saddle, smashing her to the ground, a heavy foot on her vulnerable chest.

He pressed the pistol between her eyes, with that silent, maniacal laugh. Bishop shot. Through his back, blowing out his chest. The outlaw spun on his feet, not dropping the gun. He dropped to his knees, still laughing. Shooting where he was facing now, low to the ground, striking the tombstone. The gun continued to fire in his dead finger even as he fell on top of it, flashes exploding under his body, then dying.

Bishop was steady, with the rig aimed and no slack in the trigger lines. The last gunman's mouth curled open, and he raised his pistol before the shotgun blast opened him up completely, into the dewy grass and mud beside White Fox, blood bubbling from his mouth and nose as if it were boiling out of him.

Bishop shucked the spent shells, watching them land at his feet, as White Fox rubbed her hands across the painted, checking the slash before taking him by his war bridle and walking him back.

Bishop stood by his wife's grave marble, his shoulders slack, smoke still drifting from the down-turned rig. In a moment, he was before her carved name, some of the letters marred but still legible. He used his sleeve to wipe away the blood staining it.

Bishop said over his shoulder, "You going to arrest us for this, for all what's happened?"

The deflated Duffin found a place against the apple tree and caught his breath. "Come on, Doc. This was a battle brought to us. You don't charge murder in a battle."

"Like in Good Fortune," Bishop said.

Duffin deserved that and he knew it. He looked down, then over to watch White Fox, leading the painted over. He turned, looked to Bishop, then down to the red pouring from his own leg. Soaking the ground.

Duffin pulled at the edge of his pants, hiking them over to see the bullet wound just above his knee, open and scorched by black powder. He clenched his eyes with, "Sweet Jesus, I didn't even feel it this time."

"Nerves go numb, sometimes. You'll feel it."

"Okay, Doc. But you still have to answer for the other things we talked about."

"Sure, Miles."

As Bishop turned away, Duffin collapsed.

The field medical kit was open, the surgical knives laid out on their leather apron, protecting them from the wet grass, and beside the shotgun rig and ammunition. Bishop and White Fox had Duffin under the shoulders, pulling him forward to straighten his wounded leg.

White Fox took the miniature oil lamp from the kit and lit it, a waft of black smoke churning, then curling from its chimney, before the flame settled and lit the operating area around the apple tree. The horses chewed quietly to one side, and beyond the fall of the light, in bleak anonymity, were the bodies of the attackers. The still lay twisted in the grass, and by the foundation of the old farmhouse, where they fell.

Bishop ignored all as White Fox held the light for him, and he worked through the medical kit with his one hand, picking up empty bottles, saying, "There's almost nothing here. You've been busy."

"The medicine you left is long gone," White Fox said unapologetically.

"You haven't done any surgery?"

"I've done what I've had to do," White Fox said.

Bishop regarded her for a moment, holding the light, the halo cast showing up a face that was more beautiful now because of its experience. He let that thought go, pulling out a roll of surgical thread and unwrapping a small pack of wax paper around two small brass hinges, connected with an adjustable screw.

Bishop said, "You're going to have to be my hands, like before."

"But better now, I think."

Bishop grinned to himself, gave a little smile of encouragement, then attached a small magnifying glass to the edge of the oil lamp, bringing it to him like a monocle on its own, hinged arm. White Fox held the lamp over Duffin's leg as Bishop examined it through the glass, the flesh-tears of the wound large in his vision, and the smashed, torn edge of the bullet visible just beneath the first layer of muscle above his knee.

Bishop said, "It's not swimming, so that's good, but God knows what we'll get when it's removed."

White Fox put down the lamp and threaded the only suture needle, Bishop saying, "I always liked my design for this lamp. One of the best things I ever came up with."

"Those are always your words," White Fox said. "'One of the best.' Even about that."

"I love my work," he said dryly.

She cocked her head toward the rig, put the suture on the lid of the kit as Bishop fixed the brass clamps to the wound, opening the flesh more and pulling back muscle to access the slug. He chose a short-blade surgical knife from the few in the leather sleeve.

White Fox angled the light from the lamp, finally putting it on top of the headstone, with Bishop nodding his approval, before he cut into Duffin's leg. Blood spurted, and White Fox grabbed hold of the slug with a pair of tongs, as Bishop held the artery tight, slowly closing it. Ebbing the flow. White Fox leaned in and began stitching.

"Closer together, and don't pull too tight," Bishop said. "You know what I've taught you."

"I'm better when you are not watching."

"Miles will be better if I do," Bishop said.

He meant that as a challenge, not an insult, and White Fox responded as he knew she would. She adjusted her touch, bringing the suture to the edge of the wound, lacing it together, then said, "I also know what I've learned. You can move that now."

Bishop said, "This was a great thing in the field."

He released the clamp with his one hand, pulling it away as White Fox finished sewing around the wound, using smaller pulls for the stitching, and saying, "You compared what I did to beading. Once. You are lucky I didn't have an ax."

"For the surgery or for my scalp?"

White Fox answered, "I'm civilized. Remember?"

Bishop said, "I remember, and I apologize."

White Fox shrugged but let herself have the

moment. And the relief. The surgery had taken less than an hour, but the night was almost done and the sky was breaking apart. She lowered the flame on the lamp as Bishop wiped the instruments clean, packed them back into his medical kit, precisely, and with care.

He paused, noting the worn-away gold of the army insignia across the lid, and what was left of his fractured name.

"My past life in a box," Bishop said. "It could belong to anyone now."

White Fox thought about the name and the flaked gold and said, "No. It is yours only."

"These sons of bitches aren't going to stay here and foul my land."

Bishop had rolled two of the bodies onto a ragged blanket, and White Fox picked up the other end, and they hauled them, like a travois, across the grass to the edge of a small gulley. Bishop pushed them down the hill, watching the bodies roll.

Neither he nor White Fox said a word. Just kept on with their work.

The last of the bodies was the thin scarecrow, his face still locked in a grin, lips pulled back across wide, yellow teeth in his silent laugh. Bishop turned his head to one side, seeing the extended and inflated veins, slashes of purple and blue bruising down his throat, surrounded by puncture marks from a hypodermic needle. That's how he'd kept laughing after his lungs were mostly gone.

Bishop said, "It's a new world of addiction," and

rolled him into the gulley, his body landing on top of the other corpses.

The coffee they brewed in the pot from Duffin's pack tasted like rust, but it was the only hot food Bishop had had in days, and he topped his off with some of Avery's whiskey, what little was left. He and White Fox had kept watch on Duffin through the dawn hours, building a fire next to him. Bishop thought of digging a grave for the men he'd left to rot, or be eaten by coyotes, but decided that was for someone else. Anyone else.

Duffin stirred. Opened his eyes, and immediately shut them again, wincing in pain. Bishop held out a cup that was more bourbon than coffee, with, "We're down to bones and scraps, literally, but I think we saved your leg."

Duffin sipped greedily. "Again."

"Again."

Duffin held out the cup. "I'm always thanking you, Doc. That just seems to be the way it is between us."

"Frankly, that's a relief for me. God knows, I've had it the other way too many times."

"But not with repeaters like me," Duffin observed.

"No," Bishop agreed.

"Can you fetch me my saddlebag?"

White Fox rose and took the bag from Duffin's horse, hefting it with her arm and feeling its weight. Her expression was dark when she set the bag down in the grass beside him, and he reached in for the army Colt.

"I saw you took off my holster," Duffin said, "and if I asked for it, you would've known what I had to say."

"I know you," Bishop said. "I knew what you were going to say after 'thanks.'"

Duffin had the pistol resting across his chest, aimed directly at Bishop's face. "Your rig and that bandolier, put them in my saddlebags," he said, then looked at White Fox. "And miss, I want all your knives too. And I think I saw a tommy hatchet."

There was a moment when no one moved. None of the three was sure why. Then Bishop reached for the shotgun, but White Fox had it first, held it up, and pushed it into Duffin's leather pouch. She then packed in the ammunition, took the sawed-tooth battle club from her belt, and looped it around the bag's metal catch so it would hang.

"Now, that's more than good," Duffin said. "I know this is a crazy situation, and I'm feeling halfway dead, but I'm going to do my job. And you both will ride with me."

Bishop glanced toward the gully, then looked back at the injured man. "You're damned lucky the right outlaws won."

CHAPTER FIVE

Blood and Ashes

"You're riding back into your own history," Duffin said. "How's that feel?"

Bishop's response: "How's the leg feel?"

"Like hell—"

Duffin had his answer and the words dropped off, pain scorching him as it did whenever the horse swayed a little off-center. A moment, then a recovering, holding on, his gun tucked into his belt and cushioned by his belly. Riding between Bishop and White Fox, he was keeping a few paces behind, watching their backs and moves.

"That Hospitality House, that news was sent over telegraph," Duffin said.

Bishop nodded. "That would be Avery, wanting to make the most of it."

Duffin said, "It surely came from him, but the commander didn't really care. Not his jurisdiction."

"I figured."

"No," Duffin said. "That had nothing to do with anything."

"You showed me your reason for coming, Miles."

"I guess I did," Duffin said, sucking in cool air as pain hit him again.

"Sorry we have nothing to give you," Bishop said.

"It's okay. It's okay. A few seconds, the burning passes."

The marshal marshaled his thoughts as best he could. "All right—now miss, do you happen to know what your husband was trying to do in these trees?"

Duffin was now looking up at the lengths of barbed wire in the pine tops; hundreds of jagged feet strung between dead limbs like the web of a giant insect. Long sections hung from split branches, and had been anchored to railroad spikes hammered into the trunks, bleeding the trees of sap and killing them. The entire thing, taken as one, looked like a dragon had come here to die.

"Was he planning to string telegraph wire, or what?" Duffin wondered.

Bishop said, "More like 'what.' The spikes were so the lout could rest his gun, have his drinks, and shoot steady from anyplace in these trees. Those were his turrets."

Duffin considered that. "Sounds like my grandpa's drunk logic. I guess that's one way to fight off an ambush. He was surely expecting somebody."

"Who the hell knows?" Bishop said.

"I haven't been on this road in years," White Fox said.

"Well, somebody has been," Duffin said. "Somebody's been here to do business in the last weeks. There's still a few tracks." He pointed to a spot along the side of the worn section of plain that passed for a road. Someone had tried to not leave tracks. There were flattened grasses and broken twigs.

"Business?" Bishop said, more to himself than to Duffin.

"Again, miss," Duffin said. "What do you think your husband was up to with his—what would you call them? Experiments?"

"I don't know," White Fox said.

Bishop was trying to read the feeling in White Fox's black eyes. "You know, Miles, nothing personal, but you're making me sorry we didn't let you bleed to death back there."

"I'm meaning no offense, Doctor. I truly am not."

Bishop pursed his lips, then said, "I'm sure of that. But it's being given just the same."

Miles rode up a few paces so he could address the woman in quiet earnest. "I *am* sorry. I am simply trying to get information. Information that will help a lot of souls."

"Do what you must," White Fox said flatly.

"Miss, there's no need to—"

The horses pulled up suddenly, stepped backward. Reacting urgently with a head twist. Before them, mostly concealed in a patch of high grasses, an insect-eaten pine, massive, decades-old, had been dropped to block the last turns in the dirt road, branches and trunk stretching completely across from ditch to ditch.

White Fox faced Duffin, who was to her left, while still on the painted's back. Then she dropped off, saying, "I have said I will help do what you need done. But you have the way of a mole, digging, digging, and I do not like it."

As Bishop looked over admiringly, she took the reins of Duffin's horse and walked it in, stepping over branches, smashing some down, then around the last of the tree, while kicking broken chains and large pieces of dead iron out of the way. More barbed wire was hidden within the branches, to slice anyone trying to move them, and pieces of hammered steel stuck out of the road's muddy edges as jagged teeth.

Clearing the obstacles, encountered by chance, White Fox handed Duffin back his horse. She looked up at him hotly. "So you understand it, because you say you need to understand it, that wire, all that iron from years ago, was to stop me trying to run away."

The three rode the last mile near-rubbing shoulders, tense and silent. Two were displeased with how things had gone. Bishop had expected it.

The other tall pines along this stretch, the ones that hadn't been strangled by barbed wire, were scorched to the roots, becoming something more than dead trees, but like rows of standing, dead men. Stripped husks for bodies, burned limbs now twisted arms, ending with branches that had become claws. All of it covered by white ash, the blowing remains of a recent forest fire.

"I know it's hogwash, but riding by these woods gives me the chills," Duffin said, trying to be conversational as he shook water from his canteen. "I imagine this place was a nightmare even before the fire."

"It was," Bishop said. "The kind that daylight doesn't dispel."

"Like a bad fairy tale."

"They're all bad," Bishop said, thinking back to when he'd read them to his boy. "Else they'd be boring."

If Duffin heard, the meaning didn't register. "Miss, how old were you when you came to live here?"

White Fox rode for a moment, then answered Duffin. "My fourteenth birthday. My father traded me for a freight wagon loaded with fruit trees and four cases of rifles. He wanted those guns."

"I wouldn't blame you your reaction," Duffin said, "but *did* you burn these woods?"

Bishop answered. "She did not. But she held your knee together while we pulled out that bullet."

Duffin sounded exasperated. "Doc, you fixed me better than anyone could, and not for the first time, and I'll say that to whoever'll listen. But you both have something around your necks, and my commander tells me it could kill a lot of people. Maybe already has."

"You're dancing again."

"Yes, sir. And on more than half a leg, thanks to you. But—"

"To me, a *man* is dancing," Bishop said. He wanted to make it clear the surgery hadn't created a social bond between them. "It could be any man I fixed. It happened to be you. I believe in helping when I can. I believe in protecting myself when I am left no choice. Take that as gospel—otherwise, I mind my own business. This witch hunt of yours, it's a waste of all our time."

"What would not be a waste, Doc? Tell me that."

"Looking at a bigger map than just the fort's interests," Bishop said. "Let's assume that your affairs and mine intersect. It's possible, maybe even likely. Who wanted me dead back there?"

Duffin angled his horse around a wide, spreading puddle of ruined water, top thick with floating oil. "I do not know who in hell attacked us, did not recognize them when we rode past. I know a lot of the outlaws running between these borders, I've seen the wanteds, and it wasn't any of them."

Bishop said, "I wish I could believe it's just more of the goddamn fools that come after me these days. Someone who read those damn magazines and knows my habits."

"But you don't."

"With pox in glass jars? In my backyard? There's a whole country they could have attacked. Why here? And I have to ask myself who they were waiting for—me or you?"

"Why me?" Duffin asked.

"Exactly," Bishop said. "I wouldn't've gone to the fort without you. Maybe someone doesn't want me there."

Duffin considered all of this between flashes of pain.

"They didn't seem to know White Fox was coming, was there," Duffin said.

"That was apparent," Bishop agreed. "We're lucky she was."

Duffin regarded her. "Thank you."

White Fox dipped her forehead—or it might just have been the gait of the painted that caused it. Or she might have been smelling the lingering scent of burned everything—to her, not death, not destruction, but the odor and taste and gray ruin that is the price of liberation.

"You two decorated the ground with them like you've been doing battle together since you were born," Duffin said. "Does that come naturally?"

"Did killing, to you?" Bishop asked.

"No."

"Then maybe you weren't properly motivated," Bishop observed.

"Why do you say all this, Marshal?" White Fox asked intemperately. "Why keep talking endlessly?"

"Because whatever's happening to your people, the reason you and the doc are racking up bodies like cordwood, started here," Duffin said. "With the man who beat the hell out of you until you stabbed him."

"What are you talking about?" Bishop asked. "White Fox killed the bastard. And before you open your jaw, two things you should know about that: it was self-defense and good riddance."

White Fox added, "I did it . . . I don't regret it."

"Actually, you didn't kill him," Duffin said.

The marshal was spit-roast between the gaze of the two riders athwart.

"That a surprise to you?" Duffin asked, too coyly.

This made White Fox wheel and face him, lock eyes with Duffin, who was pleased he had struck a nerve. He fiddled to keep his leg straight off his saddle.

"You better keep talkin'," Bishop said. "She don't need a knife to kill you. Just a stick up your horse's ass."

Duffin fell back a few paces without realizing he'd done so. He caught up.

"He lived after you knifed him, kept working on all sorts of weapons, for all sorts of folks," Duffin said. "At his old place . . . where we're going."

Duffin gave the two a moment to digest the information. "He is the same lout what built your arm-rig, right, Doc?"

Bishop nodded. "He had a twisted, creative bent."

"And now you two are together."

"You don't have to tell me my life story—and I don't appreciate the innuendo."

"I wasn't suggesting anything. What I mean is, would that bend him more? He survived a murder attempt by his wife—justified, yes, I'm sure—and then he hears about you and your gun becoming famous, about you riding around with his woman, and things get a little dark in his brain."

"Do you have any idea where he is?" White Fox asked.

"Do you?" Duffin asked.

"She just said she thought he was dead," Bishop said. "You saw."

"That's why I was so insistent about you joining us. I was hoping you could tell me more about him. Or at least point in some direction."

She shook her head.

"He shouldn't be difficult to find," Bishop said. "His handiwork is not exactly subtle."

Duffin was silent.

Duffin took a scouting lead of a quarter mile, brought his horse to the dirt road's widening, letting Bishop and White Fox catch up their few yards. This was the last of the road before the small house in the cutout of dead trees. White Fox put her eyes anywhere else. Scattered around, old bolts and nail heads were acorns, making a trail to a large pile of rusting iron, and beyond it, another heap of old metal. Bent, torn, and surrounding the house.

And there was more.

Tons stacked and corroding. Wagon frames and a blown-apart locomotive boiler were the big pieces, leaning against a back wall, reaching above the roof, caving part of it in. Cannon parts and slag steel were pushed to the sides of the house, also piled high, so the place seemed to have grown out of the wastes of forged metal, heaped together, and rust-bleeding.

Ash from the forest fire covered it all with a thin layer of white, turning the grounds the color of a corpse.

Duffin stopped and waited for the others.

"Just as we knew it. Nothing alive at all," Bishop said.

"I didn't say there would be," Duffin said. "The report from the unit that came out here had 'dead' or 'death' a lot."

White Fox turned her head from the shack. Defiant, she kept her hands on the painted's mane, stroking it more to calm herself, as Duffin threw out: "Do you want to stay behind?"

She shook her head.

"She's probably thinking about all the times he almost killed her," Bishop said, riding nearer to the marshal. "When I set her broken bones, or stitched up her head. Or trying to forget all of it."

"Either way, you did a good job, Doc. Let's go in."

He angled himself from the saddle, bringing his injured leg over, then struggled down. White Fox was off the painted and courageously came forward, lent a shoulder getting Duffin to the ground. He balanced against her, then grabbed a saddle fender to hold on, straightening himself. Grunting effort.

Bishop said, "This woman is special. Don't ever forget that."

White Fox said, "Wait," then pulled a piece of a wagon axle from a scrap heap. Part of a brake handle, long, with a curved, bolted edge. White Fox clamped

Duffin's hand over the top of it, her fingers completely over his, squeezing.

She said, "He broke his leg once, used this for his cane. You should use it too."

"As always, miss, I'm obliged for your concern and thoughtfulness."

She examined it. "He tried to beat me with it . . . tried."

White Fox took several steps away from the house, turning her back, as Bishop and Duffin, leg dragging, made their way around the metal heaps to the front porch. Bishop steered Duffin from a small, open pit, with stacks of barrel bands, ends sharpened to razor-points, lining the bottom.

"Traps everywhere," Duffin said. "Miss, your father has his place set up the same way, don't he? That's what I've read about, anyway."

White Fox was back at the painted, checking the horse's slash wound with her light touch, as Bishop answered for her.

"The Cheyenne didn't need a white lunatic to tell them how to rig traps," he said. "And there's a vital difference. White Claw built his snares and pitfalls to keep marauders out. These were made to keep someone in."

"Well, Doc, it didn't work either way," Duffin said, pulling a bandanna from his pocket, tying a knot, and presenting it. "You're going to need that."

"I could tell," Bishop said, accepting it and working it on with his one hand. "What else did your men find that needed 'dead' or 'death'?"

"A moment," Duffin said.

But the doctor knew the smell; a heavy decay that found its way to the bottom of his throat and settled there. This time it wasn't mixed with battlefield sulfur and black powder smoke; instead the rot in the air was the sweet, rancid taste of disease. He pulled the bandanna over his face.

Bishop observed clinically, "These rags aren't enough."

He lit a torch from a tar barrel, letting the black smoke clear the stench for a few breaths, before standing in front of the house's hard-leather door. Duffin wiped his eyes on the bandanna, then pushed the door open with the piece of scrap iron, a rush of flies bursting around them, before they stepped in.

The front room was the whole house, with stove in the corner and beds on the opposite side. Rats scuttled as Duffin and Bishop came farther in, the torch throwing yellow across the caved-in floor, not holding the weight of the metal trash, corn-whiskey jars, and infested furniture. Windows were boarded, with iron plates stacked against them, murdering all sunlight; no way to tell day from night.

Duffin said, "Like a bear's cave, isn't it?"

"He didn't believe in clocks or calendars, so White Fox wouldn't know how long she'd been kept."

"You knew this man damn well."

"That's no secret."

Duffin kicked brass fittings across the floor, hitting the toe of Bishop's boots. They clanged dully. "Those all look like parts for something he'd build for you," Duffin said.

Bishop scooped some up with his one hand. "Again, no secret." He let them drop noisily. "So this was where you got my drawing?"

"He's got more of your plans, and a diary of all the work he did for you," Duffin informed him.

"We worked on inventions to fight disease and disaster," Bishop said.

"I know. Something to breathe through smoke; a special saw you figured up, cuts through a man's chest and holds the ribs open at the same time so you can get to the heart. Never heard of a sawbones using anything like that. And all your special helmets and suits, to seal you off from the diseased while you give out medicine. Very fancy, Doc, and more than this son of a bitch could've come up with on his own."

"Again, all medical instruments."

Duffin said, "Yeah, but now being used for something else." He dragged himself around another heap of brass pipes, scraps of steel, to half a rifle stock, lying in a corner with strips of tied canvas dangling from it. Bishop held the torch to light the room. Duffin lifted the stock with, "What was this, the first try for your rig? Doesn't look like it would work too well."

Bishop said, "Marshal, this man made the first shotgun for me, and I doctored his child bride, and that's what there was to that. This is the closest place to mine, and where I ended up the night after my family was taken from me and I was left for dead. In all the stories, that's the one true thing about ever printed."

"I've certainly pursued it a few times," Duffin remarked. "Did you really tell the miss how to operate on your arm, stay awake through it?"

"I passed out once or twice," Bishop confessed, growing impatient. "What the hell has that got to do with this?"

"Because of a dying man killed with your gun,"

Duffin said. "Or one like it. Because we got a letter at the fort, were told to come here, and this place was laid out with evidence against you. Indian camps being attacked, and they're using your inventions to do it . . . little kids describing them exactly. Or as exactly as the language allows—'demons.' They've targeted the Northern tribes and they're spreading disease with those grenades, made here. There's a crate out back, and we found notes on how infections can turn into epidemics. Your notes, Doc."

Bishop fired back: "You know how many men died of epidemics along the front line, instead of by artillery? Both sides? There were headlines about it for months after Appomattox. Did you bother to read those?"

Duffin said, "Doc, we're not ready to accuse you of anything."

"I don't care what you do or don't do, you're missing the point by years. Want to stop a sickness, figure out how it works. If he had any of those old notes from me, they were about prevention. My writings when I was healing up. That's all."

"That's not the point. The point is that everything here's connected to you one way or the other. Every damn last thing. Weren't you just the one to tell me to look at a bigger map? Well, here it is."

"But every name on that map is John Bishop, and I'm telling you that's wrong."

"I hope so," Duffin said. "Maybe I even believe so, I'm no judge. I'm just the law sent to find you, to get you here, to let you look around, and I wanted to do it." Duffin leaned against the shattered-belly stove, resting his leg, the bandanna still over his mouth and nose. "I made it clear as I could, you and the miss had something hangin' around your necks. Well, this is it. Throw a light on that curtain."

Duffin grabbed hold of a curtain made from a bedsheet, hung on a length of rope to shield a small pantry.

Bishop said, "Yeah, White Fox put that up herself."

"I figured. Is the old blood yours, or hers? There's newer along the bottom, I think belongs to the husband."

Duffin yanked back the curtain, took a step, holding on to the axle, a hand clamped over his covered mouth. Almost losing balance, he choked back a rush of air thick with rot as they stood before the blacksmith.

"That's the bed you recouped in?"

Bishop shrugged. "A little different then."

The blacksmith's empty sockets were the first thing seen; the torch throwing shadows and cinders into the spaces where the eyes should be. The face was drawn back, wax-paper skin tight to the skull, with a mouth gorged by a mocking, black-swollen tongue.

The body was lashed to two iron crossbars leaning against the wall behind a metal bed, as if he'd been staked to the ground. Arms and legs were spread wide, and tied to the iron with leather thongs. The flesh of the wrists and ankles had been ripped away by his struggling, leaving only raw bone and flies that had stuck to it and died there.

"Sending a hell of a message," Duffin said. "Just like a Cheyenne raiding party'd do it. Or a Cheyenne wife who was sick to death of this scalawag."

"It may mean nothing," Bishop said. "They got a sense of humor."

"Maybe," Duffin agreed. "I'm thinking, though, that whoever did this knows how to point a finger."

"At?"

"Take a look under there."

Duffin held the torch as Bishop bent down, reaching under the bed for a burlap sack that had been put into a metal pan, filled with putrid water. Insects crawled.

Bishop said, "Give me your knife."

Duffin gave it a thought, then drew the knife from his hip sheath, handed it to Bishop, who handled it like a scalpel, careful not to touch the burlap or the metal pan. He used the tip to open the top of the sack, slitting it, before looking inside.

An old man, smiling, was looking up at him from the sack, steeped in liquid decay. Flesh peeling from a skull, and tufts of brittle hair. It was the kind of grotesquery, Bishop thought, the lurid dreadfuls never in all their dirty imagination got right.

"A pointed finger," Bishop said, and took Duffin by the arm. "You want to die for all this?"

White Fox was still by her painted, eyes away from the shack until Duffin and Bishop threw aside the leather door, stepped into the sun, and pulled away their bandannas, drinking fresh air. Duffin balanced himself on the scrap-metal cane, planted the torch in the mud, as Bishop charged Duffin's horse, flipped open his saddlebag, and pulled out the rig.

Duffin called out, "Hold on, Doc, you don't need that!"

"The hell I don't. You said it yourself, everything in that slaughterhouse points to us, and I'm not going to stand idle while being blamed for the worst crime there is. And you let that rot go on!"

"We got two murders here," Duffin said. "And no idea who that old man is."

"It doesn't matter!" Bishop protested. "Don't you see? Those bodies are there to spread infection. Even the flies are dead. That contaminated bloody water? What could breed out of there? And you've seen these goddamn glass grenades, loaded with disease, and you let this all pass. You didn't even move the bodies to clean it up."

"There was a risk, but I had to see your reaction, Doc, what you'd do. And White Fox's, too, when I asked about her husband."

"We pass your exam?"

White Fox had Bishop's right arm through the harness, tightening, and he was fitting the cup over his right, locking it into place below the elbow.

"What was it?" she asked. "In there?"

"Death, laid at my feet." Bishop's dark eyes sought her questioning ones. The doctor confirmed, "He was one of them."

"How?" she asked. "Experimenting?"

Bishop shook his head. "This was not self-inflicted."

"Good," White Fox replied.

Duffin was openly uncertain about what to do next. His expression was resolutely set on "Stop him" but his body was languid with "How?" After a minute of contemplation, Duffin moved from the porch, hobbled around the edge of the open pit. He was in a neutral state now. "Someone's going to a lot of bother to get you hung, Doctor. Or at least hunted down. Thoughts on that?"

"Yeah." Bishop was tight-lacing the bandolier with,

"Willing to start an epidemic makes them lower than horseshit."

"I mean about naming you—"

"Not now," Bishop said. "I'll face down whoever, or whatever, I have to, but something's got to be done here. If this is still an active site . . . that bucket gets tossed into a water hole . . . goddamn, you understand what that could mean?"

Duffin was choosing his words. "I goddamn do."

Bishop kicked over the tar barrel, the liquid rolling out spattering the porch, slopping against the wood and old steel. He smashed a window with the double-barrel, reached through the glass, and grabbed two oil lanterns from a pile of stacked junk. Bishop threw both against the porch, shattering them and letting their oil run to the floor, mixing with the tar puddles.

Bishop said, "Let's see how it burns. Clean it to the ground."

Duffin protested weakly, "We get everything we need in there?"

"I don't care," Bishop said. "This place gets shut down."

He picked the last of the torches, a broken ax handle, from the emptying tar barrel, pulling it out of the thick black, and lit it with the torch Duffin left burning. The two flames burst together.

Duffin limped closer, lay a hand on Bishop's arm. "Booby traps," he said. "The man was a master, you said so yourself."

"And you saw yourself, he was not subtle. He wanted to kill us; we'd've stepped on a charge under a plank, blown up in a doorway. Tripped a wire that lit up a cannon. Fallen in a barbwire net or had one fall on us."

Duffin released the arm.

Bishop looked to the marshal, the rig locked downward, and said, "You're the law, and this house, those bodies, are an unknown danger to the territory. Any evidence in there—how long will you take to find it versus the risk? And a blaze—any living evidence in there, someone we mighta missed, it'll flush him out."

"What about after?"

"We hunt, starting here."

"After that," Duffin clarified. "There'll be a trial, a jury trial, a hanging for *someone*." The pronoun was vague but the look pinned the charge on Bishop.

"I don't care if it clears or convicts me, this place has to go," Bishop said. He added, "And how do you know it'll be a hanging?"

"Eh?"

"Military men get a firing squad."

The implication was surprising and daunting to the young officer. He stood dumbly trying to mentally expand the scope of this thing, whatever it was.

"Now, Marshal," the doctor said. "Do your duty."

Duffin regarded Bishop. "Your rules. Help or survive."

"This is both. Burn it. I can't. Makes me look guilty."

Duffin hesitated, still. There was too much to contemplate.

"Dammit." Bishop did not waste time with further debate. He held the ax handle, its tar burning, and faced White Fox. She took the torch, bringing all of her strength back from her shoulder, and sent it careening through the front door, setting the oil streaks on fire. Bishop dropped the second onto the rest of the spattered oil and pools of tar. Hot orange and yellow sprung up, small bits of flame growing, then spreading across the wood and crawling through the stacks of iron to more wood beneath them.

Bishop shouldered Duffin away, and the three stood by their horses, the place burning before them. Now, White Fox wouldn't turn away, as the porch and frame were eaten, piles of metal collapsing into the fire, sending plumes of flames, wild sparks, and thick, oil smoke into the air.

For this moment, White Fox stood motionless. The heat scorching the air around her, she stayed with eyes fixed, as if making sure it was all truly burning into nothing. She was on the wrong side of him; Bishop wished he had an arm to put around her at that moment.

Black-powder ammunition, stacked behind the back walls, exploded in the flames, throwing steel and iron pieces that crashed back into the fire, splitting more wood, collapsing more of the house.

White Fox and Bishop backed away, held their horses, and turned the animals away from the heat and smoke, which rose, arching over them like a hellish rainbow. They were shielding their mouths with fabric when the first gunshot rang from a hilltop behind them, above the smoke. The air was alive with burning noise, and the occasional big drum boom of ordnance, but this was a high-caliber weapon, and its sound was thunder.

Duffin drew his pistol, looking up, balancing himself and trying to see. Anything. Through the blowing smoke. There was a second muzzle flash. Distant, but a bolt of white in the gray-black.

During the interim, Bishop had started moving to the edge of the road, facing the burned trees, the rig moving, locking into place, as he extended his arm shoulder height. He aimed, shooting into the smoke just below the second flash, and to the center. A gut shot, if it hit. He waited a moment for any return sound; a man screamed, loud enough to be heard over the roof collapsing.

CHAPTER SIX
The Confederate Sailor

Just a few minutes earlier, Cavanaugh had been watching as much as he could from the hillside. He had been sitting, legs ahead, on a slope of rock, elbows hugging his sides for support as he adjusted the brass focus ring of the Broadhurst spyglass, clearing his sight line through the burned trees and to the blacksmith's shack. Then he lowered the metal tube. He'd targeted what he needed to see. Taking a cigarette from a silver case in the coat of his old gray uniform, he lit it, cupping his hands to hide the flame, then propped the spyglass against a hip of his extended legs, right next to a Colt's Dragoon pistol. Both within instant reach of hands as familiar with both as if they were body parts.

His back pressed against a cropping of moss-covered rocks, Cavanaugh twisted his marionette body around, bending as if his joints were loose springs and old leather, extending his neck and head and looking over the edge of the small rise. He watched White Fox salve the cuts on the painted's sides, thinking for a moment he'd wish she was doing the same to him. Not her especially . . . any woman.

He shook it off, murmuring as he always did, "Son, them thoughts is why you never made the grade. Why you never saved a penny of any nation."

He kept the cigarette between his lips, drawing deep, and rubbing his temples with his eyes closed. Thinking about the mission. His orders. Getting it all clear in his head.

Cavanaugh sat up straight, chest-buttoned his Confederate Navy long coat with the lieutenant's braids, smoothing the front and pulling at the cuffs to even them, then picked up the telescope. He focused on Bishop and Duffin stepping from the house; small figures tearing away their bandannas, and with their mouths flapping silently.

Cavanaugh grinned, easy and lopsided.

Bishop raised his voice from below, the words echoing against the rocks around Cavanaugh's ears. The puppet-like figure retrieved the spyglass, stood up halfway, hunkered into his bony hips. The spyglass focused on Bishop, now taking the rig from the saddlebags.

"Ho," was all the former Confederate officer said, the word a cross between an exhalation and speech. The weapon was as formidable as the magazine drawings depicted.

Cavanaugh moved forward toward the ledge, crouching, and reached for the Dragoon. He stopped. Still watching through the spyglass. The torches were lit. Watching, hammer on the Dragoon being cocked back. Torches thrown.

Cavanaugh retracted the glass, letting it drop into

one of his coat's deep pockets. He held the pistol down out by his side, in a near-formal stance, eyes still on the shack below, watching the fire and waiting for its smoke to cover his position.

Oil and powder exploded in a flash, though the boom came a heartbeat after. He felt the heat.

The smell of the burning followed quickly, wind-borne, then the choking, rolling black. Cavanaugh had a window of opportunity before it grew too thick. He raised the pistol and fired toward the treetops. A flock of birds broke. He couldn't really see, so he waited. The tar smoke was a roiling ocean and blocking him from below. He turned away, lungs hot, to catch his breath. Got it, stood, saw a break in the black sea, and shot again, aiming at the shack.

Just as the shotgun barrels flamed directly at him.

The echoing crack and the blast of iron pellets struck simultaneously. Cavanaugh howled louder than all the sound around, staggering on independently functioning marionette-legs to the far side of the ledge, then diving down a small grade, tumbling forward. He landed on his feet, though not upright. He used a nearby rock for support getting up. His boots were filling with blood when he limped onto the road. There were trees here, sloping downward, and he literally stumbled from one to the next to the next, hitting an ugly, painful *oof* before dropping, knees into the dirt and hands up as figures approached. In a moment he found himself before the double-barrel rig and Duffin's Colt.

"This is full sur*ren*der *gen*tlemen!" he said as if it were a single word. Breath didn't come easy. The men didn't move. He spoke again, with effort. "I've been *shot.* I'm *giv*ing. Myself *up*. To my *bet*ters."

Cavanaugh's words were gurgled with the mellow residue of a Chesapeake waterfront accent, stressed with new pain. Even kneeling and stooped over, he was taller than most, and his head seemed larger than a bison's; mismatched pieces sewn together, shocks of thick, prematurely gray fur.

The pie-faced boy came forward cautiously. Too slowly. Cavanaugh fought to keep from twisting and falling to his side.

One hand up, one hand lowering slowly, the one-time Rebel called, "Look there!"

Heaved by its polished grip, the Dragoon landed in the mud at Bishop's feet. Duffin stopped as though waiting for it to discharge on its own.

"There are . . . there are . . . a handful . . . .44 balls . . . pocket. And . . . a cigarette if . . . you wouldn't mind? Already rolled. May I?"

"Don't move." Duffin came forward again.

Hands back up, waving long, thin arms, Cavanaugh said, "That's an ex*pen*sive weapon . . . that you boys . . . know well. I wouldn't be . . . giving it *up* . . . if *I* wasn't giving *up*."

Cavanaugh fell forward from the effort and loss of blood. He was conscious enough and gentleman enough not to want to lie on his face in the dirt. He twisted his jointed body at the waist to put the weight of his torso on one arm. He was still able to look at the men if he rolled his eyes toward his forehead.

Bishop put his foot over the pistol, staying in the center of the road with Duffin. Cavanaugh kept his smile, but was watching the inescapable gun barrels facing him, eyes darting between them and White Fox, the war ax angled at her hip. Behind the three, the shack was flames . . . orange, and yellow, and crawling blue. No wood or metal now, just an outline of fire. The smoke still churned overhead, but the air was clear enough down here.

"This is quite a *thing* . . . I'm seeing," Cavanaugh said, changing his focus, wiping the sweat from his face on the sleeve that wasn't under him. "It's like . . . a biblical vision . . . you three. You could make your own army."

"I'm a territorial marshal," Duffin said. "Why did you shoot at us?"

"Too far . . . to . . . shout."

Duffin didn't believe that, but he let it go. The man was wounded, perhaps mortally; the marshal did not want to come away from this encounter empty-handed. "I want your name and everything about you."

"First . . . like I said . . . I'm the fella who knows . . . when he's been beat."

Bishop, who had been looking at the man's right boot, smirked mirthlessly. "That's too easy. A Trojan horse."

Cavanaugh's brow arched admiringly. "A scholar."

"Who are you?" Duffin repeated, standing over the man.

"I am . . . the gentleman . . . you've been looking for," Cavanaugh said. "I'm part of the crew . . . what set Doctor Bishop here . . . up for the raid on the Indian camps . . . and all the rest that's gone with it."

White Fox tied the painted to a tree, moved forward as if to check the man's wound, but Bishop stopped her with his human arm.

Bishop kicked the Dragoon aside and took another step. Cavanaugh saw the lines from the triggers, going back along Bishop's arms like nerves, tense as Bishop moved, his eyes narrowing.

Bishop said, "Explain yourself."

"See," he said to Duffin, his voice weakening into loud whispers, "now *there's* . . . an executioner. Who wouldn't . . . believe him . . . capable of . . . terrible things?" Cavanaugh couldn't look away from the rig as he spoke. "You could . . . kill me now, Doctor . . . and I personally . . . would not . . . put any blame on you. You're a stranger to me . . . and this was about nothing but cash."

"So you *were* shooting to kill," Duffin said.

Bishop demanded, "Who paid you?"

Cavanaugh nodded toward the flames. "That one, burnin' up right now. Said you stole . . . his wife . . . his home . . . his life."

"I took his home," White Fox said.

"His words . . . ma'am. I didn't listen too much . . . after he paid . . . just let him prattle on."

Duffin said, "Tell me what you did to frame this man."

Cavanaugh struggled to rise on a stiff arm, but it caved at the elbow and he thudded to the ground, kicking up dust. "Aw . . . hell." The Confederate looked at Bishop. "The blacksmith . . . he gave us special equipment he said . . . was yours." He breathed for a moment. "We attacked some Cheyenne camps . . . some Arapahoe . . . and soaked 'em down with . . . bottles of blood . . . if you can believe it. Like some . . . unholy . . . conse*cra*tion. Other stuff too . . . we spread . . . globes . . . all carrying disease."

"You knew what you were doing?" Duffin said with disgust.

The man did something with his upraised shoulder that resembled a shrug. "Indians . . . sorry, ma'am . . . don't mean nothin' to me. Money . . . in the rubble where I live . . . is everything." He snickered, winced from pain. "This smell . . . I know . . . too well."

White Fox scissor-stepped around Bishop's arm toward Cavanaugh. This time Bishop did not arrest her.

She moved over to the pistol in Duffin's hand, which hadn't moved a fraction of an inch. Her brown eyes were bottled fury as she glared down at the Rebel.

"You're wearing a Confederate Navy uniform," Duffin said. "From?"

"South Ca'lina," Cavanaugh said. "Poor . . . ruined . . . Charleston. I consider myself . . . a man of the sea . . . but lean times bring . . . desperate measures. This came up . . . so we took it."

"You're just full of lost causes," Bishop said. "Who is 'we'?"

White Fox moved an arm. In a moment she was turning the ax handle over in her palm.

Cavanaugh, watching her, said, "My men . . . the ones that you took care of . . . this morning. Dumb clods . . . the lot of 'em. You got it right . . . lost causes. I don't think there's any left . . . is there?"

"Lost causes or men?" Bishop asked.

"Not men," White Fox answered. "They are all dead."

"So . . . she can speak," Cavanaugh said.

She spit at him. "That too."

"You must be quite a package, dear . . . because . . .

there're a lot of dead men . . . on account of you . . . and your rat-crazy husband."

"Dead husband," Bishop said.

"Dead." Cavanaugh's watery eyes shifted to the rubble behind them. "And . . . cremated."

White Fox had the ax, slightly behind her hip, ready to throw, her face giving away nothing.

Bishop said to Cavanaugh, "There are a lot of dead Cheyenne women and children. They're just lying in the plains. Carrion. Yes?"

"Maybe. Like I said . . . they don't mean nothing to me." He blew out what he'd been holding in his lungs to speak. "Can I . . . try to . . . stand?"

"If you can do it on your own," Bishop said.

Duffin nodded in accord, and Cavanaugh began moving his four limbs. He made a hash of the actions, ungainly shifts and bends, but using every joint at his disposal, including the stiff knee-high boots for support, he got his feet under him and rose like a ghost from a grave, slowly and in waves. The red splotch in his center was actually comprised of several smaller holes, scattershot that had merged. Finally standing, albeit lopsided to the left, a complement to Duffin listing to the right, he towered, grinning, over the marshal. Breathing came a little easier, at least. There was no ugly raling.

Duffin adjusted the aim of the Colt at the center of Cavanaugh's chest, almost pressing the gun into him . . . wanting to slash the chronic smug set from Cavanaugh's face with the barrel sight but holding back.

Cavanaugh looked down at Duffin, like a parent at

a child. "So you're . . . the law . . . to whom I'm . . . turning myself in?"

"Which I don't quite buy either," the marshal said.

Cavanaugh shrugged the same shoulder as previously. "Rather do this . . . then get chased down . . . bleeding out. Don't know the country . . . well enough . . . and better to spend the time I got left . . . with some hot food and a bed. Before the big day."

Duffin said, "You're making this too awful easy."

"My old pap always said . . . I was born to be hung. Who am I . . . to cross him up?"

"Why did he say that?" Bishop wondered.

Cavanaugh looked at him. "Because . . . everything I did . . . was a lost cause."

Bishop kept the rig steady as Duffin locked restraint cuffs on Cavanaugh, the metal cutting his bony wrists.

Cavanaugh winced. "Tight enough for you, Marshal?"

Duffin said, "You surrendered. These're a part of that."

"Don't worry . . . I'm not going nowhere," the prisoner said. "A couple of the doctor's . . . shotgun pellets . . . also bit my right toes . . . maybe taking a piece of one off."

Bishop said, "There's blood on the front of the sole. Saw it before. Pressure stopped the bleeding."

Cavanaugh tried to whistle, mostly sprayed spit. "You *are* as good . . . as they say."

Duffin cocked a head toward the ruin. "Walk."

"My nag's . . . on the other side of that hill . . . unless we're going to ride double."

"I'll get it," White Fox said.

Duffin thanked her with a nod though she didn't move, yet. The marshal looked to Bishop.

"I have to take this man in, find out if any of this flapdoodle makes sense. But we also have an understanding, you 'n' me. You're under arrest."

"I want to find out what he knows too," Bishop pointed out.

White Fox stepped in. "And me?" she asked.

"I have to ask that you come along," Duffin said. "'Cause of your relation to and knowledge of the deceased."

"You say the sickness started here, in this house," she said. "All right, so you found out what you needed to. I came as I said I would. I will remain with the doctor. But you promised me medicine, and I gave my word we would have a doctor who knew the best cures. We did not know such sicknesses before. You brought them, but we will die faster. I'm not going to throw away my people because they've been exposed. We need someone who knows the treatments. You're keeping your word to me, Marshal, so I can keep my word to them. After the cure, I don't care what happens to me."

Bishop regarded Duffin. "There is an urgency, like she says."

"I saw the little girl, I am aware," he said. "But nothing can happen without first going to the fort. All orders will issue from there."

Cavanaugh said, "You don't need to be doin' anything . . . with these two good folks. I'm the fella . . . and I'll say it a hundred times if need be. Tell everything . . . you ever needed to know."

"The fort," Duffin repeated. "That's where we all need to go, regardless."

"The trading post," Bishop countered. "That is where the medicine is."

"But you will need an order requisitioning it."

"We will be there when you send it, and White Fox will be ready to move out," Bishop said. "I will come to the fort and shc will follow."

The doctor looked at her for confirmation. She gave it.

"Your oaths," Duffin said, as though it was a bad deal in the making.

"Did you even need to ask?" Bishop said.

"I will get the horse," White Fox told him. "We must hurry."

"I will . . . do my best . . . to keep up," Cavanaugh said.

"No," she said. "Bishop and I go ahead, quickly."

Duffin was about to protest but stopped himself as he considered the odds. Right now it was three-against-one. If he turned on them it would still be three-against-one . . . but the wrong way.

"I will keep you company," Cavanaugh said. "I promise."

"Oh you're going to ride beside me, all right," Duffin said. "Draw one breath I don't like, I'll kill you."

"Marshal," Cavanaugh said, and near-laughed, "I swear to believe you, but you still look like my baby cousin in short pants."

Bishop shook his head. "Don't test him."

"This little fella, he'd kill me quick?"

Duffin corrected him. "It wouldn't be quick."

Bishop looked to White Fox, who was walking to

the painted, hooking the ax back onto her belt. She gathered the reins around her fist and brought herself into the saddle, her back always to the men, the single braid to the waist tied off in blue. She galloped away to retrieve the Confederate's mount.

Behind her, the last burst of fire and smoke from the wreckage as she brought her painted around, starting back down the dirt road, and away.

CHAPTER SEVEN
The Traders

They were miles out, Bishop and White Fox, taking a long slope through a field of tall flowers, riding quickly to its edge, then slowing, and following a small creek. They'd ridden mostly in silence, exchanging only a few words, with White Fox not looking at him.

She did not have to. Her set profile told the epilogue to the story Bishop knew well.

Bishop, forward in his saddle, the rig in its special sling, noted the brightness of the day and the sweet smell of the air, which he needed to fill his lungs to recover from the night before.

"You never have to go back to that shack again," Bishop said earnestly.

White Fox nodded. "Now it's just a grave. A monument to evil."

Bishop could not help but flash to the paper monument Avery had constructed in Good Fortune. That was a monument to evil as well, in a way; but not the same. Bishop did not believe his own heart was as black as that of the blacksmith. And yet they had both been driven to their acts by the loss of a loved one, however grotesquely that love was expressed in the case of White Fox. Bishop knew in his soul that the two were different. But how? That was bitterly elusive. Maybe there was value in Duffin's way, taking things piece by piece, one step at a time. This way, the thought was once again too big for Bishop's own learning to put in any kind of context.

"Part of not going back is to let the memory die too," the doctor said. Only when he heard it did he realize he'd said it aloud.

"We are beings of spirit simply having a human experience," White Fox said. "Spirit and memory do not die. Just bodies." She looked at him, finally. "But the bodies of the young must be saved."

"That is my priority," Bishop said. "You people have been thanking me for what I have been able to do, but—this is different. By God, this is my past come to haunt me."

"Haunt you?"

"I always feared this. Disease on a grand scale. I saw it in the war. We lost more people to sickness than to injury. One to the other to the other to doctors to nurses back to patients. Illness moving indiscriminately from Yankee to Rebel. It is why I sought other means to cure. And then . . . Beaudine. Devlin. They turned me from what mattered."

"You can go back."

"How? I would always think of the workshop I just destroyed. The perversion of everything good."

"Don't think like that, for my sake," White Fox said.

"I need you to doctor. You must be able to draw on everything you know."

"Of course," he said. "But I just left a man bleeding back there."

"To hurry and help people who deserve your help. He was shot because of money."

"You always think the reason for killing makes a difference," Bishop said.

"It does."

Bishop shook his head. "I helped Confederates during the war too. My job was healing. *Was.* I'm executing by my actions or inactions."

"You were also, lieutenant, a warrior. As am I. Neither by choice. You must live like a wolf or an eagle. You hunt, you care for your nest or pack, you kill or you nurture, depending on what is before you." She looked at him. "Instinct. That is your guiding star."

White Fox rode on, and Bishop couldn't find his next words. He kept the reins drawn, drifting back from her a bit but staying to the edge of the creek, which was running clear, cold, and deep. He looked down to it, the water finding its own place, and let the cool drift against his face. He took another deep breath for more needed cleansing.

White Fox said, "The trading post's a half-day from here. I do not want to wait for the marshal."

"I had no intention of," Bishop said. "They will have everything we need and will sell it to me without trouble." He laughed, thinking of Avery's wall. "My credit will be good. If not, the rig will co-sign."

White Fox failed to see the humor in that. "The world is a rotting carcass and we are all maggots."

They continued for a mile, and Bishop broke the silence. "Is Edgar Allan Poe still in your saddlebag?"

White Fox looked back at him and said, "'The viol, the violet, and the vine. Resignedly beneath the sky, the melancholy waters lie.'"

Bishop said, "I don't know that one."

"'The City in the Sea,'" White Fox told him. "I've read it all year and I still cannot understand it."

"I don't think it's meant to be taken as a real place," Bishop suggested.

"That is clear," she said. "Real or not, I'd like to find that city someday."

Bishop was struck by the insight in that remark. "Some private place hidden from the world."

"Yes."

"That would be a fine thing." He thought back to his lost home, the tombstone where his wife was buried, their boy with her so he would not go alone into the afterlife. The voice of White Fox, her longing; this was the first time since he lost his family that the idea of home did not bring up bile.

They paused at the shores of a river. Bishop was nearer the shore, trying to lean out of his saddle for a taste of fresh water, the rig and sling fighting him, his hat just skimming the top of the running creek. "Well, these are melancholy waters."

White Fox, beside him, held out her hand without glancing at him. She knew where he was. He handed her the filled hat, she drank, he scooped the Stetson again, and then they rode on together. Hate for what the blacksmith had done to her rose but, as he drank, he swallowed it down.

He wondered, for the first time, if it were truly possible to heal.

* * *

Side by side, at long miles of right angle to the other two members of their party, Duffin and his prisoner rode at a reasonable pace toward the fort. The marshal had opened the Confederate's coat, stuffed it with the bandanna that smelled of corpse anyway, and buttoned the garment tight around the wound. The wounds weren't deep. That, and leaning forward in the saddlc, would keep him from bleeding out.

Cavanaugh said, "I know you're not really a young'un, but how'd you get to wear a marshal's badge? Your pap a lawman?"

"How's the belly?" Duffin asked.

"Holdin'," the Confederate replied. "I really want to know. I've seen things at sea. In other lands. I'm naturally curious."

"Actually, he was a minister. Retired now."

Cavanaugh howled; laughter starting painfully in his belly and traveling up, and out, in a high-pitched burst that shook the marionette limbs and threw his head to the sky. Duffin would have been insulted if he weren't busy watching his prisoner twist about in the saddle, as if it were a cover for some move to slip his cuffs. But Cavanaugh kept his hands in front of him, even lifting up his wrists to show Duffin, as his laugh became a quiet body-shake, then a dull ache from too much jiggling of the wound in his abdomen.

"How was that funny?" Duffin asked at length.

"The joke's on me," Cavanaugh answered. "*Your* daddy might not approve of your profession—"

"He was, is, fine with my choice."

"Then we got that in common. Seeing me in these bracelets would've made my old man proud as a puffed cock on egg-layin' day, all of 'em his."

Duffin was confused. "Prouder than when you joined the Rebel Navy?"

"Oh, I don't think he cared one bit for that. He was southern born, but only that. He wanted me to follow his profession. Housebreaker. He was a good burglar, made the papers as 'The Plague of Charleston,' got himself shot breaking into a church kitchen. But if he weren't in his grave, he'd raise a glass to my current situation. Believe me."

"I believe you," Duffin said. "And for what it's worth, you bested him might'ly."

Cavanaugh's lips pursed, then opened. "That I did."

They were angling their horses through a small break in the rocks that led to the main, cleared trail near the Sweetwater Fork—a small sloping of gray that gave way to a plush run of grass and a patch of blooming, full dogwoods. The surrounding greens becoming orange and tinged yellows, all leading to the river.

"You know this country, Marshal. I don't think I could've found this cut, even with a map."

Duffin kept his horse in pace with Cavanaugh, saying, "When you were a sailor, did you do any navigating?"

"Plenty," Cavanaugh said. "It all depends on what you're used to. I'm good at finding my way on the water. Stars at night, wind direction in the day, sextant when I had one, coastline whenever possible. Here? I could ride all day and into the next, it wouldn't make any difference. I'd just as likely end up where I started."

"So how did you end up here? I don't mean this place, I mean this 'profession'? You needed the money, you said."

"I did, and piracy—well, that's got too many people

already both for and agin'. Let's put it that the oceans led to the rivers."

Duffin's glance was sideways, and had the pistol aimed at Cavanaugh's spine. "That's not an answer."

"All right. Let's put it that after the war, the only job I could get was pulling lines on a riverboat. Met a gentleman who wanted to know all about ironclads. I had crewed one of the last . . . I understood his passion. Together we went looking for the remains of the submarine *Hunley*, and he paid to hear everything I could recall."

"You didn't find it?"

"Not a speck of her rust."

"You said 'gentleman,' a gambler?"

"Actually," Cavanaugh said—suddenly a gambler himself, drawing the word out as though he were laying a full house on the card table—"he's a doctor. Later, he hired me to push a broom at a sanitarium. It was honest work anyway."

"That's who's paying you now?" Duffin asked obliviously.

Cavanaugh said, "Indirectly," he answered. "I was working with the man you turned to ashes."

Duffin had the gun braced against his leg, pointed up at Cavanaugh's chest, or neck. He didn't care. "Remember what I said about you breathing wrong? That's what you're doing now."

Cavanaugh said, "See, Marshal, I think that's the pain talking. The gentleman doctor *I* know would fix up that leg."

Duffin said, "It's already been fixed."

"Doctor Bishop and his squaw, but did he give you anything for pain?"

"What he had in his kit, which wasn't much."

"My Lord, a doctor without tools, without medicines, without a goddamn arm." Cavanaugh laughed easy. "You know, since the war—"

Duffin said, "I'd tread lightly."

Cavanaugh extended his cuffed hands completely in front of him, palms up. "We're just having a talk. I'm still your prisoner, and I'm saying the world's turned upside-down, and you think it hasn't? Look at you. Leg paining, and the man that shot you, he was full of cocaine and morphine, and you could use either one. That's upside-down to me."

"How do you know who shot me?"

"He was one of the ones I rode in with," Cavanaugh told him.

"Who was he?" Duffin urged.

The Confederate sailor shrugged, again one-shouldered. "Names don't make a never-mind. Cannon fodder. They followed orders because none of 'em had their minds right anymore. You fail to notice they didn't make a sound? Even dying?"

"I was too busy surviving."

"See, that's where you and the doc—*your* doc—differ. He don't miss a thing. You ask, I bet he noticed. Cocaine and morphine needled directly into the voice box, maybe a little taste of laudanum. That's how they kept them from screaming in the crazy houses. The doctor—*my* doc—showed me. You never heard of any of this before?" Cavanaugh stopped his horse, mostly using his legs, looked to Duffin, grinning. "Marshal, I was right. Jesus wept, you're still in your short pants."

Duffin stopped, turned the horse when he was sure

of his seat, and aimed again at Cavanaugh's chest. Then the world turned red.

The whip slashed across Duffin's face, splitting his nose in half, peeling back, blood pouring over his mouth and chin and also splashing his vision. His horse reared back, legs chopping, as a lasso dropped around Duffin's shoulders, yanked tight, then catapulted him from the saddle.

Pulled into the air, Duffin landed on his back. Dazed. Bones unbroken, unless a rib or two had cracked, but the pistol lost in the grass and his leg felt like it was between a log and a saw blade.

Smith was stepping from the cover of the dogwoods, taking in the rope's slack, tightening the lasso, when Cavanaugh brought his horse around. "Where the hell have you been? I was running out of things to say to this asshole."

"Never happen. You were just changing tones, I heard it."

The bullwhip hanging around his neck, Smith coiled the lasso with his massive hands before hauling Duffin to his feet, saying, "You're not where you said you would be."

"Blame the preacher's son here. At least you found us. Where's the wagon?"

Smith said, "Over next rise," then fist-smashed Duffin in the temple. A single blow with the fleshy anvil, sending his head lolling forward and to the side, like a broken doll.

Cavanaugh said, "Easy, big man, you just near took his head off."

"It's what you always say."

Cavanaugh held out his hands. "What about these?"

"Knees," Smith said. "Get down onto them."

Cavanaugh swung one of his puppet-legs wide over the pommel and dismounted. He settled to his haunches, awkward moves, followed Smith's thick, pointing finger and placed his hands on top of a long, flat rock protecting a gopher hole. Smith stood over him, a wide-blade hatchet raised, and brought it furiously down. Metal sparked. Rock chips flew. The gopher rustled somewhere.

Cavanaugh yelped and stood, his cheek bleeding from a splinter of granite under the skin, the links to the cuffs nearly cut. Smith grabbed hold of Cavanaugh's wrists and pulled his thin arms away from each other like a huge wishbone, finally splitting the handcuff chain.

The former prisoner walked in circles, rotating his arms, working his joints back together. "Sweet Jesus on a crutch, son. You almost pulled me apart."

"Nah," Smith said, throwing Duffin facedown across his saddle. "You just didn't know you had the strength to beat the chain."

The Confederate found the cigarette he had wanted earlier, lit it, inhaled hard, then looked from Smith to Duffin to his horse. He swore he didn't know which was dumber.

It was shaping up to be a bad day, continuing.

The old woman outside the trading post looked as if she were made of clay, with brittle straw for hair, and eyes that were completely veiled by yellow cataracts. She sensed White Fox riding toward her, but didn't move from her place on the long sun-blanched bench next to the trading post door, as she hadn't moved for the previous twenty-five years. She nodded her head in greeting, hearing White Fox tying the horses to the single hitch rail.

White Fox nodded back, though she knew the woman to be blind. She noticed the bold red nose sniffing, tugging at wrinkles all around. The smell of the burned forest had come along for the ride. But that was not all White Fox noticed.

Bishop drew the rig from the saddle-sling and dropped to the dry ground, dust rising, before chambering two shells. His eyes were elsewhere as well.

White Fox knelt before the old woman, taking her hands and speaking in an almost-whisper of Northern Cheyenne. The woman smiled, her face breaking apart, while Bishop moved around the side of the post, noting that both of its windows were broken and their frames fire-blacked.

Bullet holes pocked the log and mud walls.

The old woman, her narrow eyes an opaque white, slipped her arms beneath the blanket that draped her, then came back with a flat-blade knife and a small, carved figure. The knife was a pounded iron edge, with no handle, and the figure, a perfect Cheyenne maiden that was cut from hard, red maple, with exquisite details decorating her dress and eyes.

She held out both, and White Fox reached for the carving, but the woman pulled it back, blindly slapping the iron knife in White Fox's hand instead.

White Fox looked at it, said to Bishop, "A sign left for others. She heard the leader say his name. It is Walter G. Dent."

Bishop went through the door first, letting his eyes adjust to the heavy smoke and flour dust that was the air of the place. He passed the dead-cold iron stove, walked to the main counter, and leaned across it like an old, familiar customer, calling: "Dent, greetings from the high country!"

No answer. Beside the counter was a gun case, glass sides gone, with only ghostly impressions of pistols left in its green felt lining, and not a single weapon. On the stock shelves, there were no airtights, just empty tins dumped with a pile of slashed flour sacks.

A single bison hide hung from a hook in the ceiling, the squeak from the support chain as it moved freely back and forth, the only sound. Something had recently collided with it, sent it spinning.

Bishop took a step from the counter, the broken glass from the gun case under his boots, blood spatter across the pieces. The brown hide was still moving, the chain crying. Back and forth.

White Fox was now through the door, grasped the hide and stopped it, the iron knife in her hand. Quiet. Bishop regarded her where she stood. Not moving. A jar of peaches rolled from a shelf, shattered on the floor. Bishop jerked his look to the counter, the rig swinging up from his waist. It was just the wood gave way, weakened by gunshot.

As in Avery's place, but longer ago, slugs had been fired from across the room, ripping the shelves. Wood splintering. Empty jars exploding. There was a creak that wasn't the bison.

Bishop dropped, pivoted, the double-barrel turning toward the movement on the far side of the trading post; what he'd caught from the corner of his eye was enough. He fired, not a killing shot. An outlaw screamed out, diving from behind a stove, blood striping his legs.

The gunman ran low, trying for the cover of some stacked crates. Trying to aim his drawn Colt. Bishop fired again, the thunder sending the first gunman spinning against a wall, his chest opened wide by buckshot and powder.

Bishop, holding his place, called out, "Whoever you are, I don't give a spit. We just want to do some business! We intend to. You want to get yourselves killed over that?"

A second gunman charged through the door, his arm instantly around White Fox's neck, pulling it back, knee into the small of her back. She strained, but without calling out. He pulled tighter and whispered a threat into her ear. He couldn't see over her chest. She used that, fitting the blade between her fingers, then, yanking her arm backward, jammed it into his thigh. To the bone.

The second gunman cried out. A howl. His grip went limp, then went away entirely. White Fox broke her stance, turning in place, and pulled the blade from the leg, then brought it up, all speed and force, through the bottom of his jaw and into his mouth, the knife point pricking the bottom of the gunman's tongue.

Blood geysered, filling his mouth and throat to overflowing. White Fox wiped a spot from her cheek. He collapsed, eyes surprise-wide, trying to comprehend as he hit the floor, unconscious and on the way to dead. White Fox clamped a foot over his throat. Silencing any last screams.

It was over in simultaneous moments; Bishop reloading, and two more guns diving from behind the main counter, firing. White Fox spun to the earthen floor, the slugs ripping the wall behind her, punching the corpse with the blade in his throat, moving its arms and legs herky-jerky.

More shots from behind shelves and around corners filled the room with smoke and noise, echoing, deafening. Bishop held to a far wall, not wanting to draw the fire toward the blind woman, the rig leveled and steady on the back door, the only other way out.

Five quick shots through the broken gun case from a back room brought Bishop up from his cover, turning his aim and firing. A third gunman was blown back against empty shelves, then lurched forward onto the case's metal and glass, landing hard on the sharp ruins.

The dead man's partner hit the back door, turning to lay cover fire, then running.

Bishop loaded shells from the bandolier, closed the breech with a quick move, then silently went for the front door, signaling White Fox to stay low with a gestured wave. He walked the opposite way from where the old woman was still serenely seated and stayed by the frame, shotgun gyroscoping from his shoulder, as he looked for a target beyond the horses tied at the rail.

There was nothing.

Bishop cocked his eyes toward the old woman, who let one hand drift out of her blanket and to the right. She had heard what he had failed to see. He shouldered the rig, stepped out and to the right.

"White Fox!" he called firmly, not a warning but a summons.

White Fox shut her eyes, calmed her breathing, before working the flat blade from under the gunman's jaw and pulling it free. She wiped the edge clean on the corpse's shirt, before following Bishop back into the bright noon.

The wagon was an old freighter, with dynamite fuse strung along its sides, wrapped around powder casks, and then connected to six-stick bundles at each corner. Additional dynamite was set on top of a barrel in the center of the medical supplies that loaded the wagon down, and Dent was braiding that fuse with the other pieces hanging from the tailgate.

A large bandage, soaked reddish brown, hastily applied, covered Dent's thick neck, and he didn't even glance at the feel of the Smith & Wesson jammed into his ribs by the last surviving gunman.

The new arrival was panting from the run, swore as much from momentary relief as fear. His back was to the no man's land he had just navigated.

Dent wrapped fuses, saying, "Who's left alive?"

Bishop stepped from the sun's glare, the double-barrel aimed directly. "You two are the last."

The last gunman turned with an expression of monkey-faced horror. Dent, sporting a bowler and waxed-up mustache, smiled at the silhouette and continued doing what he was doing.

"Doctor, you think being here changes anything? Make a move with that hardware, the wagon goes up. Don't make a move, wagon goes up. Want to guess what happens if I kill you and that bitch?"

"You just made a hell of a mistake," Bishop said.

"I think not," Dent replied. "I've been out here, waiting since we took the place, knowing you'd come." He cocked his head toward an arroyo. "Bodies're over there if you're interested. Four. I was the only one hit. Flesh wound. They just weren't prepared. Like my four, just now."

"We couldn't fight *that*!" the fourth gunman said, retrieving his gun but fearing to point it in the direction he was looking, at Bishop's rig.

White Fox was now at the edge of the trading post, standing under the long shadow from the roof's eve, keeping her hands down, with the knife hidden, aligned behind her wrist.

"Get off the wagon," Bishop ordered.

The gunman said, "Why, because she's killed some men?" He shrugged. "I've already been paid, took care of my kin."

"Boss?" the gunman said anxiously.

Dent ignored him. He looked from his work, swallowed in pain, then struck a sulfur head on his heel and touched it to the fuse. It sparked, then burned. The still-panting gunman didn't know if this was a bluff or if he should run, and if he ran if he could get far enough before the wagon blew up or he was shot or knifed by the man with the gun-arm or the Cheyenne, or maybe by Dent if he got annoyed. The gunman stayed, shaking.

"Won't be nothing but ashes in just a few breaths," Dent said, the sizzling of the fuse behind his words. "This is the job, making sure nobody gets their hands on what you want. Feel bad for this sack, though. He always wanted to dog-hump that one you brought. Got drunk, claimed she'd been coming to see him for years, but was now with a famous one. Guess that's you, ain't it?"

Bishop felt the double-barrel's weight, the tension from the trigger lines, not hearing, but watching the fuse burn across the wagon, toward the dynamite bundles. Then, with a quiet sound of sliced air, the blade whipped from White Fox into the gunman's shoulder, the one attached to the arm with the hand with the gun.

He squealed once when it went in, once when Bishop yanked it out, tossed it to Dent. "Cut it!"

The gunman brought his pistol up with his other hand but a shotgun blast from Bishop spread him across the dirt.

Dent flipped the knife so it faced Bishop. "Why?"

"Because you don't want to die."

The man had a long, narrow face that grew longer at the top as his brows arched, almost touching his hat. "Oh?"

"You didn't get that wound in a fight." He indicated the man's throat. "Someone cut you, along the jawline. To convince you to sit here and do this if your moron gang failed, which they weren't supposed to."

"You are guessing."

"I am not guessing about the basic yellow in your backbone," Bishop added pointedly. "You pissed on that rock"—he cocked his head to the left—"shat behind it. For a couple days, I'd say. You did not want to go to the outhouse back there, or anywhere near the place where bullets were sailing." He toed the soil. "Ants eatin' your crumbs. Too many to have gathered in just a day or even two."

Dent didn't move. Until he did what he was told and cut the fuse. The fire reached the end of the line and perished.

Bishop walked over, rig still alert, and pulled down the edge of Dent's bandage, stopping where it had stuck to the skin by clotting. It revealed a string of raw, ragged stitches along the front of his neck, slashed from one side of his jaw to the other. "Who cut your throat?"

Dent pain-swallowed. "Someone—someone who wanted to remind me of our business together."

Bishop lightly touched the stitching, taking back his fingers to check for blood on the tips. "Not the work of a surgeon." He stepped back, motioned Dent from the wagon. The man eased off. "Were you really going to blow yourself apart?"

"I guess I was. I'm pretty used up."

White Fox was walking over, her hatchet in hand.

"You let the old woman live," Bishop observed. "To warn us?"

"To warn you," he agreed. "And . . . I have a mother."

"So, a beau geste," Bishop said.

Dent held up his palms. "If you like."

Bishop said, "You were waiting for us? For me and White Fox?"

Dent adjusted against the wagon wheel. "We were told to. The papers are always full of how White Fox used to trade here, so they figured one or both of you would end up here, no matter what."

"Now the big one, Dent," Bishop said. "Who are you working for?"

"I don't know. I don't know a name. German. Good with a scalpel. Not so good with thread."

White Fox moved to Dent with, "This German did your doctoring?"

"His heart really wasn't in it," Dent said. He looked back. "Like mine, here."

Bishop pulled Dent to his feet with one strong hand, then shoved aside the crates in the back of the wagon, checking for labels. "Field kits, for doctors riding out to the reservations."

Dent said, "The blue crates, I think."

"We'll get you cleaned up," Bishop said. "Give you a drink you can swallow, then you can try to be a little more complete with your answers."

"Doctor Bishop—yes, I knew your name and I read about you, which is why I was dynamite-sitting here—I've told you much of all I know. We, this bunch, been here a few days, using up the one whore I got and all my corn liquor. We got paid to take the place and then wait. Then a fella showed with more money, and they paid me out for everything in the place. Weren't even going to go to the black market, just blow it up or burn it so it wouldn't reach them ailing tribes. They paid me to sit here, like this. I sent the cash home to my old mother in Littleton by post. Things haven't been the same since the Pike's Peak gold played out. That's all I know."

White Fox said, "They cut your throat."

"Yeah." Dent held his bandage with his hand. It was loose from everything he had done just now that wasn't sitting still. He swallowed painfully. "Wish you had your chance?"

"The way you helped rob my people makes you one of the worst men I've ever known," White Fox said. "If I wanted to end you, I would rub your skin raw with a stone, then cactus, everywhere, then take you to a salt flat to die."

Dent had paled under his sunburn. He turned from White Fox, breaking her gaze. Bishop pulled a blue crate from the buckboard and dropped it, splitting the sides. Rolled bandages and bottled medicines poured onto the bloody ground.

Bishop said, “I’m with White Fox. There’s a lot of help in this wagon you were going to destroy.”

“But I didn’t,” Dent said. “Hell, before they kilt—I don’t know his name, the owner.”

“Grant Foster,” White Fox said. “You killed Grant Foster. Who is where?”

Bishop told her. She gripped the hatchet harder.

“Jeb . . . Mr. Rawlins,” he corrected himself, “he told me he’s been here more than twenty years, and nobody trades no more. Land’s been picked clean by the railroad hunters, and the army moved the tribes, and I can’t live off the dog-eaters who’re left. You don’t think he would have taken a deal to get out of here clean, forever?”

“He got out of here clean, forever,” Bishop noted.

“All right, okay,” Dent said. “I’ve been a bad’n forever; they bought me and my gang, and I didn’t even get a name of who hired me or who I kilt,” Dent said, watching Bishop unpack bandages one-handed. “You’ve done the same, and for no reason other than to kill. Kind of makes me the better man, don’t it?”

“Don’t believe the crap you read.”

“You shot Leech, here.” Dent looked at the mess on the dirt.

“Before he could shoot,” Bishop said.

That ended that. Dent eyed the bandages covetously. “You still going to doctor me up proper, Doc?”

“Better than proper.” Bishop popped the cork on a bottle of iodine, gesturing to White Fox. She yanked the kerchief off, causing Dent to yelp, then to yelp louder as Bishop splashed the antiseptic across the crude stitching on Dent's cut throat, burning it clean. "Because you're going to send a wire to Marshal Duffin at Fort Collins about what happened here, that we've got the wagon and supplies to move with your help."

"I'm not going," Dent replied.

"You are," Bishop said. "Looks like you have an infection. It needs treating. They can't amputate a gangrened head."

Dent cried out as the burning went deeper . . . wiped tears on his shirtsleeve.

Bishop unwrapped a clean bandage, handed it to White Fox. She tore a section with her teeth, lay it on the wound, turned the section once, then tucked the end behind the gauze behind the neck.

The old woman called just then. White Fox turned to see her, now leaning against the trading post wall, egg-yolk eyes toward the sun, and holding out the tiny Cheyenne maiden for White Fox to take.

CHAPTER EIGHT
The Lady Freemont

I know you can't be angels; the stench here is too great. He thought a long moment; at least, it felt long. *And it isn't brimstone either.*

Avery's words, spoken in his head, were magically written in the dark, drifting from the direction of his mouth, actually moving in front of him like smoke signals, when he saw the two men enter the tiny room. He thought he was speaking, but there was only paralyzed silence from his throat. But he was still seeing the letters swirling in the air, then dissolving away. It probably came from the Bishop Memorial Wall. Seeing headlines all day and night kept them with him, announcing the events in his own life.

He smiled. He couldn't help it. Hallucinations, a quiet, opium-like haze, were something he'd enjoyed more than once. The only difference was, he didn't hurt then. He hadn't been beaten, and scabbed blood wasn't loosening from his scalp and floating into the sweat pouring down his face. The metallic smell was in his nose, the scent of rot.

Still drugged, Avery didn't have the strength to move and plead at the same time. He tested the ropes chopping his wrists and ankles, then gave up, the cot sagging under his enormous weight. He tried to wiggle his fingers, to assure himself he could, but they wouldn't move.

A wide, leather belt, with steel hooks, held his bruised head in place, as if he were being prepared for surgery.

His eyes blurred when he opened them, tears welling, struggling to focus on the figures moving about the room; brown shadows in front of dim light. He tried to give them faces but couldn't, even as they stood close by and spoke.

"How much longer do we have to wait on this one here?"

The Southern-scented voice was answered the way the felon Smith answered everything: "Until the doctor tells us."

Avery didn't know what they were doing, other than talking. He could hear but not see them as they carried Marshal Duffin by his ankles and shoulders, dropping him on the cot opposite Avery, scattering insects, and tying him to the headboard and footers. That much the sheriff-mayor could determine by sound alone. Smith yanked the belts into place across Duffin's head, buckling tight, as Cavanaugh double-knotted his slack arms and legs, anchoring him to the cot's frame, then gave the ropes a little tug to make sure.

Cavanaugh said, "The marshal won't last 'til morning, and I'll wager good silver against it. Good silver."

Smith said, "You don't need your nose to breathe. Just the slits."

"True, but he's damn, damn near," Cavanaugh said, coughing up at the smell of the room. "I know the boss wants a few more blood draws, but these boys smell like rotten meat."

Smith said, "Quiet your mouth."

"Fine, fine. You're not going to take the bet?"

"I am not a gambler," he said. "But if you want box—?"

"The injury," Cavanaugh said. "The injury."

The men left. Avery could hear, now, the rasping breath of the other man. He was mouth-breathing, apparently having lost his nose in some manner.

Avery's takeaway from the visit was not complicated. If the others weren't angels, and there was a still-breathing—barely—man beside him, then he was still alive. And being alive, he must be needed by these people, whoever they were. Weiber-Krauss the German. And Smith—the pig. And the man with a Confederate voice that he didn't recognize.

Avery had to smile—that, too, inside, since his mouth didn't seem inclined to move. Here he was, a man who was no way a hero, splayed like the star of a penny dreadful.

No angels, but there's a God for sure and he's laughing at me. Me and—

That brought him to the other captive, who he

couldn't see, whose smell was lost in the mustiness of the room, whose breathing was like an accordion without the music.

And we are going ripe, he remembered. The other man must be injured on more than just his face.

As his brain came slowly to wakefulness if not focus, Avery recalled fragments of the assault that brought him here, thought with a sense of deep futility the useless discharge of his derringer. He felt betrayed by the little firearm. All those years, never having had to fire it, and the one time he did—

Bishop. That is why Bishop is such a man, he thought. He doesn't carry what belongs in a woman's handbag.

His roaming mind anchored itself to Bishop. Avery wondered where the doctor was and whether he would think the barkeep had received his just rewards. And then he remembered the German better—

It was your *victims they were after, Dr. Bishop!*

Avery considered that, in as much as he could consider anything. The victims—okay, the bodies for display or interment. Then why take him? Why not Homer? Where *was* Homer?

The man beside him moaned. In a way that said he hadn't been cut in the throat or bashed in the mouth but had gotten hurt somewhere else. Probably the head. He sounded like any man Avery had ever heard crowned sideways by a bottle.

The moan came again.

And then so did the man with the voice like a cherry blossom. By now, Avery could crack his eyes. He watched the man, who was wearing Confederate pants, no shirt, and a swagger. It looked like he had on a cummerbund, but Avery decided it was a bandage taped carefully across his belly.

The Southerner turned up a lantern. Unless it was Avery's imagination or the lingering effects of a drug, it was swaying a little.

No. The Confederate had bumped it with a shoulder, that was all. Yet the man could not be that big; the ceiling had to be that low.

The newcomer stepped around the cots, to where a dentist's chair, outfitted with leather and steel restraints, was surrounded by shelves of antiseptics, glass bulbs, and beakers of various sizes. He selected a small bottle.

"Smith, did I ever tell you my mama ran a pest house? Right in the middle of Savannah. Rooms full of terminal cases, bedpans of infection emptied over the back fence. And the neighbors had no idea."

"So, you know how fevers work, how infections spread," Smith said, following him in. "Maybe you shouldn't mouth so much, Cavanaugh."

"I know more'n that," the Confederate replied. "I've learned when folks are ready to die, so we can get maximum use from these, take the blood before it stops bein' made."

Smith eased his mass on a stool behind a rolling porcelain table covered with hypodermic syringes, amputation blades, and blood-collecting equipment all precisely laid out. He filled a surgical pan with carbolic solution, saying, "The doctor decides what happens here, not you."

"I'm just telling my experience."

Smith rinsed his hands in a pan of alcohol, then

dried them with a towel he dropped into a wire basket. "I don't think. I do what I'm ordered."

"Unless it's putting down a horse, right?"

"Horses are pure and good," Smith said. "We are not."

Cavanaugh snickered, uncorking some violet water and holding it under his nose to break the smell. He saw Smith's hands curling, face turning beet red, and said, "Easy, big man. You need to learn how to take a joke."

"You need to learn to make one."

Cavanaugh looked toward the door and froze.

"*Ja*," Smith said. "I heared it too."

Dr. Weiber-Krauss's buggy was a so-called gentleman's carriage, with a folding top that he'd pulled up when he felt the first spittings of the afternoon shower. The wheels were as tall as the doctor's chest, and handled the road to the Lady Freemont by bouncing over ruts and scattered mine debris, then landing hard, their shock-absorbing springs offering nothing.

He had trailed behind Smith and Cavanaugh, watching for danger. He had also been going slower than they, keeping one hand on a leather pouch on the seat beside him, holding in place fluted glass containers of blood and clouded water. Each bump brought down his hand, keeping the bottles from colliding. He rounded a bend in the old mine road, and was waved on by a man in muddy linens, perched on a slag ledge with a rifle cradled in his arms. The Muddy Linens man saluted the buggy as it passed, which Weiber-Krauss half-returned—more like a wave—before snapping his horse toward the Lady Freemont's mine shack and tower.

Patches of snow laced the hills around the mine; frozen white sliding into the gray rock that had rolled down from the mountaintop, forming its own barrier around the ruined stables, shack, and laddered entrance to the shaft, which was blocked with rubble. The churned earth of the place was the color of old metal, with no plants growing at all. There were a few hardy weeds, and whatever fed on them moving low to the ground.

Weiber-Krauss circled his buggy around the buildings. The horse clopped loudly on the hard ground and occasional wood plank that had come from something once standing.

The office shack was on huge supports, built against the mountainside, that were collapsing inward but holding. The mountain itself was doing the heavy lifting. The corral was below and to the side, canvas nailed into place to cover where its walls had once stood, and the miners' quarters were now an open pit, filled with blowing trash and the rusting corpse of a hand-pulled mine elevator. If this were a tale by the Brothers Grimm he had so loved as a boy, gnomes would live here.

They do, Weiber-Krauss thought without amusement or irony as he considered his two workers.

The Lady Freemont reminded Weiber-Krauss of ruins he'd seen on his travels throughout the South, homes and ports and factories and mills left skeletal and useless by Sherman and Lee, except there was no battle here, only abandonment. Now, these many years later, all of them that had not been torn down or rebuilt were simply rusted.

Cavanaugh stepped onto the deck outside the old office, leaning against a weather-beaten railing, lighting an already-rolled, and watching as Weiber-Krauss stopped the buggy next to a new, polished steel hitch in the shape of a wolf's head. The sprinkling of rain picked up as he tied his horse, the storm rolling in across the Rockies carried by a snake of cold wind.

Behind Cavanaugh, Smith jumped four stairs at a time, then down around the Confederate and running around the side of the shack to the corral to unhook the hearse team, and lead them under the canvas and scrap-board shelter he'd hammered together.

Cavanaugh spoke from the deck. "We'll be hearing about this one, Doctor, packing that marshal inside but letting our horses get their rumps wet. Smith complained all the way."

Weiber-Krauss didn't bother to answer. He came up the rickety stairs, satchel tucked under his arm and holding the leather pouch, which he placed by the shack door.

"This is difficult, gruesome work for most people," Weiber-Krauss said. "Smith isn't human, I don't care, but you—I still do not understand what a man of your refinement is doing here."

"The pay is good and the entertainment, sir—you cannot beat it. We lost every man you gave me. At least in the war, the crews of the ironclads had training or skills or passion. These men had the ability to stop bullets with their bodies."

"That was their purpose, if needed," Weiber-Krauss said, opening his satchel with a snap of wrist movement.

"Well, they sure fulfilled it, and without a single scream," Cavanaugh said, relighting his rain-dampened cigarette with a grin. "But one of them put a slug into the marshal's leg, and he howled like a bayonetted dog."

Weiber-Krauss said, "Where were you?"

Cavanaugh half-edged the spyglass from his pocket. "On watch, as ordered, after taking care of those crazy bastards in the junkyard, just like a Cheyenne would."

"What happened after?"

"Bishop and the marshal blew it up, as you expected," Cavanaugh said. "No more blacksmith. No more chubby man from Good Fortune."

"Again, my confidence in your dead soul has been rewarded," Weiber-Krauss said, handing Cavanaugh a small, tied sack.

The Confederate gave it a shake, hearing the jangle of the gold inside, saying, "I watched that Bishop, doctoring the marshal's leg, that Cheyenne there too. Later, when he had me on the ground, it was quite a thing to look up at that shotgun, pointed at my face like a twenty-four-pounder cannon. Seeing it for real, it's quite a weapon."

Weiber-Krauss said, "Not as effective as ours."

Cavanaugh looked at him. Weiber-Krauss was right, though the Confederate had never looked at a disease as a *weapon*. Not exactly. But it was, wasn't it?

The rain was falling steady as oversized drops now, splattering the ground like bullet strikes against the slag and mud. Weiber-Krauss and Cavanaugh pressed themselves against the shack, under its bent-back tin roof and out of the afternoon shower.

Weiber-Krauss said, "This will pass in a few minutes."

Cavanaugh closed in his shoulders, slumping, but

still towered over Weiber-Krauss. He was still thinking about sickness as a weapon.

"If you had your way, every drop'd be deadly, wouldn't it?"

"Use what we're gathering from the diseased, and they will be. One day. It will be so that every town in every state will fear the rain."

Cavanaugh said, "After what I had to do with that bucket under the bed, I read up on Doc Blackburn, assessing why you hate him so much."

"Luke Blackburn was a *schande*—a disgrace to the cause, and to medicine," Weiber-Krauss said, voice rising. "Yellow fever epidemic with infected clothes and bedding? This attempt, trying to expose the enemy to the disease without actual contact with the pestilence, this was idiotic in the extreme."

"His amateur mistakes," Cavanaugh said. "But you're taking the direct approach, sir, sailing into your own port."

Weiber-Krauss acknowledged the compliment with a tilt of his head. "Exposing tribes to infection through their water, with blood, we can ensure they'll be thinned out. Savages are roadblocks to progress, and better to have them gone than scuttled away where they can mutiny. You're a naval man; you understand this."

"I understand gold."

"And expansion. And the gold *that* brings. And," he added with some relish, "progress. Medical progress. To understand disease, one must exploit it. Witness it. Field-test cures."

Cavanaugh smoked, nodded toward other men below them, men of the Muddy Linens Brigade who were scattered around the mine, ignoring the rain.

Walking their guard posts, or taking a stance as sentries, they were all blank eyed and silent, sported linen trousers and shirts and kept their rifles to their shoulders. A small group sat under an old army tent, shredded, letting in more water than it kept out, playing cards with their weapons propped next to them. Waiting for orders. One was away from the others, hunched down on his knees, head down, staring at the ground, rifle in the mud.

"The pray-er," said the Confederate. "Asking God's forgiveness for his every sin."

"There is nothing wrong with earnest repentance," Weiber-Krauss said.

Cavanaugh flung his cigarette sizzling into the air. "I wouldn't crew with any of 'em."

"Your judgment."

"Why'd you have me recruit these damaged souls?"

"For one reason only," Weiber-Krauss said. "They are loyal to me. You were never a patient, but even those in the general ward could talk to these men, on their level. Simply, they trust. That is their need. I intimidate them. The desire to please, above all, makes a good soldier, makes a good soldier brave. They are different from you. Your thinking about the mission was clear."

"For a janitor."

"No matter. When we sought the *Hunley*, and I heard the ideas you proposed to Admiral Buchanan—innovations for warfare that should have been implemented—I knew you were a man for this team."

Cavanaugh said, "Ideas that got me flogged twice for insubordination and theft."

"Still, sound thinking. To have a self-propelled torpedo—"

Cavanaugh cut in, "I just improved on the British, French, and German designs."

"If the South had those instead of what you used, the *Hunley* would now be a victory ship, not a sunken hulk."

"Admiral Buchanan was another South Ca'lina boy, so his rebuke had that extra sting. The old bastard wasn't going to be defied," Cavanaugh said, lighting a match, flicking it into the rain, watching it travel to the ground. "When I was at sea, I know my captain regretted not hanging me."

"Some men are just too useful to hang."

"No," Cavanaugh said. "Some are better stuffed with poison and oozing blood."

Weiber-Krauss took out a pocket watch, angled it so he could see the dial.

"We have time," the Confederate said. "Smith still has preparations with what I brought."

Cavanaugh shuddered slightly. The Indians and the diseases were one thing. The next step in the progression was more wholly damning.

Weiber-Krauss regarded the men below and said, "Do you regret anything you've done for me?"

"No worse than in war. I can sleep at night."

Smith stepped from the corral carrying Duffin's saddlebags, and Cavanaugh called, "Hey, big man, toss those."

Smith looked to Weiber-Krauss. "Doctor?"

Weiber-Krauss nodded. Smith tossed the bags, and Cavanaugh stretched over the railing to snatch them out of the air. He took the Dragoon from the leather, checked its action, saying, "It hasn't felt right since the marshal took it off me. Ah, I'll fix it later." Cavanaugh put it under an arm, held out the notebook that had been stuffed into the bag's deep pocket. "A gift from the great one-arm. More of Bishop's plans, I'm supposing. The marshal was going to use whatever's in there against him."

Weiber-Krauss thumbed the pages. "Special equipment for treatment of disease in the field," he said, not hiding his excitement. "These can be of tremendous use."

"There were more in the shack but I had to leave those . . . evidence."

"Of course," Weiber-Krauss said. "Do you think he is in the clear, Bishop?"

"I don't know. I don't think the marshal's disappearance is going to help him any. That was his main defense from blowin' up the blacksmith's place. That and the word of a Cheyenne."

"He will be tried by what he did and what he hasn't done," Weiber-Krauss remarked, momentarily cherishing the book to his bosom as if it had been written by the finger of God before putting it in his satchel.

Cavanaugh laughed. "You mean the *Police Gazette* headlines?"

"An infamous man is a better scapegoat than an innocent one."

"Then we are damn well protected," Cavanaugh said, still smiling.

Weiber-Krauss took a last look at his motley troops, who were nonetheless out in the rain, before turning to the shack door and pushing aside a section of rotten board to reveal heavy armor underneath, and three deadbolt-locks in the hammered steel.

The keys Weiber-Krauss used to open them were on

a large rail conductor's ring inside the satchel he held, and he turned each lock before signaling Cavanaugh to hand over the pouch with the bottles of infection. He placed his own satchel inside the door, against the wall, then held out his hands.

"Doctor, you for sure don't want these breaking."

Weiber-Krauss took the pouch carefully, saying, "Not until I order it."

The waterfall over the sandstone ledge was snowmelt: narrow, running streams of cold from the mountains, pouring over a jag of black rocks and forming a shallow lake surrounded by rain-bent grass. Colors in the lake's surface broke apart as White Fox dipped a small wooden box into the water. Holding it with both hands, she filled the box to the brim before dropping in a piece of lake ice.

Packing a handful of medicines, she had gone on ahead to the nearest village, leaving Bishop and Dent to make the best time they could with the wagon. She had left while they were still unloading the dynamite, agreeing to meet here at the lake. It was a lake she and Bishop knew well, from one of the few leisure times they had enjoyed together.

White Fox had actually gone to two villages; they were close enough. She wanted to come up with a plan for dealing with the illness. She had returned, told Bishop she was still working on it, then come here—congested from the hard ride, the damp morning, the unpleasant air of the forest of evil.

The ground was still rain-wet, and the horses drank from the edge of the lake, as White Fox sealed the box lid, fitted the brass nozzle on its side with a celluloid anesthesia cone, and breathed deeply.

Bishop was on the back of the wagon, checking the blue crates. "That the one I made?"

"No." White Fox drew from the cone, taking in oxygen from the ice water. "My father, following your plans. The old one was given away."

"They have cigarettes for asthmatics now," Bishop said, opening a crate with a blood smear across its lid. "Herbs from China. It's the newest thing."

White Fox still had the cone pressed against her mouth, "I could never smoke a cigarette or a cigar or even a pipe. I always choked."

She breathed into the device, the air calming her lungs, steadying her, the coolness settling inside. She met Bishop's inquiring eyes, finally said, "We have a day's ride to go."

"Then we'd better leave soon," he said. He looked over to where he'd tied Dent to a tree. "Do you know how many cases were yellow fever? Anything else?"

"Children and the old ones. Hundreds. I lost count. John, this is monstrous. It spread so quickly. I did my best."

Bishop said, "I know."

"But not good enough," White Fox said, pulling off her buckskin jacket, tossing it aside. "Now it's up to you, Doctor."

"Keep your jacket on. It's going to be frozen around here tonight."

White Fox put aside the cone. "The jacket has too much blood on it."

Bishop pulled a folded blanket from a medical crate and tossed it to her. Then he went and untied

Dent, who had been told to speak very little to keep from opening the wound along his jaw. He had complied amiably, even holding his head very still as he climbed onto the wagon.

White Fox came over with the painted and Bishop was about to settle into the back of the wagon, when a stuttering voice from the edge of the meadow made him turn, bring up the rig. He snapped it into place, then stayed by the wagon, aiming down at the man who was climbing off a red, dog-eared mule, his hands in the air.

"Dr. John Bishop?"

"That's a pretty foolish question, under the circumstances," Bishop replied.

"Yes . . . yes, it's certainly you, but may I ask again, so you can confirm?"

Bishop bowed a little at the neck without taking his eyes or rig off the man.

"Dr. John Bishop?"

"I am he." He added, pointing the rig at a saddle scabbard. "Step away from the carbine."

"Oh of course. Thank you, sir."

"Who are you?" White Fox asked. "We haven't time—"

"I understand. My name is Innocence Lee," said the other. Lee, skinny, all Adam's apple over a starched collar and with thick spectacles, took a few more steps, not lowering his arms, elbows crooked to his sides and palms out. "Please, don't shoot. I'm not here for any nefarious purpose."

"Who are you?"

"Innocence Lee, hailing from Potter, Nebraska. I'm involved with physical therapies, specializing in the healing of bones. That's not precisely right, I'm truly a librarian with an interest in orthopedic medicines, but the closest thing to a doctor my group has."

Bishop kept a foot on the tailgate, the rig locked. "I've known you less than a minute and you've already lied once. Not a good sign."

"I what? Lied?"

"Your belt buckle says IA."

"Oh." The newcomer laughed nervously. "My full name. Innocence Lee Atwood. I–I saw no need for formality."

White Fox had moved her steed to the side of the wagon, catching sunlight in her face. She was watching the beanpole with his hands still raised and stuttering away: "I went to the trading post for supplies, and a woman told me of the recent, frightening occurrences. She had been drinking, so maybe—I didn't know."

White Fox smiled a little at that.

"Go on," Bishop told him.

"But she said I might find you along the river, or next after that on this lake, as she thought you were going to a Cheyenne camp. I didn't know how she knew but she seemed to and, well, here you are. She was alone out there," he added.

"She can take care of herself," Bishop said.

Bishop said, "You're holding up necessary healing. Get to the meat of things."

Innocence Lee pushed his glasses up on his nose with his middle finger, then snapped them back to peaceful intention. "The woman I saw, who is blind as you know, but I still took her word, said you had medical supplies and might sell some. I'm from a small settlement, Nebraskans moving for the mountains, and the children are sick with measles. You know what that can mean, Doctor, and we have no way to treat them, which has slowed our little wagon train to a stop."

Bishop said, "We're on our way elsewhere."

"I understand, but thought you might let me have something from the wagon. Anything that might help."

Bishop looked to Fox, who made no expression, didn't move, just watched with a hand on the knife handle. His brow furrowed as he looked at her. She didn't seem to notice his expression and didn't pull the blade as Innocence Lee took a few steps forward.

"Please, sir . . . madam," he said. "Anything you can spare."

There was a deep draw of air, stirring some courage, as he made his way to the back of the wagon, hands out at his side, eyes on Bishop and Fox and occasionally on Dent, who sat still as a dead man.

"Open the red box in the back," White Fox said. "Take as much as you can fit in your pockets."

Innocence Lee came to animated life. "Thank you! Bless you!" He moved to where Bishop was seated, unafraid despite the rig, and used a small pocketknife to slit the cord. He gently removed the bottles, and even more gingerly put them in his pockets as if they were newborn kangaroos. "This is very kind. I can administer it myself. I know a thing or two from reading the medical texts. That's my interest."

White Fox said, "So you claimed."

"Why did you ask me to say my name in direct response to the question?" Bishop asked.

"I have a book of common law on my reference shelf," he said. "That makes things legal, you see."

"Ah."

Innocence Lee finished taking medicines as he was instructed, hesitated as he seemed to consider asking if he could carry one or two or three.

"Be on your way," Bishop said.

"Already going," said Innocence Lee, his relieved smile splitting his thin face, his eyes crinkling to nothing, and said, "Thanks so much for your generosity, Doctor. And best of luck. To you both. On your journey. I know you're on God's mission."

By the time he'd finished speaking, Innocence Lee had climbed back onto his mule. Bishop kept the rig trained on him as if he were Dent, healthy and armed. The skinny man waved, as he brought the animal around, rode away.

The rig had quietly elevated, steady on Innocence Lee's back. They were still within range of a good man with a carbine.

White Fox said, "You always do that now. Keep the gun on everyone."

"Habit. I don't even think about it anymore."

"You'd kill him?"

"If his hands left the reins or he turned too quickly," Bishop confirmed. "I would have cut him in half."

Fox said, "Odd words, standing beside all that medicine."

Bishop dropped from the wagon's gate, walked to White Fox. "It isn't congestion," he said.

She sat stoic and still.

"How long have you been fever-sick? In the light, I see yellow along the edges of your eyes."

White Fox looked away.

"We're not going until you answer me," Bishop said.

"It hasn't been too long," she said, watching Innocence Lee cut the mule toward an open spot in a gathering of cottonwoods. Then she replaced the celluloid cone over her mouth and nose. "Just my trouble getting a breath. The fever, not so bad."

"Yet," Bishop said, also watching the trees, the rig still leveled and pointed at their distance. "After Innocence on the mule, we're not staying here."

"I know," White Fox said, letting down the cone. "Give me two more breaths." After she had inhaled, she put the cone back in a pouch slung over the pummel.

And gasped.

"Dent's gone!" she said urgently.

"As I expected," Bishop said. "Take the wagon, go to the camp."

"What are you going to do?" she asked.

He answered, "I'm going to find out what Innocence Lee wants with Walter G. Dent.

CHAPTER NINE
The Forest Primeval

Dent looked like a thick-bodied ostrich as he rushed along the lakeside, his head held stiffly atop an artificially stretched neck in an effort to keep it still. He wasn't sure what to expect: the gallop of a horse behind him, dying before he heard the boom of Bishop's rig, or neither of those. Bishop would be angry but not careless, and he had noted Lee owned a carbine. He might even have noticed that the scabbard was well worn, the sign of a hunter or a sharpshooter. In either case, not someone you wanted firing at you from a place of concealment.

Which is what the woods alongside the water offered, and which is why, following the trail Innocence Lee had left, Dent now ducked in among the cottonwoods. The branches were low and Bishop would have to dismount to make it through here.

Considering there hadn't been a plan until the marksman showed up, pretending to be a librarian of all things—right down to that comment about the book of common law, brilliant—the improvisation now was a good one.

Dent had not told Bishop about the sixth man at the trading post because he was there for exactly this reason: to find out where the disease had gone after being disbursed, and how bad. White Fox had provided that information. Now Dent had to get it to Innocence Lee, who would protect him as they made their way to the Lady Freemont.

As he hurried along, Dent did not expect to encounter anyone. He stopped short as he practically ran into a wide man standing just behind a tree, a cowboy in a torn shirt and a torn grin with a cigar that wasn't lit so it wouldn't draw anyone to them. The man held a Spencer Repeater in his two hairy fists and wore a Remington revolver on his side.

"Walter G. Dent?" the man said gruffly.

Dent nodded.

"Innocence wants yer report," he said. His pale blue eyes looked past Dent. "And I want the legend."

"Fine, good," Dent said through a nearly closed mouth. "Straight ahead? Yes?"

The cowboy spit. "Unless you want to go back to yer friend with the gun-arm."

Dent snorted like a bull and hurried on with his odd, stiff-necked gait as he tried to keep his head from bobbing while he traversed the uneven wooded terrain. Fallen branches under fallen leaves were the real danger, and he stepped high to avoid them.

The oncoming informant was a comic sight to Innocence Lee, who was no longer a comical sight himself. His collar was on the ground, along with his eyeglasses, along with the broken bottles of medicine he had pulled from his pocket. His thin expression was no longer as innocent as his name.

He was standing beside his horse, holding his carbine, waiting to see if Bishop got past his grizzled sentry.

Dent said, practically through his teeth, "See? I steered you right to them."

Innocence Lee said, "You did, Dent. What can you tell me?"

"There are two Cheyenne settlements, a day's ride, hundreds of Indians ill, many of them women and children," he said.

"That far, that fast," Innocence said. "The doctor will be very happy to hear that. The Indian took the wagon? Bishop's on the painted?"

Dent nodded.

Innocence cocked a head over his shoulder. "Well done. You've got a palomino behind that outcropping. The gold is in the saddlebag. Take it and don't come back. If the doctor needs you again, he knows where to find you. If you say anything, to anyone, *I* will know where to find you."

Dent nodded, just a little, but it was an enthusiastic little. He scurried off as Innocence watched him go. In his other life, as a buffalo hunter for the railroads, Innocence met a lot of little men. Most of them carried pocket watches and had fat red cheeks and earned a lot of money for taking things that did not belong to them, like land and labor and sometimes lives. Walter G. Dent was not as bad as they were. They were snakes that swallowed prey whole . . . Dent just gathered nuts.

Neither had any real courage. Not like the inaptly named Randy Coward who was the first line of defense against John Bishop. There was a man, a steel driver on the railroad, who was worth every pound he weighed and then some. There was a brawler who used a gun because it was efficient, not because it gave him any particular satisfaction. Whether it was his arms against thc spikes and hard ground, or facing down any Indian brave who had ever crossed his path and got his back broken in the process, Coward was the battering ram of civilization.

Innocence would have been happy to face John Bishop first. But Coward had insisted. The only reason Innocence stayed was in the event the man fell. It would not do to be running after a slow Cheyenne wagon with a fast John Bishop on his tail.

Bishop had not been surprised, so far, but neither had he been satisfied at the pace of things. It was like rooting out bees from the house, when he had one. They got in where woodpeckers drilled, then you could kill them and kill some more and there were still a colony's worth somewhere.

This crew was not like the others he had faced. There were separate teams, independent leaders, all working under a man whose master plan was known only to him and to those who were fighting with him. It had taken an entire military garrison, a marshal, and God knew how many civilian informants for them to find out what little information they had. And it still led them to the wrong conclusion, that John Bishop was poisoning Indians and had killed the husband of his lover—who wasn't his lover. It took bureaucratic skill to be that thoroughly and consistently wrong.

Bishop was not accustomed to the painted, and the painted was not accustomed to the weight of a man. There hadn't been time to swap the horses out, but he didn't like rough-handling his mounts and he was not able to go as quickly as he liked. The painted was also unused to Bishop's one-handed control, which made a necessity of sharper pulls to execute quick turns.

Riding along the mushy lakeshore, he found it easy to follow Dent's tracks—which may have been the point. Bishop also spotted, easily, the hoofprints of Innocent Lee's horse. The parallel path may have been a coincidence but he didn't think so. The librarian wasn't a librarian; his hands were too calloused for that. The carbine had not worn its shape into the scabbard, which meant it had gone in and out so many times the leather had lost its stiffness. The opening on the bottom was worn wide from the rifle being drawn and redrawn. Equally telling, Innocent Lee knew how to stand like a man reassuring you he wasn't going to draw. Hands out, floating alongside his hips like little hummingbirds.

No, Innocent Lee was out there, probably waiting for Dent, possibly in ambush—

Bishop reined to a stop, did not reinforce it verbally. The trail of both men turned into the woods. The branches were thick and low and that meant dismounting.

He did so, turning the horse sideways as a shield so he could peer into the semi-daylight of the shaded, uneven expanse. There were boulders ahead, fat cottonwoods with foliage so low to the ground they looked like shrubs.

He listened, heard nothing but the chatter of leaves and the occasional crow or American dipper. But those were all to the north, his right. There were no birds calling from ahead.

Because someone or several someones are there.

Thinking of White Fox, Bishop tied the painted to a tree. If something happened, she would come back for it. A killer, a good one, wouldn't be stupid enough to take it. Not anywhere it might be recognized.

This wasn't like preparing for the three cousins, Tommy, Vance, Edward. Innocence had staked out his quarry, come close enough to read the rig firsthand, assess its firepower. And Innocence might not be alone.

Bishop was surprised to ask himself a question he had not yet asked: why was he doing this? Dent meant nothing, except bait. If he went on, followed White Fox, he could help her cure the sick—including herself. Innocence might not follow him, and if he did Bishop would be no worse off than he was going blindly into the eternal twilight of these woods.

As a medic, even though a lieutenant, Bishop had not been involved in strategy and tactics. But there was one thing he had learned, which was that you don't leave an enemy at your rear to nip and pick at you, at their leisure. That was why, forty years ago, the Mexican general Santa Anna had to bring in thousands of troops to crush a hundred-and-thirty-odd men at the Alamo. He had to protect his rear.

If only the penny-dreadful writers could see him now. Not afraid. Cautious. He didn't cherish this life enough to fear death. But he didn't want to die stupidly, carelessly. There was no going around the woods to the north; he knew they spread for miles. And to the south was the lake, too muddy and deep for the painted, and his rig wouldn't survive.

Which gave him a sudden inspiration.

Randy Coward was not a patient man. Anyone who swung a mallet for a living learned to expect instant gratification. You bring the hammer down, something happens to whatever it hits. Happened for the years he was with the railroad, happened before that the years he was a roustabout on the Mississippi.

It wasn't happening now and though the Spencer wasn't a sledgehammer, he wanted to swing it. At something.

The big man had been there three hours, had emptied his canteen, but he did not want to leave his post. Or rather, he did not want to turn his back on a direction from which John Bishop might be coming. He didn't mind putting down the Repeater to urinate, because even then he had a hand full of Remington.

Coward allowed himself to sit. He did do that, his back to a tree, facing east. As the sun moved to his back, seeing was easier as it lit the way that Dent had come, the way that Bishop would come—if he was even coming. The stories could be wrong, lies. Innocence could be misinformed. Maybe the man was all gun, no bullets. Maybe the firepower was just so much warm wind.

He pulled jerky from his pocket and tore at it. He watched a pair of chipmunks running up and down a tree. He wondered what Innocence was thinking, what he was doing. He hadn't heard any shots from back there, so he knew Bishop wasn't circling around. The big cartoon. The big P. T. Barnum size—

Was that splashing?

Coward held his breath. There was sound from the direction of the lake. If it were a bear, it would make noise, a lot of it. If it were not, the water would slosh, being pushed instead of struck. A lone rider wouldn't be in the water, not with good shoreline.

The sloshing stopped. Then started again. Something was right *at* the edge of the water.

Coward was itching and bored and it wasn't far. His heart started to dance as he wondered if it might be Bishop at long last. Maybe watering his horse.

A buckskin jacket hung from the nub of a branch that had broken off so long ago that the limb itself was gone. Coward put what was left of the jerky in a vest pocket, pulled it once—careful to keep a finger on the trigger of the leveled Repeater at all times—and, drawing a long breath that filled his barrel chest, he decided he had to see if it was what his sentry grandpaw used to call during the War with the Mexicans, "*Foe or go.*"

Palming the revolver in his right hand, he turned toward the glinting lights of the lake. He used the Spencer, held tight in his left, like a poker, pushing aside fluffy branches so he could survey the terrain ahead. Each step took him a little bit to the east or west, giving him a slightly different sliver of lake. He still didn't see anything.

And then he did.

There was a painted in the slanting sunlight. It was just standing there, half in the water, half out, facing south. The reins were hanging over the neck, the loop dangling just above the waterline. He took that in between blinks. What interested him more was the hint of clothing he saw under the surface, bobbing there like underwater plants. Shirt nearest, pants farthest. But what interested him more was a slash of bright gold or brass or something of that hue on the narrow, pebbly beach. He'd seen it before, in magazines that got passed around at the rail sites. The cannon-arm, the limb of death, the sinew of God, the other names he'd heard read aloud around the campfire. The rig of Dr. John Bishop, the creature known as Shotgun. The name appeared so often that it was the only word Coward learned to read.

"Lord A'mighty," he muttered.

His eyes shifted back to the painted and he saw how things had come to be. There were Injun decorations on the horse. Not his—the squaw's, whose name Coward didn't bother to know. The saddle was lopsided, toward him. The cinch was loose underneath. Shotgun, the killer, the legendary immortal, must have taken her horse and fallen. Tried to hold on, went over anyway, landed in the water, and drowned. His arm was off; maybe he couldn't one-arm-push his way from the muddy bottom.

"Aw, shit," Coward muttered. "The bastard kilt hisself."

But then his next thought: the arm would be worth a fortune. Couple of bullets in a dead man, Randy Coward would still be the man who did him in. The metal arm *was* gold after all. He'd just take the horse, shoot it later, and it would be a victim of the mighty Coward fusillade.

His heart beating faster, now from riches just within reach, the big man moved ahead—still furtively, looking toward the still lake, trying to see a body beneath the sun-polished surface. A horse's hoof came up, then down languidly. *Slosh.* Then again. *Slosh.* The end of the tree line was just a few paces away. Coward could see to the east and west—a few yards both ways, then a few yards more, then he was on the dry, open stretch maybe seven, eight yards wide. Crouching, revolver at the ready, he turned to one side, then the other, then back. There was no one in hiding.

Standing tall, remembering to breathe, Coward allowed himself a half-smile and moved toward the pants and shirt just bobbing there. Air kept them up, but there had to be a body below to keep them from drifting.

He pointed the Spencer ahead, watched the lake for any sign of movement that wasn't a fish or burble that wasn't a frog, just in case Bishop was hidden 'neath. He reached the edge. He looked down at the clothing, squinting through the light. There was no arm on one side and—

No arm on the other. No feet either. But he did see rocks, big ones, pinning the two sleeves to the lakebed.

He heard the rattling sound behind him, slightly to the west, the left, and turned. There were other stories in the penny dreadfuls. Stories about things they called ghouls . . . dead men that rose from their graves to eat the flesh of the living.

At first Coward thought it was a ghoul rising before him, just four feet away, shedding rocks and dirt, but it wasn't. It was a one-armed man, bare chested, barelegged, with something glinting in his good arm. The sun shining from the polished edge of the tomahawk momentarily blinded Coward. Which, added to his confusion, delayed him from swinging the rifle around.

He stood there, dumbly, momentarily helpless in his confusion, as the blade came up, then swung down in a sharply angled diagonal line, cutting him from his right clavicle to south-left of his navel. He felt the punch of the blade but not the slice, felt the warmth of his blood as it went from the inside to the outside, felt the horror of the snarling face in his own stupefied one as the attacker's chest hair was coated with the gore of Coward's vitals.

The single cut of the hatchet was followed by a slight turn of the blade and a lateral cut along the waist. The slash was deep and fine and guts spilled over the lower edge, sections of intestine that had been sliced free in the same cut.

Coward dropped in sections, vaguely conscious as his knees fell forward and his half-severed upper body listed at right angles and flopped to the side. His viscera went in all directions. And the brief, glowing future of Coward died in a gory heap along with its dreamer.

Bishop stood over the dead man feeling about as much as the dead man felt. There was some satisfaction of the plan having worked. Weighting down the clothes, quietly hacking out a shallow grave for himself, struggling with his one arm to conceal himself under the rocks he had piled beside the hole before digging. All of it quietly, quietly, so as not to attract attention. If he made any noise, he tried to keep it the volume and pitch of one of the frogs that inhabited the still line of the lakeshore. Until now, he had never realized how much a bullfrog made a sound like rocks clunking in their hollow way.

He was gratified but there was no time for reflection. There was still a gunman out there. And there was still preparation to be made. Kneeling beside the dead man, Bishop took the revolver, tucked it in the band of his knee-length long johns, and went to work.

Innocence Lee was not Randy Coward. For one thing, he could read. A trainman's son raised in Baltimore, he had been educated through high school. For another, because he was thin as a sapling, he had always relied on cunning and marksmanship more than bulging bull-muscle.

But Innocence Lee was also an experienced stalker. And he had a sense, born of a score of years plus two in the West, of hunting game and at times being hunted by game, when something wasn't right.

Leaning against a tree, twin Colts in his gun belt, Innocence Lee chewed tobacco and mentally put holes in wildlife and thought. What wasn't "right" was Bishop not having come through yet. He had to have known or by hours ago figured out what was what with Dent and Innocence. Innocence believed, since Bishop was no dope, that he had let Dent go because Dent *was* a dope and couldn't have gotten away from a man like Bishop. Unless permitted.

So where was he? Bishop would not leave *this* unfinished. He would not leave a trail unfollowed, especially since there had to be so much he did not know about what was being blamed on him. Not knowing what was on Bishop's mind was only part of the problem. It was already becoming nightlike in the woods. Innocence had not made provisions to camp here. He had planned to dispose of the shotgun, grab the mechanical contraption as evidence, deliver that and Dent's report to Weiber-Krauss, and then return to the railroad with Coward.

That was still the plan, though the timing was now a full mess. He couldn't see the squirrels and hares he was mentally picking off; in the hunter's world, that was a sign to go to camp, have some coffee, call it a day, fall asleep dreaming of showgirls instead of deer.

A crunching ahead caused Innocence to become fully, instantly alert. It came from the direction of where Randy Coward had been stationed. The skinny man had the Colts out and aimed midriff-high, wide spread . . . he could see down the center of them, shoot at anything that moved peripherally. And he would. At anything that wasn't Randy Coward. Or if it was Randy Coward he might shoot anyway, since the son of a bitch was told not to leave his post until John Shotgun Bishop was cold.

Twigs cracked lightly, like the bones of little girls. Innocence Lee was focused on the dark ahead, watching for a familiar shape. He himself was under a large canopy, lost in thick shadow. He stopped chewing but did not spit. He would allow himself to dribble down his chin rather than spit. He did not intend to speak or breathe or swallow or do anything to give away his position.

He wouldn't hail Coward and, until Coward knew where Innocence Lee was, he wouldn't speak either.

The two had partnered enough to know that the team leader believed in absolute invisibility above all.

There was a darker shadow upright in the dimmer shadow. A hulking figure with a rifle in one hand, a revolver in the other. The weapons were pointed down.

The bastard. The dolt. Had he given up? There was still daylight out there, by the lake. Innocence Lee screamed inside. *Had Coward abandoned his post?* If he had, these would be the last steps the big man ever took. The contract killer could not do his job, uphold his reputation, if he could not count on his people. As he counted on Dent to run, he counted on Coward to stay.

The silhouette of the buckskin and guns was Coward's, and Innocence Lee spit now. He moved the twin Colts to center and fired—

At the tree line, as he slapped backward, spine first, against the cottonwood. The gunshots had come too close together for him to tell them apart, but Innocence Lee had fired second. The man emerging from the shadow, the one with the severed arm tucked up a sleeve and "holding" a Spencer, had fired first. The Remington had discharged into the chest, twice.

Momentarily pinned to the bark by the impact, Innocence Lee sucked down air as if he were a gasbag trying to float himself. But it was a failed effort. He slumped down, streaking blood, eyes staring into the dark face of a man who was not Randy Coward.

Dressed in Coward's clothing, Bishop kicked the Colts out of reach with the toe of his right boot; the boot and the long johns were all that remained of Bishop's clothing. He squatted in front of the dying man, tucked the revolver in his a-little-too-big blue jeans, and reached across his own belly. He pulled the severed, still-bloody arm from the sleeve of the buckskins, the arm he had fixed there with parts of his rig harness. The Spencer was set in a fist tied tight around it with the dead man's shoelaces. He plopped the tomahawk-hacked limb across the legs of the failed assassin.

Dr. Bishop, a man of acute medical knowledge and skill, had struck breastbone to dull the impact of the bullets. The lungs of his victim, both left and right, would still drown in blood, and soon, but not too soon. Not soon enough for Innocence Lee.

Bishop crouched and put a palm to the two wounds, which were essentially one. He applied pressure, not to stop the bleeding but to cause pain. Innocence Lee screamed deep in his throat, the awful sound staying there.

"Who are you working for?"

The question was calm but the need was urgent.

Innocence Lee made an effort of shaking his head, managed impressively if briefly. Bishop leaned into his palm a little. Innocence Lee screamed again, this time the sound rising about to his tongue.

"It will take you, I'd say, another half-hour to die," Bishop informed him. "I can probably draw that out. I can certainly make it hell. Or you can talk and die now, without any pain."

The head shook again, a little.

"I'm guessing there's evidence of some kind in your saddlebag," Bishop went on. "I doubt that other lunk could write or read, but you can. Maybe a letter with a postmark? A map in handwriting I'll recognize? Notes you made when Dent passed through?" Bishop pressed again. "I am sure, very sure, Walter G. Dent did not cover his tracks, because he did not expect anyone but you and your partner to follow them."

Innocence Lee was panting to keep from screaming and also to keep from speaking.

Bishop covered his mouth with a bloody hand. "Oh no. You don't hyperventilate yourself into oblivion. You will live and feel the full term of your injuries unless you tell me what I want to know." Bishop waited a moment. "Maybe it will help if you think of this as 'last rites.' Are you remotely religious, Innocence Lee? Secretly devout? If you confess your sins, God may yet forgive you. Thirty, forty minutes is a long time for Him to make a final, eternal judgment."

This was something else that had played through the mind of Innocence Lee before sleep. Maybe a self-hating part, he didn't know. But it was: how will you die? If dying was the only thing left to do, would you stay true to your life or repent it all in an uncharacteristic act of terror? And most of all—this had to do more with being caught by the Indians, who were known to delight in torments of the flesh, of others—would you have the resolve to take your own life by direct action or as a result of direct action?

With supreme effort, Innocence Lee rolled his spine off the cottonwood and reached to where Bishop had kicked one of his Colts, not because he expected to reach it but because he expected Bishop to stop him the quickest way possible. The only way a one-armed man could be sure of stopping him.

As Innocence Lee rolled-flopped toward his right, Bishop stepped back with one leg, still at a crouch, drew the Remington, and shot the man in the side of the head. Innocence Lee jumped back, into the tree, wrapped around it slightly from the impact, stiller than the dying crack of the firearm.

Bishop exhaled. The man had principle. And in the end, he died in a quasi-religious state. The bullet had struck him in the temple.

CHAPTER TEN
Divide and Conquer

The helpless mass that was Joseph Daniel Avery had used the inattentive comings and goings of Cavanaugh and Smith to rally his wits. The man beside him was still unconscious, as whispered *pssts* had determined whenever the others were gone. Smith was the one who came in, mostly, working over on his little table. On what, Avery had no idea. Except that it smelled like compost.

He tried not to be scared, but that was increasingly difficult. No one abducted men, locked them to a bed, and experimented in a corner with rot unless he had malicious intentions. Avery recalled some of the blacks in New York, the ones from the islands, who had potions and animals and put the two together in bizarre ceremonies, with dance and blood. Voodoo, they called it. The Municipals had called it "Caribe Kick-a-row," when the immigrants all went mad.

These men were not mad, far as Avery could tell.

They were quiet and methodical and for that reason, frightening. They had a plan and he was a part of it. The fact that he was being forced to participate was not a good sign.

Someone entered and the man in the bed looked over. It was a dark but familiar shape—the hat. He recognized the homburg. The wearer came over, to the far side of the bed, away from the other prisoner.

"Good day, your excellency," Weiber-Krauss said, leaning over the bed, one hand on the wall. "Or should I say, more formally, 'Mr. Mayor-sheriff-bartender . . . opportunist'?"

Avery continued to breathe through his poorly coordinated mouth, which was about all he could do with it.

Weiber-Krauss continued to peer down through the darkness. "Mr. Avery," he went on smoothly, "how would you like—to remain alive?"

The man in the bed looked up. His eyes, which had been struggling to see in the dark, relaxed. So did the rest of his face. It wasn't until that moment Avery realized there were choices.

"I can see that you would, and I suspected as much," Weiber-Krauss said. "Which is one reason you are here. I think you would rather live and be quite well-off instead of dying and being merely and conclusively—dead."

Avery nodded weakly. Weiber-Krauss motioned him still with a little downward wave of his hand.

"Can I assume we have an agreement?" Weiber-Krauss asked. "A nod will do."

Avery nodded once. It was only when fear started flowing away that he realized how tense he had been.

Bishop had said he'd sell his grandmother; he was ready to listen to terms.

"Very good," Weiber-Krauss said, openly pleased. "We are partners, then, and I will tell you now what I want you to do. You are going to be set free. Not just from this bed, but . . . freed. Liberated. You will be given a wagon. You will drive it to Fort Collins—with one passenger, the gentleman to your right—and then you will return here. You return the wagon, you receive one hundred dollars in gold. How does that sound for three days' work?"

It sounded, Avery thought, too good to be a sincere offer . . . but it was the only offer on the table and he knew he was going to take it.

"To spare you the effort of speech," Weiber-Krauss said, "I will answer questions you probably would ask if you could. First, why did we abduct you? Well, honestly, I did not want you distracted, I did not want this to be a negotiation like the one about the three cousins, and I did not want anyone else involved. Except the gentlemen who we also abducted. Second, what about your friend Homer? He is dead. Smith killed him. You will never find him. We did that to convince you that we are in earnest. You betray me, we will kill you—but not as quickly. Third, you will be hearing about John Bishop, no doubt. He is involved. *How* he is involved is not your concern. By now, I am certain he is also dead. Fourth, what is this all about? Why am I doing this?"

For the first time, Weiber-Krauss rose, hooked fingers in the pockets of his black silk vest.

"I am seizing power," the German said. "Power and wealth. I am going to run this territory and, from here, the rest of the nation. Those who are not part of my movement are in the way. They will be destroyed. You are being offered passage on that train, Mr. Avery. I advise you to keep the ticket with you at all times."

Avery nodded again and, with an encouraging smile and a hand laid reassuringly on his shoulder, Weiber-Krauss left the man to his visions of freedom and riches and, perhaps, even a thought or two about the dead man Bishop who he had once called a friend.

"Do you think they'll make it to the fort?" Cavanaugh asked when Weiber-Krauss returned to the adjoining office.

"Who can say?" Weiber-Krauss replied. "All that matters is they get close enough to be found, isn't it? The marshal's uniform will do the rest."

Cavanaugh gave his puppet's-head an acknowledging tilt as they waited for Smith to finish mixing his chemicals, precisely to the formula Weiber-Krauss had devised and tested on mice in this very place. Though Avery would not be here to witness it, what the German had said was not a pipe dream, not the reverie of an artillery-maddened veteran of the War Between the States.

It was going to happen and it was going to happen in a way that would make said war perhaps the last that would ever be fought on American soil . . .

Bishop returned to the lake to set his clothes out to try and to recover his rig and White Fox's horse. He had, with him, the saddlebags of Innocence Lee and his partner, whose name was Randy Coward. Their horses he left behind, as he would do with these items and most of their contents when he was finished going through them.

The first things he'd checked were the bodies of the two men. All he learned from them was that Coward had once worked on a Mississippi Steamboat named *Nelle*, according to a tattoo . . . Innocence had been shot in the neck, which was probably why he wore a high collar. It was an old wound, indicative of nothing. Considering how few people there were in the West, a high percentage of them got shot somehow, somewhere.

The contents of the saddlebags were equally unhelpful. No travel documents, correspondence, souvenir wanted posters of themselves, bankbooks—aught. Just chewing jerky, chewing tobacco, a local map, a newspaper from Denver that was two weeks old and unmarked, and a copy of *Infamous Crimes and Felons Magazine*, with Bishop's picture on the cover. Though his rig was discharging and his expression grim, the text made a point of noting that Bishop was defending himself. It was libel to imply that he was an infamous felon.

Bishop repacked everything and left it as he found it, except for the men. He dragged both men to the pit he had hatcheted out for himself, and, stuffing them more or less inside, he kicked rocks over them, hat-scooping pebbles as fill, added a few branches as cover so the birds and cats wouldn't get him. He left the horses untethered. Eventually someone would find them; at least they wouldn't be eaten.

It was nearly nightfall, and without a moon to speak of Bishop decided to make camp farther back along the trail. He would set out after White Fox in the morning. There was certainly no point going after Dent. The bastard was long gone and probably too frightened to stop anywhere, even in the dark.

Bishop rested where he had spent the previous night with White Fox. He didn't light a fire; he'd rather deal with predators circling him—they never did more—than moths swatting their dusty wings on his face. He closed his eyes thinking of the Cheyenne woman, her long onyx hair flying behind her, war club tethered to her belt as she rode the painted, this painted, to fight or to heal. He remembered the time and way she had first said his name.

"Bish-op." The syllables equally accented. The lips pursing and ovaling. They had become so close in spirit as to be soul mates. Not less, and not more. His own losses made intimacy impossible, at least for now. Unless he considered the torture of Innocence Lee intimate—which he supposed it was. The Chinese cook had told him that enemies create their own "whole" in the same way lovers do. Attentive, intense, and ultimately achieving a climax.

He fell asleep on his back, on White Fox's saddle, his rig attached, propped and angled low on a rock, ready to fire if he heard anything that sounded anything like a hammer, trigger, cylinder, or some combination thereof.

The syringe was the size of a six-shooter. It was adapted from an Indian enema syringe by Weiber-Krauss, not just for its volume but for its metal casing. The contents were too dangerous to trust to glass. If the living patient flailed and it flew, and it broke, it would have the same effect as the glass globes filled with toxins.

The man in the marshal's uniform was still not awake, though that wasn't because of his injuries. He had been given opium, injected with a medical syringe, both of which were stored in a large tin that had been hand-carried from Germany. That injection, like this one, was administered by Weiber-Krauss and not Smith. Smith held the lantern that helped the doctor find the vein.

Avery watched it all from his cot, where he had been allowed to sit, unshackled, provided he did not move. He did not move. He did not speak, though he was curious as all get-out what was going on. Weiber-Krauss being a doctor, he assumed it was an experimental treatment—one that the medical profession would not have sanctioned had he asked. So he didn't ask. Outside of prisons, volunteers for new medicines were also probably scarce. Perhaps it was a miracle cure. That might have been what Weiber-Krauss meant when he said they would all profit from this enterprise.

Avery didn't know. He was guessing. The entirety of his experience with science came from the dreadfuls, where things like this usually created a monster or a lunatic.

In addition to his other titles, Joseph Daniel Avery, medical pioneer. Weiber-Krauss was correct. That it might be illegal did not matter. And immorality depended on who was judging. Like that shoot-out with Bishop and the cousins. Ask ten people and you'd get ten different views of who was in the wrong. Though

Avery did wonder why this marshal had been selected for this, whether the injury to his face had occurred before or during his selection.

It was not his problem. Come daylight, all he had to do was sit on his ass and coax a horse along. Though he had to say, in addition to curiosity, he was plagued a little by Smith. The man looked bad, felt wrong, seemed soulless. He had felt that back in Good Fortune, the little muleteer with his whip.

Now that he thought of it, Avery wondered why the *driver* wasn't driving? Probably because he was needed here. Maybe driving was just something he did in public. If Weiber-Krauss was a doctor, maybe this man was a chemist or a botanist. In dreadfuls, the mentally twisted always traveled about in a profession people paid no heed to.

Weiber-Krauss gave Avery a brandy and told him to rest, since he'd be leaving in a very few hours. The portly man nodded, his three chins agreeing, and lay back enjoying the feel of not being tied to the bed. As he lay there, he heard quiet conversation about "Someone" Lee being late, and a randy coward being late, but Weiber-Krauss didn't seem overly perturbed. It was night, after all, and even snakes stayed put in the dark, he said.

Cavanaugh chuckled but there was no humor in it. There was no humor anywhere, Avery thought, and he missed that. He always tried to be, at least, jovial. Like with Bishop.

Bishop. He couldn't grasp the implications of the man's death, if it were true. He didn't press Weiber-Krauss on that either. The Shotgun had made a lot of enemies and, again, there was no saying which was bad and which was good. He would miss the man if he were gone, but Avery couldn't even think about that now. Those were thoughts for the Hospitality House, the memorial wall. The legend and the man were all part of that other world now.

The brandy had its way and Avery slipped into slumber with the image of the penny-dreadful front pages plastered across his mind's eye, the words floating as before . . .

Long before darkness fell, White Fox had stopped by a creek to water the horse and make a torch. The horse was skittish and she saw why. They had come upon the remains of a black bear, its carcass picked nearly clean. Used one of its leg bones, packed on still-damp patties of the coyotes that had eaten it, and lit it with a match. Then made a second. She stuck them both at the side of the buckboard and hurried on. As night came the malodorous lamps were both light and distant signal that help was coming. Her clackety arrival was met by an elder's croaked cries of *a'o'sémėstaa'e, a'o'tsémėstaa'e.* Ground owl.

The shouts of the sentry woke the Cheyenne camp, the few who could walk emerging into the light of their own few campfires. The tepees of the sick and dying already stood like grave markers. White Fox continued on to one in particular before stopping. She had already marked, in her mind, the box she would need and went to it immediately after leaping to the soft ground. Her knife stabbed through the cord of a box marked the same as the one that Innocence Lee had selected from. He seemed to know—she didn't wonder "how," not too deeply—what medicine was needed. A bottle in one hand, a torch in the other, she ducked under the flap of her own doeskin tepee.

The girl and an old woman were there, beside a little fire, the former very still, the latter attentively applying a wet cloth to her brow. Having known many illnesses over many scores of years, the white-haired woman seemed untouched by this one.

What passed for a smile bent the toothless mouth of the leathery face and the woman scooted back.

"The wagon," White Fox said in her native tongue. "See that everyone sips once from each bottle. Healthy first, then the sick. Use only half. I must soon go to another settlement."

The woman grunted understanding and rose.

"Snow Getting Deep," White Fox said after her. "Where is Firecrow?"

She made signs as she backed through the opening. The two gestures were ominous. They informed her: war party.

"Why?" White Fox asked as she opened the bottle.

"*Hávêsévemâhta'sóoma*" was the hushed reply.

The men were going after the Demon. John Bishop.

That was not something White Fox could do anything about. Not now. She silently prayed that he did not follow her, even knowing that he would. That her very tracks would lead the braves to him and him to them.

"The girl." White Fox focused herself.

Through the open flap White Fox heard tribe members already gathering, opening the boxes. They would do as she asked, do it cautiously, understanding what the old woman repeated to them.

Her shadow animated and distorted on the skins behind her—like a demon herself, she thought—White Fox parted the girl's lips carefully with one hand, poured the bluish liquid with the other. The barely conscious girl, blotched and awash with perspiration, coughed weakly as it went down. A *hmmm* came from her throat, then, as soothing liquid settled in.

Capping the bottle and setting it on the ground, White Fox eased under the child, slender fingers combing through tangled hair. As the fire burned lower and the sun rose higher she dosed the girl again. This time the girl swallowed of her own accord. The sounds of the settlement were muffled, seemed far away. Exhausted, White Fox shut her eyes, allowed her head to sink until her strong chin fell to her chest.

It was dark in the tepee, bright outside, the painted face of the fox on the outside seeming to stare down and watch over the occupants. There was no noise inside, no movement, save for small breaths until a soft voice caused White Fox to start. The girl was looking up, her eyes clear and wide. The woman smiled down at her and was met with a tiny, healthy grin.

"Did you have a nice rest?" White Fox asked.

The oval face nodded. She understood. She was Cheyenne. The medicine woman touched a cloth to the remnants of sweat from the broken fever, saw the spots that were already fading. "Can you tell me your name?"

"*Naesetsestôtse,*" she said, pointing.

"Blessing Medicine?" White Fox said, following the finger. The girl was pointing to the jar. "Oh yes.

Yes. This is the medicine that blessed your life and returned it to us."

The girl's smile widened. "*Naesetsestôtse,*" she repeated, turning the finger toward herself.

White Fox was uplifted. Raised and touched by innocence in a way she had not been for too, too long. "You will have a new name," she agreed. "But—your parents? Your tribe?"

The girl shook her head.

"Were you in migration? Your tribe?"

Another shake of the small head.

"Lost?" White Fox asked.

The girl shook her head again.

"Were you carrying things?" the woman asked.

The girl nodded. White Fox felt her heart tear in two. She had been sent away. Possibly to avoid sickness from the other settlement. Perhaps to escape a conflict between the Cheyenne and the Arapaho. The tribes, long allied, had been fighting for territory of late as settlers seized their lands. It was the inevitable result of the failure of Red Cloud's War, a recent and foredoomed struggle between American Pony Soldiers and braves of the Lakota, Cheyenne, and Arapaho nations. The Oglala Lakota chief Red Cloud struck in response to miners, but the struggle flowed south and spread and soon turned brave against brave as they competed for a limited amount of game and land. Blessing Medicine could have been sent away or hidden by her parents to escape capture by Lakota or Arapaho.

"Blessing Medicine," White Fox said. "It is very, very fitting."

The camp was still . . . too still. It told her that

only the ill and the healers were here, the men having departed.

"Blessing Medicine," the woman continued, "I want to ask you something. Something important. All right?"

The girl nodded with a little more enthusiasm now, having been addressed by her new name.

"When you came to us, brought by the constable Firecrow, you spoke of *Hávêsévemâhta'sóoma.* The Demon. Do you recall?"

The girl shook her head.

"Let me try and help you," White Fox said, wiggling her nose at the girl, getting her to laugh a little. "You told us you saw someone who was half a man, but also half a gun. Does that—"

"Yes, I saw him," she said in a musical little voice.

"Can you tell me?"

She pointed to the tepee. "Like that."

White Fox followed the skinny little finger. "Like—deerskin?"

The girl tittered a little. "No. On it."

On it. White Fox was puzzled until her eyes settled on the fox that Spirit Eyes had rendered on the skin. "Tell me more," she urged.

"He scared me."

"Did he move or say anything?"

"No," the girl said. "And he was like my father's great father when we found him in his blanket, gone from his body. He had no color."

And then White Fox understood. The girl had not seen John Bishop. She had not seen the man at all. Before hiding in the rotted log, she had seen something else, something far deadlier than the man with the gun-arm.

* * *

The carthorse was grazing and White Fox did not want to take him. He had done his work for the day. Armed with a blanket, her club, and her knife, and a half-full deerskin water pouch slung over a shoulder, she went to the small corral and then to the tent of Young Bear, a bold youth in his tenth year, still shy of proficiency but with a magnificent painted.

"I wish to borrow your horse," she told the sulking boy who was squatting nearby and chipping stone for arrows.

"To go where?" he asked, eyeing her hands full of weapon.

"Did you see the war party?"

He stopped chipping, nodded glumly.

"Headed east?"

He nodded again.

"I must go to meet them, quickly," she informed him, already moving past him back to where the animal stood nuzzling another mount.

"Take me," he said, rising and putting his shoulders back.

"You will slow me," she said, adding critically, "as you do now."

She hurried on, the boy running after her. "I can fight!" he insisted over a shaking fist.

White Fox ducked under the single log rail, threw the blanket on the horse. "I do not need a fighter," she said, hooking the knife to her belt and pulling herself onto the painted by the dark mane.

"But you go to join the war party!"

"No," she replied. "I go stop them!"

With a deep, firm "*Hyaah!*" White Fox wheeled the horse to the east with a strong, certain pull on its mane and heeled it in the ribs. The animal neighed, stopped, stood its ground, and got the two heels again, harder. Twice. With a whinny it bolted forward, responded to a pull to leap the fence, and kicked up a cloud of dust as it galloped away, leaving the sullen boy holding his flint and standing bony-shouldered in the late morning sun.

CHAPTER ELEVEN
No Man's Land

Loping. That was the word that best described Avery's day.

He loped from the room to an office to a staircase to a buckboard. The horse came loping from the makeshift stable that used to be a large storage shed, from the looks of the axes and shovels and other rusted implements still hanging from the wall. There were over thirty animals in all, fed by a man who forked hay from one to the other to the next. Avery could have kicked himself. His instincts had been right when he first asked Weiber-Krauss about horses. He thought back to the riders who came to town with ponies to sell to "some European" who had purchased the mine buildings and planned to turn them into a ranch. He had never been able to find out anything about the man, because all the documents on file were with a shipping concern in Germany. He had never been able to ride out here because the property was private and he had no cause to obtain a warrant.

Avery could not get out of there fast enough. He knew all these implements well, and from this very bloody mine. And finally, after the man in the marshal's uniform was carried to the cart, blanketed and sweating, and placed beside a sack of food and a water barrel, Avery loped to the step-up, sat, and with a map handed him by Cavanaugh, started loping to the road.

"You didn't look at your chart," the Confederate sailor noted.

"I know the way to Fort Collins, friend," Avery insisted.

"You sure? You took a good blow on the head."

"I'm seein' a little bleary-eyed on my left side," the man acknowledged. "Didn't affect my memory."

"Good to know," the Southerner said. "Because you know that Weiber-Krauss meant what he told you."

"I remember everything he told me," Avery replied. "Loyalty, rewards."

"Right. Don't think for yourself."

"Never do," the man replied. That was what got him into trouble in New York. Shaking down one too many establishments, thinking his fellow Municipals would support him instead of concluding they could have more themselves if he were gone.

Cavanaugh backward-leaped to the ground as Avery loped on. He didn't ask about it, didn't say anything, but he noticed that there was no one new at the mine office. He had seen Smith and Weiber-Krauss outside, had waved to them but got no return, and suspected that the men they were waiting for did not arrive. If they were out hunting John Bishop, as Avery had surmised, he was not surprised. That was one of the reasons he did not give too much thought to the possible loss of his other meal ticket. Bishop hated this about him, but Avery had recognized the value in having feet in both camps of a struggle. Whoever came out on top, he'd be right there bringing the other foot into alignment.

The sun felt good on his bald, throbbing skull. Even the clouds above had a lope to them, drifting in the way he was headed, company. They were certainly livelier than the man on his back, who didn't make a sound. Cavanaugh had told him to water the man's mouth once every hour, as though he were a houseplant. He was to pour the water and massage his throat so he didn't choke or drown but swallowed.

Avery would mark the time with the sun. It would take him at least until the late afternoon to reach the fort; he would certainly be there by dusk.

The plains sun was hot, but Avery knew it was not *that* hot. He reached around to ladle water from the barrel, poured it over his head. He noticed, then, that his passenger was shivering with dark spots forming on his face.

"You ain't healin'," he said. Spoken aloud, the words carried a frisson of concern. It gave him his first hint that either the medicine was not working—or it was not medicine.

He kicked that thought from his mind. Booted it hard. This was just a kind of cycling-through something, getting the disease so it *could* be cured. He loped on, pausing to cut himself bread from the loaf they had given him, slapping on a thin slab of the boiled ham they had included as well. He was perspiring and the thought of a salty lunch sounded right. The plain was flat, a well-worn straight ribbon of dirt leading to distant mountains in whose foothills—like those he had recently departed—lay the fort. To the south of them, Cheyenne territory. There was no path in that direction. No one from the mine or from the town had a reason to go that way.

He chewed loudly, which seemed to enhance the taste. Avery had thought that hunger was the reason he had been feeling a little faint. When the ham didn't improve his condition he decided it had to be the sun and took another ladle of water, this time to drink. Halting the horse, he slid from the seat to relieve himself. He watered a scorpion, as much to keep it back as to keep from wetting his boot; he *was* dizzy. Climbing back on, Avery filled his mouth with the last of the meat and leaned back to see if there was something he could use to cover his head. He was annoyed that he hadn't thought to ask for a hat.

He reached for the blanket to see if the marshal were wearing a neckerchief.

He was, a yellow one. It was stained through with perspiration. But that wasn't what arrested Avery's attention. The man was now covered with pocks, with pox it seemed to him.

"The bloody maniacs," he muttered. He was still chewing the last of the ham and flecks flew. He swallowed, trying to get his suddenly scattered mind to make sense of this. To give this man a fatal disease and then not monitor the cure? How was that any kind of research?

The feeling of discomfort rose, along with the beat of Avery's heart. He couldn't fathom reasons. He couldn't concentrate hard enough, woozy in the seat, to try to *fathom* reasons. His passenger needed medical help. Prompt attention. He shook the weathered reins hard, lurched back as the horse moved, and while he was leaning back searched around for a buggy whip. There was one behind him, halfway under the marshal. Avery used extended fingers to tickle the handle and pull it over; then he grabbed it, turned swinging, and snapped the horse to greater speed. He rocked back again, but this time had taken the precaution of bracing his fat palm on the seat back.

There had to be something at the fort, something Weiber knew could help. That was why he had been sent there. They had to be working together.

Sweat filled his eyes, stinging them, as Avery cracked the whip again, then fumbled it as he tried to put it on the seat. It fell and he left it, the horse swaying before him even though it was trotting straight.

"Go," he told the animal quietly. "You just go."

And then the sun and clouds swirled together as he slumped over on the side of the bumping buckboard.

Bishop was up with the birds and on his way before the sun had done more than peek over the horizon. Reigniting the campfire, he caught a fish using thistle, as White Fox had shown him, the pink flower acting as bait. He gutted it with her knife, and while it cooked he changed into his dry clothes, stiff from the river but a better fit than Randy Coward's wardrobe. Bishop did keep a bandolier he found on the man's horse, slung it over his shoulder. He wouldn't use the loops for shells. But he had an idea for a new medicine kit. It would be more efficient, he reasoned, if a doctor did not have to carry a bag, if tools and vials could be tucked in a strap. Bishop didn't know, but he suspected this. Seeing his old drawings had rekindled that spark he once had. The spark of invention. It was a good feeling.

Bishop rode off, chewing casually on the lake trout, spitting its bones from the tip of his tongue.

There was no reason to rush. The ride would take a half-day at least and there was no reason to push the painted. He was enjoying the uncustomary quiet, the unchanging view, the sunny fleece above and the reasonably green grasses ahead. His thoughts were still rich with White Fox and their time here. Their connection enriched him. It may well have saved him. He let that, like the warm sun, roll around him as he rode.

He was hungry again shortly after noon, and used the hatchet to dig out a rabbit warren. He caught the male, broke its back, and cooked it over a fire he built in a natural circle of rock. The painted chewed grass, occasionally looking to the west as though wondering where his mistress had gone. Bishop had removed his rig, relaxing his shoulder along with the rest of himself before he set out.

It was shortly after his meal that Bishop noticed the line of braves coming toward him. He counted ten in the wavering heat that hovered near to the ground. They weren't just riding. They were heading. They were not pushing hard, but they were moving quickly enough to suggest a mission. A purpose.

The purpose might be him, though he could not understand why Cheyenne, to whom White Fox would have brought the medicine, would mean him any harm.

But Indians were strange. It was easy to rile them with a good deed that insulted their manhood or interrupted a ceremony or diminished a shaman who felt that healing was his job and his alone. Bishop did not understand Indians, and he did not understand very many women. It was his misfortune to be able to read mostly people who wanted to kill or exploit him.

He tried not to think the worst. They might be a welcoming party sent by the tribe to escort him to the settlement. It was not. It was the worst. The men were painted for war. Red lines across their upper arms. White lines down the face. Full array of warbonnets.

There was not enough time to slip into the rig, and he wasn't sure he wanted to. Though he could cut them all down in moments, he did not want to do anything belligerent if it wasn't necessary. He had the hatchet and he had the knife and he had Randy Coward's Remington. All were within easy reach. Bishop rose to face them, walking over and taking the reins of the painted so it would not be spooked.

Bishop stood on the side of the horse facing the Indians. He wanted to show them he was not afraid. He did not have to hide behind the horse of a squaw. He remained in place, sucking rabbit grease from his gums as he waited. He did not like what the men did next. The line widened, arced, and they came around in a wide circle. Bishop did not look around, did not watch them. The leader was the one in the middle, the brave who continued to ride straight toward him as the circle closed behind him. Bishop kept an unyielding gaze on that man.

"You," the man spoke when he was about fifteen yards distant. "Bishop."

"Yes. I'm Bishop."

"You kill many."

"You do not bring me fresh rain," Bishop said, the closest expression the Cheyenne had to "news."

"You kill many *Cheyenne.*"

"No."

"They die in the settlements, in their tepee."

"That's not my doing," Bishop said. "I am a medicine man—good medicine. That is bad spirits. Not me."

"You!" the man said again. "Little girl see you. Spread sickness."

"I don't know what little girl you're talking about and I do not spread sickness." Bishop wondered just how thorough this campaign against him must be if the perpetrators had poisoned the Indians against him as well as the fort.

"You will come with me," he said.

"I know you," Bishop said as the man was finally close enough. "You are the constable. Firecrow. Your friend is my friend, White Fox. I helped her get medicine for your people."

"She brought it. Not you."

"I had other business."

"You will come with me."

"Where? Why?"

"To the tribe, the elders."

"I was headed there anyway," Bishop told him. "If you'll just let me get my things—"

"No things," Firecrow insisted. He threw a hand toward the rig. "It stays."

"It does not stay," Bishop replied firmly.

"You come *now*! Mount!"

Bishop shook his head. "Firecrow, we don't have to scuffle over this. We want the same thing. But the rig comes with me."

The brave pulled a bowie knife from the sheath on his belt. He pointed it at Bishop. He gave a command. "Mount!"

Goddamn it, Bishop thought. This was the third day running that someone wanted to kill him. Someone so different from the others that it would be comical if the situation weren't so grave.

The revolver was in his waistband but even if he were uncommonly lucky and hit an enemy with every shot, there were only five bullets, which would leave five very angry braves riding him down. Plus: these were White Fox's people. Killing them would put a chasm between them, one that might never be broached. Besides. If, as he expected, she were a part of this—unwittingly—there was no avoiding the struggle.

"Firecrow, if I must fight you, I will. But that is not what I wish."

The Cheyenne dismounted. He removed his warbonnet. Handed it to the mounted brave to his left. "Then fight."

Firecrow stood a few inches taller than Bishop, powerfully built. And he had a pair of arms. He strode forward with a hip-forward swagger that was meant to impress his warriors, not to frighten Bishop. The knife was supposed to do that, held blade-backward. The Cheyenne did not stab when they fought, they slashed. Raising his arm to the opposite shoulder, Firecrow would be able to cut down diagonally across Bishop's chest.

Bishop had already shifted to kill-mode. The doctor in him: studying the body, looking for the most vulnerable patches. A rack of beads hung from Firecrow's narrow neck. The girth of that neck meant he could move his head out of danger with a jerk here, a dodge there. His wrists were thick, biceps powerful. From riding, not from fighting; the equestrian muscles were the most finely developed. His legs were not unusually strong. He rode with his arms, not using his legs very much. He did not walk a great deal. A constable, responsible for tribal law and order under the terms of the white man, would be accustomed to giving orders as Firecrow had done just now.

Bishop handed the reins of the painted to a brave. The horse was led to the outside of the circle. He put the revolver and knife on the ground. He palmed the hatchet, holding it loosely. Tight sinew inhibited the flow of energy. He was going to attack with fluid blows, not savage chops. Bishop was not a proficient fighter with the tomahawk, but he had cut wood at his homestead. The moves were familiar. The angled blade. The efficient downward stroke—short down, then lateral. The motions between his own chin and pelvis, so that a blow could also be used as a block, protecting his vital organs.

"If I fall, they will take you," Firecrow advised.

It was a caution, not an attempt to avoid a fight. He wanted Bishop to know this was a losing struggle.

"If you fall, there will only be nine to try," Bishop replied.

Whether or not the others spoke English, the

remark drew no response. Bishop didn't expect it to. But he wanted them to hear his voice. Unafraid.

The men were only a few feet apart when Bishop brought White Fox's tomahawk up so that the head of the blade was facing his nose. He was staring right across the edge, at his opponent. Firecrow did as Bishop had anticipated. He brought the blade up diagonally, prepared to cut downward. The Cheyenne's left arm lay taut at his side, slightly bent at the elbow. He did not intend to surrender the advantage of possessing an extra limb. That was fine with Bishop. He was accustomed to doing everything with one arm. Except killing. He had explored movement, change-ups, foreign to most men. They were second nature now. Instinct.

Bishop surprised Firefox by taking a big crescent step forward, up the center and planting his foot wide, to the left. That moved his entire torso to the right of the knife. When it flashed down, Bishop's body was already not there. Firecrow cut air. At the same time Bishop made a small circling, outward motion with his wrist. The little ax flipped to its side, just beyond Bishop's shoulder, and cut horizontally from the outside in. It met the flesh of Firecrow's upper arm. The left arm, the spare. Firecrow shuddered, momently freezing in the position of his downward slash: bent forward, his momentum having carried him down.

The gash in his arm wasn't deep, but it was enough to distract him while Bishop took another step to the side. Now Bishop was facing his opponent's right side. Firecrow was facing only the outer perimeter of braves.

With a cry, Firecrow did not bother to rise but cut

laterally back, low along the line of his hips, to where Bishop was standing. The doctor brought the tomahawk down to meet the bowie. There was a clunk as metal struck wood. Firecrow pushed the blade against the carved oak handle, trying to muscle the blade into Bishop. The doctor used the other part of the weapon. He brought the club-back straight up. Firecrow's force carried him in a semicircle while the blunt metal mallet struck his chin. Snapped his head back.

The Cheyenne roared, stepped back, charged forward with the bowie over his shoulder. The gleaming point was aimed at juncture of neck and shoulder. It connected by sheer, savage force. But the knife struck the leather bandolier and, apart from a punch in the clavicle, Bishop was unaffected. And Firecrow had left himself vulnerable. Not to the hatchet but to his adversary's powerful human arm. An arm accustomed to doing everything.

As the Indian struck, Bishop circled the tomahawk and his arm around the neck of the Cheyenne, from the back. Circled it so that the back of the weapon was on the other side, then encircling, then reaching the Adam's apple. Bishop closed, choking with strength the Cheyenne had clearly not anticipated. One painted hand reached up, was unable to get purchase. Firecrow was forced to drop the bowie and bring his second hand up. But Bishop had already put his knee in the small of the Indian's back, wrestled him so he was arched backward, then bent so his weight was on the throat of the off-balance man.

Bishop did not look at his opponent. His steely eyes were on the circle of braves. If they moved, he would be forced to use this man as a shield. He felt they would be less likely to attack if their leader might be the first victim.

Firecrow was gagging. Bishop pulled him a few staggering steps to the side so he could plant his own heavy foot atop the bowie. Then he said, "I want to talk, not kill."

The Cheyenne continued to pull at the powerful forearm up against his windpipe, artfully cutting off the flow of air and blood.

Using surgically trained fingers, Bishop skillfully turned the tomahawk so it was now the blade, not the club, against the man's throat.

"Do not make me cut," the doctor warned. "I do not want this!"

Firecrow did not yield. Bishop fought the urge to draw blood. He thought again about White Fox—

"*Pa'èséèstsèstse!*" bellowed a familiar voice. "Stop this!"

The cry came from across the prairie. A freakish coincidence or demented fate. Either way, Bishop did not have to look to know who it was but he did look anyway. And what he saw was a punch in the belly. White Fox was galloping forward . . . but not. The horse was moving hard and fast but she was slumped onto the animal, one fist full of mane, the other arm wrapped around the great neck for support. After the effort to shout, the woman slumped toward the side holding the mane.

Bishop dropped the half-conscious Firecrow and ran toward the circle of braves. They seemed hesitant to let him out. But did, at the last moment, seeing that he would have pushed through. None went to help their leader, who was on his knees. If he rose it must be of his own effort. A leader who could not help himself was a former leader. That was ancient law.

Bishop flung the ax into the soft ground so he would have a hand free. The horse slowed as Bishop approached. It had been looking for guidance for miles; the hand on its mane had been less and less in command. It trotted toward the man who extended his hand, palm out—a target for the big brown eyes of the stallion.

He turned his armed side toward the animal as it slowed to a walk. He caught White Fox as she rolled from the strong back like a sack of grain whose ropes had snapped. Bishop bent under her weight, slowing her fall and laying her on the grassy earth.

"Oh no," he said more to himself.

White Fox's eyes were closed. Her brow was beaded with hot sweat. Her breathing came in quick, sharp gasps. He placed his palm on her forehead, was alarmed at how feverish she was.

"No," he said again. Without looking away from her sweet, bloodless face he partly turned and shouted, "Water!"

"Bish . . . op," she said. "Another. Not you. Little . . . Hen . . . saw . . ."

"Hush," Bishop urged.

White Fox closed her eyes and her mouth, in that order.

One of the braves wheeled his mount and covered the few yards in moments. He passed down a water skin while at the same time taking the mane of the other horse. Bishop reached across his chest to take the pouch. He undid the leather knot on top with his teeth, emptied the contents in splashes onto White Fox—her face, her neck, her bare arms, her shins. He rubbed the cooling liquid in and she stirred, a little. Her eyes opened dully.

"Bishop," she said with a broken smile.

"Don't speak," he said. He rose and turned to the disrupted circle. Firecrow was standing uncertainly in the middle. "Come around here. Create shade. At once!"

Rubbing his throat, the Cheyenne leader translated for the others. They did as instructed while Bishop went back to retrieve the bowie. Firecrow made as if to protest but said nothing as the doctor turned and hurried back to where White Fox lay. He immediately began hacking the ground. Hacking with a fever of his own, the need to get her into cooler earth, out of the afternoon heat, as quickly as possible.

"Firecrow! I want a blanket and long sticks," Bishop yelled back. "Four of them!"

The Cheyenne told a man to dismount and bring his warrior's blanket over. He told another to take two spears to the doctor. With uncertain expression, the braves did as asked. It was not unusual for a tribe to limp home from combat. The act of having fought was more important than whether or not a victory had ensued. Courage was all; skill was relative; death proved nothing. And enemies one day, gathered around a pipe of peace, could be blood-brothered allies the next. Still, they were not used to so rapid a turnaround.

Bishop hacked out a trench, gently lay White Fox in the dark soil. He tried not to think of it as a grave, as it had been for Randy Coward and Innocence Lee. It was the womb of Mother Earth where White Fox could be reborn. He stood and with powerful drives he plunged the native spears into the earth—top, bottom, sides.

"Tie the blanket on top," he instructed.

Firefox translated but the Cheyenne had understood. Their expression now showed admiration. They did not know of this man and this woman, other than what the constable had said of the Demon. What they saw now did not appear to be any kind of a monster.

Bishop stood back from the makeshift field hospital. He faced Firecrow, who had come over to assist.

"I will need more water," Bishop said. "And send a rider back to the settlement. Quickly, before the medicine is used up. Bring me a bottle from a blue box, with blue water inside."

Firefox moved as if to go himself but Bishop grabbed his arm.

"No. I'll need you to talk to the others."

The constable understood. He sought, selected one man. Short, light, eager. His name was Knob Pipe, and he smelled of tobacco. He was up on his steed and turned to the west even as Firecrow was finishing.

Then Bishop, not content but content with all he could do at the moment, turned back to White Fox, sat beside her with his legs crossed, and took her hand lightly in his.

"Major!"

The man on the wall had let the binoculars drop across his chest, turned to cup his hands around his mouth, shouted again into the compound.

"Major Terry!"

Major Burton Terry was taking his three-o'clock circuit of the compound, with his three-o'clock cigar. He turned his gray eyes toward the private who had shouted down. Bellowed around the rough stogie he had rolled himself, through his neatly clipped beard, "Yes, Private Ford?"

"There's a wagon just sitting on Ingham Hill," he said. "Just sitting. Driver asleep. Looks like a man in the back. Possible uniform."

The tall officer, a battle scar from forehead to cheek, barked orders for two men to bring it back.

"Search for explosives, first," he said cautiously. "And tricks." He was thinking first and foremost of that crackpot place they had investigated, with designs for booby traps and explosives and unearthly new devices. John Bishop was still out there, still free to work madness on the civilization he clearly hated.

The gate was opened by the sentries there, and the men rode out on puffy clouds. Both approached wide, their sidearms drawn. There was always a chance the men were not unconscious or asleep, were not even white, were Cheyenne with a new and devious trick. Terry remembered one instance, during the war, when a pale Apache named Powder Face had infiltrated a Union camp in a Union uniform and shot three men before he was killed with a picket post shoved through his back.

Terry watched the dust billow and fade, the gate close, the sounds of the hoofbeats swallowed by distance.

"Private?" he shouted up at the wall.

The observer was back behind his binoculars. "No movement yet, sir," he reported.

Movement within the fort had slowed—imperceptibly—but apart from routine drilling and patrols, so little ever changed in here that any new business was met with a blend of anticipation and readiness. Terry was one of those Easterners, a Bostonian, who had been with the 1st Massachusetts Volunteer Cavalry Regiment from 1862 on. He had taken his saber wound in the Battle of Secessionville, when the Rebels stopped the Union's only attempt to seize Charleston by land. After six months in the hospital, Terry took to the field with a vengeance—quite literally. He hated gray. He hated treason. He hated, period. It probably had not been the best idea to read what he thought was a seafaring adventure while recovering. Growing up, he knew about whalers. Injured by "the Confederacy" he learned about white whales. But a flimsy bed in Hagerstown, Maryland, was also where he learned to make his own smokes to help fix the sight in his right eye. That was his own therapy, his own determination to work around the scar tissue that had formed on the upper and lower lids.

"Sir!" the private called down, watching for hand signals that were crafted for and unique to this unit. "Party signals that—sir, Marshal Duffin is the passenger in the buckboard!"

"Alive?"

It took a moment for the private to respond. "Yes, sir!"

"The other?"

Another moment. "Alive—no identification. A wound on his scalp."

Terry's first thought was an Indian attack, but then it wasn't likely the two would have gotten away in a wooden cart.

"What else are they carrying?"

"Cargo—buggy whip. Blanket. Water cask. Some food supplies. No weapons."

"Undercarriage?"

That took a longer moment. "Clean, sir."

"Horse?"

"No markings, sir."

It was a standard checklist that the sentry could have answered without being prompted. But the major liked to keep an orderly flow to things, with himself a part of it.

"Bring 'em in," Terry ordered, patting his pocket for a match to relight the dead cigar. "I will see Duffin in the infirmary."

"Yes, sir!"

The major returned to his office. There was a detail to investigate unscheduled arrivals and sanctuary seekers. It was led by Sergeant Manat—who had been a sergeant over Terry when the young man had enlisted, stayed a sergeant after supposedly raping a Southern girl. There was no proof, though, and—Terry had investigated—no youthful issue nine months later. Manat was slavishly loyal to the man who had rescued his career from safeguarding a shuttered Union bullet factory in upstate New York.

The giant of a noncommissioned officer strode out like Paul Bunyan, followed by four much smaller men carrying canvas bags for contents and stretchers for the two men. They walked through the open gate. The wagon would be cleared before being allowed inside. As with captured Cheyenne, even wounded men were not permitted to stay together inside the fort. Nor with whatever they carried. Quarantine was a regulation, and Terry was all about the rulebook—

unless it conflicted with that other book, the one about the whale. Out here, as on the sea, he was the injured commander who established and enforced policy.

Terry went to his office but left the door open so he could hear and see what was happening outside the gate. The unit moved methodically. The two inactive souls were removed, carricd at a fast walk to the doctor, who stood shielding his eyes from the slanting sun, watching from his command. He stepped aside to admit the bearers, motioning where the new arrivals were to go. Terry could not see that, but he could see Manat taking his big steps back with one thinly stuffed sack and the bullwhip, which he cracked to check its operational status. Details like that would have to go in his report. Terry liked details. Like how to turn a whale into lantern oil. Details were the true stuff of big pictures. Pull the right peg and even something as large as an Indian nation could topple in on itself.

Pull the wrong one and it could drag you down, the Pequod *with it,* he reminded himself.

Manat saluted at the door, ducked to enter.

"Is Duffin awake?"

"Mute as a flapjack," Manat said. He hoisted the bag and whip. "Nothing too interesting here, as the private said. But I think you ought to go to the infirmary."

"When the doctor—"

"Pardon, but before then, sir," Manat interrupted.

Terry sat back, puffed, waited.

"The time you spent in Hagerstown," the deep voice said. "You saw a lot of bad health. I want to know if you saw anything like this."

CHAPTER TWELVE
Exodus

The Cheyenne brave, Knob Pipe, scudded his horse to a stop, dismounted in the same movement, and unshouldered a horsehide pouch as he ran over, his stumpy legs churning. He went to hand the bottle to Firecrow, who was squatting beside Bishop. Bishop remained half under the blanket holding White Fox's hand. With a grunt and a sweep of his arm, the constable indicated that the bottle was to be handed directly to Bishop. It was a show of respect—and submission, as the defeated party—which the doctor had not been expecting.

But he had also not been thinking about Firecrow or his status or the charges that had been falsely leveled against him. He was watching the young woman for any signs of deterioration or improvement. He saw a little of both. The fever had not risen, but color had not returned to any part of her. With the help of Firecrow he had removed her garments to put her in closer contact with the cooling soil, laying the clothing on top of her for the sake of modesty. His own, he suspected, more than hers.

Bishop had scrubbed his hand with the moisture and skin of a cactus. He used his index finger and thumb to gently part her lips, make sure her teeth were not locked. A small opening remained and, pulling the cork stopper with his teeth, holding it there, he poured a few drops of the blue formula into White Fox's mouth. He saw her gullet move very slightly.

"Good girl," he said in a soothing voice. She might not hear the words, might not know it was him, but patients, even unconscious, were known to respond to tone of voice.

Assured that she could swallow, he heavy-dosed her with half the contents, poured slowly in little tips of the bottle but following hard-upon so that one would pile on the next and force her to swallow.

She did, coughing lightly. But the curative went down.

All the while Firecrow was watching the doctor, not the treatment. Bishop did not know what was on his mind. It could be humiliation. Hate. Suspicion. Anything. Cheyenne were easy to read if you were a Cheyenne.

When he finished, Bishop replaced the stopper by mouth, with a tigerish parting of his own lips.

"You care for her," the constable observed.

"Very much, Firecrow." Bishop watched for any reaction from the girl. He was hoping she did not regurgitate. In her state, vomiting was always a risk.

"Even without an arm, you are a doctor as you are a warrior."

"A warrior by necessity," Bishop said.

"Nuh-cessity?"

"Need. I had to become one," Bishop said. "I wish—Lord, how I wish—I could still be just a doctor. With my wife and son and an oath to heal still my highest priority. My . . . reason for living," he clarified for the Indian.

"White Fox has told me your life," Firecrow said. "I have seen the pictures. I heard what she said to you"—he hesitated, hating to admit his error—"I think I understand."

Bishop did not ask him to explain. He didn't care. Not right now.

"A girl saw a demon," the Cheyenne went on anyway. "With a gun-arm. Spreading sickness. We came to stop this. It may be she saw someone showing pictures in those books."

More false evidence, Bishop thought. Convincing people of something that wasn't true. It was easy. All you had to do was say it over and over. And with authority. He had heard it in the army, had seen hysterical sickness in the medical tents. One person suffered an amputation, suddenly everyone was fearful and planning for a life with one arm or one leg.

It was ironic. Bishop had never done anything of the sort. But here he was, a hollow sleeve pinned to his lapel.

"One thing I learned in the army," Bishop said, "you don't attack strength. You go around it. This lie about me. That has been supported here and there and has taken on the likeness of truth. Like the dancing shadows of hands around a campfire, now an eagle, now a horse."

"Stories for children," Firecrow said reflectively.

"Very much so." Bishop adjusted his seat, stretching a cramped leg without releasing White Fox's hand. "I did not attack the lies because more flow in to fill that space. Only the truth is a beaver dam. I have sought that."

"What is truth?"

Bishop snickered. "Greater men than you and I have asked that very question. I don't know, exactly. All I do know is that someone is trying to blame me for the spreading of disease. Why they are causing widespread illness I do not know. But I will find that out."

"We," Firecrow said.

Bishop regarded him. "Thank you. Yes, we. For this is our fight now."

Off beyond the blanket, at Firecrow's direction, the braves had been using the remaining spears, other blankets, and tumbleweed—softened by kneading fingers, then crushed into doeskin sacks—to create a stretcher. Others were making torches. As soon as the sun went down, when the night air was cool and invigorating, White Fox would have to be brought back to the settlement for her tepee and rest. Since she could not sit a horse, a comfortable carrier slung between horses would be used to transport her.

The men sat in silence while the others worked swiftly but efficiently. When they were finished, all but two of them plus Knob Pipe were sent back to the settlement to prepare for the arrival of the patient. Through Firecrow, Bishop had given the little man instructions about caring for the woman. He also said that none of the healers, himself included, should remain in a tepee of the sick for long. No one in camp should drink from a skin that has touched the lips of the ill. The exceptions were those who were recovering. Their bodies would be strong enough to fight new illness. He also said the open air would help to heal and carry away the evil spirits.

"These spirits must not find a new place of rest," Bishop said simply. No slight was intended, but this was not the time to explain about communicable diseases.

The sun dragged itself along the sky, bright blue turned to purple, and as the sun set the Cheyenne woman seemed to find new life. Her head moved; there were sounds that were like those of a sleeper, dreaming, and not of a patient in pain.

"This is good?" Firecrow asked.

"It is," Bishop said, a choke in his voice. "It is very good. We have to listen to hear breathing. She has trouble even when she isn't sick."

"Her mother told her it was the work of *Wihio*, the breath-stealing spider."

Bishop made no comment. He did not want to contradict an elder, an insult to a Cheyenne. Not when they were getting along so well.

The men watched as the night bloom seemed to come to life. And then, distant thunder.

Firecrow turned to the northeast, his eyes scanning the skies.

"No storm," he said.

Bishop had looked as well. There was a second boom. There was not a third. He felt sick inside.

"What then?" Firecrow asked.

"It's a signal, probably from the fort."

"Fight?"

"Not as you mean it," Bishop said. "That is a signal for no one to approach."

* * *

Weiber-Krauss sat alone in his office, medical texts stacked to one side, drawings scrolled tight on the other, tied with red tape. In the center was a Bible, in German. It was open to Exodus 15. He was puffing on his meerschaum pipe, reflecting on the book and its wisdom.

The doctor was not a man of faith. Even had he been so inclined, wars and suffering had made the idea gagging. To believe that anyone other than man had dominion over Earth and fate was disproved by the state of things. He had become a doctor to heal, but then a service he had chanced upon at that camp outside of Gettysburg gave him a new idea just how to do that. You don't keep fighting disease. You eliminate it. In this case, the disease was greed and the carrier was men. He saw that in his own day-to-day life now. Pay men to do evil and there was never a shortage of takers. He needed them. He didn't like it but they were necessary—like marksmen were necessary in combat, like scalpels were necessary in the hands—hand—of someone like John Bishop.

The sermon he had heard was about the great flood, and the preacher had been equating the war to a wiping-clean of the continent beneath the foundations of Union. Lincoln was Noah. The ark was the Constitution, and it was reinforced later in the Proclamation freeing the slaves. More oarsmen, liberated in the South to carry the flood to Georgia and the Carolinas and eventually to Richmond.

Weiber-Krauss bought a Bible in Philadelphia and read it page by page. Therein lay the answer. The word of God Himself. A flood had cleaned away one kind of sin. One form of rotted growth and fruitless ground. The answer was in the story of Moses and Pharaoh. In the plagues.

The part beyond that, in the Wilderness of Sin, was not for now. Those rigid laws provided no room for the action that needed to be taken. One line had told Weiber-Krauss what must be done, Exodus 15:7: "And in the greatness of thine excellency thou hast overthrown them that rose up against thee: thou sentest forth thy wrath, which consumed them as stubble."

Great wrath had Weiber-Krauss. Great majesty had Weiber-Krauss and the noble line that had been descended from the *Alter Adel*, the ancient nobility that dated to the fourteenth century. The House of the Count of Rotwang. Weiber-Krauss had come to America as a boy to study with his uncle Franz, who ran the shipping enterprises. Though the formation of the German Confederation in 1815 had cost them some of their autonomy in their state of Hesse-Kassel, the true ruin had come in 1866. Weiber-Krauss had been about to return home, having completed his medical studies and field education in the war. He had been about to go back when a new German unification left Hesse-Kassel absorbed by Prussia, denuded of many holdings, and retaining titles only in name.

Weiber-Krauss stayed. He was established. He had skills. And after reading of the work of an Austrian geneticist, in particular his methodology more than his findings, Weiber-Krauss had a vision that joined both disgust with the world and the loss of familial prestige. He would loose his own plague on the world. One that he could release. Or cure. One that he would constantly refine so that any solution crafted by other doctors would avail them not at all. He would always be ahead of them. John Bishop had been his inspiration that way. His mind never rested. His desire to help was a mission.

If anyone was a threat, it was that man. Which was why Bishop had to take the blame for this. Weiber-Krauss had not wanted to hurt him. But there was no one else who had the genius for such a scheme. The publications had seen to that. He was a perfectly suited scientist. A perfectly outfitted killer. Everyone would believe those grotesque stories . . . the satanic images.

Weiber-Krauss lay a hand on the thin page of the Bible. As much of the words he liked the feel of the paper. It was such a thin fiber to carry such a great message. It hadn't needed the stone tablets of Moses. Just mulched, pressed slivers from trees. That is how mighty were these ideas. And in the back of the book, written at the foot and backside of Revelation, beneath the very name of Lord Jesus, amen, was irreverently written in a small, cursive hand the names and addresses of those whom Weiber-Krauss had employed—willingly, and not. With any pertinent information he might need to reference.

There was a rap at the door. Weiber-Krauss turned in the candled light.

"Doc, we got some news," Cavanaugh said.

The medical man raised his eyebrows to encourage the man: speak.

"Two o' the linens I sent out—they encountered Walter G. Dent. They brought him here. They also found Innocence Lee and Randy Coward. Dead."

"How?"

"Not by the shotgun of the Shotgun," Cavanaugh said. "They were shot or gutted. And—." He hesitated.

The German's eyebrows went up again.

"Randy's arm was cut off," Cavanaugh reported. "Left with him, courteously, but axed clean off with a couple chops."

"Bring Dent," Weiber-Krauss instructed. "And get the men ready to ride."

Bishop did not want to leave White Fox, but she was on the mend. That told him so was the tribe. He would not be needed there. A fort under quarantine was a different matter.

"I come with you," Firecrow announced when Bishop told him his plan.

"You must look after White Fox."

"These men can see to this," he assured the doctor. "Knob Pipe is the mate of my sister. I trust him with her life." He retrieved one of the torches, which had been lit with the coming of twilight. "And one of us must carry these."

Bishop considered this. The last statement was true. But it might do to have another with him. Someone who might not be shot on sight.

Walter G. Dent had been relatively serene sitting atop a cart laden with dynamite, the fuse lighted. As he made his way upstairs, a surly man to his front and another to his rear, he was not serene. He was terrified. The terror was like a serpent's tongue, two-forked. First, he was going to see the man who had hired him. Second, he was going to see the man who hired him on the heels of bad news. He had been with the men when they had uncovered the bodies of Innocence Lee and his brute of a partner. Dent had been a detonations expert during the war, had worked for the mines afterward. He had seen people blown apart. Blood and the body parts whence it spilled did not alarm him.

But the man who killed them, the man with the gun-arm . . . he did. Especially if he had survived, as it appeared, the carefully laid double-walled ambush. Dent did not doubt that his employer was even more deeply dismayed. What he feared was that he had no information to add. Not really.

The wound in Dent's neck troubled him. Throbbing. Behind tightly closed lips he cursed the man working for this man, the driver, Smith, for having given it to him. As a warning, because savages like Smith put no trust in words, only action. He couldn't tell if the stairs were wobbly or if that was his legs. Probably both. His lower half was not used to riding so much, and the pressure on his backside could not have done him any good. He smelled the candles and lanterns, mixing with odorous overkill. At least the wafting, oily stench killed the reek of his own unwashed body.

The chief was seated alone behind a desk as the men showed him in. Dent caught the glimpse of two others in the shadows outside. There had been a lot of those . . . mysterious shades doing the master's bidding. He assumed, but could not be certain, that one of them was the mentally deranged Smith.

The leader motioned for the door to be shut. Dent stood just inside, deciding he would neither speak nor move until instructed to do so.

"What can you tell me about your time with John

Bishop and your last meeting with my two assassins—who have heaped disrepute upon that good name?"

After a deferential, "Mr. Weiber-Krauss, sir," Dent told him. About the meeting at the trading post. His willing capture. His ride with Bishop at shotgun in back. The Indian maiden. The spiel of Innocence Lee, which was so over-the-top as to be riveting. Riveting enough for Dent to slip away from Bishop and White Fox.

"White Fox?" Weiber-Krauss interrupted.

Dent told him about the Cheyenne woman. Strong, caring, beautiful. He said everything he knew about her, then resumed his narrative, spoke about his encounter with Randy Coward and his meeting and payment by Innocence Lee. He paintbrushed every detail he could remember, since the German did not stop him. He recounted his departure, his ride, his having heard nor seen no one or nothing until the two Muddy Linens met him in the foothills where he was moving slowly, cautiously, because he would rather risk a gopher hole than the possibility that John Bishop would come after him.

When he was done, Dent stopped. With a clap of mouth and teeth that was not only audible but comical in the small, dark, quiet room.

"What was your assessment of John Bishop?" the German asked.

"The shrinking fuse of my dynamite did not faze him," Dent said. "He observed things."

"As?"

Dent raised a stubby finger and pointed to the bandaged wound. "He knew I did not get this in a fight. From the way it was cut."

"Impressive. Anything else?"

"Ants," Dent remembered. "He saw where they were eating crumbs from my meals. Where I dropped my drawers. He smelled that. His senses were like little machines, seeing everything." Dent swallowed his own excited admiration as he said again, "*Ants!*"

Weiber-Krauss closed the Bible and leaned forward, his hands folded upon it. "He was brilliant during the war and he is—well"—Weiber-Krauss sat back—"he is now man plus machine, as you say." His eyes drifted to Dent. "And he is still out there."

Dent didn't speak, again.

"The ability to observe," Weiber-Krauss went on admiringly. "During the war, he saw that men with typhoid, in the tents, died. When conditions became too crowded and the sick were placed outside, they often got well. The communicable nature of disease. His observation. My benefit." He tapped a thumb thoughtfully on the cover of the Bible. "He has the help of the Cheyenne, you say?"

"He does, Mr. Weiber-Krauss."

"The victims themselves, helped by his skills and medicines, will help to clear his name."

Weiber-Krauss flipped to the back of his Bible. He took a look, shielding the page from Dent's view. Then he closed the book and took paper and pen from his desk. He held up an empty, unaddressed envelope.

"You will receive this at your home perhaps a week hence," the German said. "When you do, you will put it in a safe place, unopened. I will ask for it back. If I do not, you will bring it to a newspaper office in a city—not in your town."

Dent was so relieved that he wasn't going to die here that he did not ask for payment.

"There will be script inside," Weiber-Krauss added. "When you open it, that money will be yours. Again, only if I do not call for it—in, say, a month?"

"A month," Dent repeated.

"Have Smith take you to your horse," Weiber-Krauss said. "You may stay tonight in the stall or you may go. Just be out of my way. Yes?"

"Yes, Mr. Weiber-Krauss," Dent said, his voice high. He had to fight to keep from laughing.

"Smith!" the German yelled.

The burly driver had been right outside the door. He leaned in with the informality only a trusted confidant would dare.

"Accompany this gentleman to his charger and then come back with Cavanaugh," he said. "We will be leaving. At dawn."

A crooked smile broke the stubbled jowls of the man. He stepped back, motioning to Dent, who followed. The explosives expert stopped.

"Good evening, sir. And good luck."

But Weiber-Krauss was already dipping his pen in the inkwell and thinking about his words. He raised two fingers of his left hand without looking over, then motioned with those same fingers for the door to be shut.

Weiber-Krauss was neither surprised nor particularly saddened by the turn of events. It would change nothing in the end—but only if John Bishop were removed. There was a part of the German that had always been troubled by the proxy war he was waging against the surgeon. For half a millennium, the family did not hang to the rear of battle or strife. He had done so now only because it was expedient. He was not a family of educated noblemen, all of whom had a military background. He was one Weiber-Krauss set on a chessboard of pawns. Damaged, mentally incomplete, and often unruly pawns. It had been necessary for him to delegate.

But, of course, the risk of that was the result he had now. The pawns had fallen before the Bishop. Now he had to take to the field.

"But not without this," he said as he began to write. He affixed the date. The place. His full title as it appeared in the ancient grants and deeds: *The Count Anton Weiber-Krauss III of the Landgrafschaft Hessen-Kassel, Ruler of the Jurisdiction of the Imperial Immediacy.* He wrote with a welling of pride, and with a fierce hope flaming in his breastbone. The hope that this document would never be seen and that the title he had inscribed would soon be amended to include, after Hessen-Kassel, ". . . and the landgraviate of the Central North American Continent . . ."

Riding side by side through the dark, Firecrow felt a special bond with the man to his left.

The Cheyenne had watched with a mixture of curiosity and admiration as the one-armed warrior slipped on his mechanism-arm. The white man had defeated him, one-armed, an impressive enough feat. With this attachment, he was in some respects a creature of legend, like Nonoma—the Spirit of the

Thunder—or the great horned serpent Mehne. Firecrow sensed, very strongly, a change in the man when the gun-arm came on. Nothing having to do with stature or balance, though it added both. It was not the transformation of a powerful warrior to a mightier one, though that was true. It had to do with *óe'e'ohe.* The tree that is chopped down. What results is not just a canoe or tepee supports or fences. There is also new growth. The one fallen creates many new things, all great and essential.

Bishop was the living form of that idea. It was as if the spirit of all things had come to abide in this one man. The constable was not ashamed that he had challenged him. Or that he had doubted him. To the contrary. He was proud to have learned from the encounter. He had grown as a human being, the goal of all Cheyenne.

The flame bounced. The light on the ground shifted. To Firecrow, the shadows around them were like ghost-lives living apart from their own. Yet all were they. The two men who rode were an army. The fight was not yet known, but whatever it was they would be ready.

Bishop spoke, quietly. It did not sound like him. Perhaps it was one of the ghost forms.

"I wanted to ask you something, Firecrow," he said. "Earlier, when we fought—right before that, actually—you did not merely want to take me to trial. You were angry?"

Firecrow did not like the question. It took him to a ghost-self. A Firecrow that no longer existed. When a time was passed, it was passed. But this man's way was not the way of the Cheyenne.

"I was mad," he admitted.

"Because of White Fox?" Bishop pressed.

"Because of she."

"It's important that you understand, Firecrow. White Fox is her own woman. She and I are like family. We are so close. Yet not in every way close. Who she chooses to be with—that has nothing to do with me."

"You are the better warrior," Firecrow said.

"That is not true. And it has nothing to do with White Fox. Do you understand what I am saying? To win her love and respect takes more than a badge of office or a headdress of many feathers. It takes more than a strong arm. Or a great horse. Or a wall of scalps. She . . ." Bishop sought for an explanation. He settled on: "She reads. She thinks."

"She is different," Firecrow agreed.

"Very," Bishop concurred. "It is not by my actions that she turns to or from any man. You and I can be brothers."

"I understand," Firecrow said, although he wasn't sure he did. Bishop had an arm that was a gun. Any woman would be won by such as that. Even a woman who possessed books. The Cheyenne would consider what Bishop had said, though. And he would embrace the idea that they were brothers. At the moment, that was more important than the thoughts or feelings of a strange warrior woman and her spirit guide Poe.

There was a hint of ruddiness on the horizon. Torchlight in the fort. The wind was blowing toward them.

"Whoa." Bishop stopped to sniff.

"What is it?"

"Only smoke," the doctor replied. "I wanted to make sure they weren't burning anything else."

Firecrow did not understand but he respected the man's caution. They continued at a trot, a little faster than before. Bishop looked ahead but the Cheyenne watched the ground, mindful of gullies and rattlesnakes and other dangers of the open prairie.

As the contours of the fort came in view, the new arrivals noticed that there were more men on the wall than usual.

"For you?" Firecrow asked.

"I wouldn't think so," Bishop said. "Most of them are not at attention."

"Ah. I see now."

"I think they are up there to put distance between themselves and whatever they are trying to get away from."

"Like the Cheyenne settlements?" Firecrow asked.

"I would guess there is disease, yes," Bishop replied. "Though the settlements were polluted by water. Though that does not explain how White Fox got sick."

Firecrow thought for a moment. He rubbed a hand on his forehead. "Water. I watch as White Fox put her lips on girl."

"Kissed her. On the forehead?"

The Cheyenne nodded.

"Right. That could do it."

A shot kicked up a clod of grass several yards in front of the riders. Both men stopped. The doctor locked his legs around the horse, held up both hands. "Lift your torch and bring it closer so they can see me," he instructed.

"This is John Bishop!" he shouted. "I wish to speak to your commander! We are coming closer to talk. Do not fire."

The two started ahead at a canter. Bishop's eyes never left the speared tops of the fort. There was movement on the barricade. Muted voices that were probably shouts into the compound. And then a wait that seemed like a very long time. More movement on the wall.

"This is Major Burton Terry," a voice shouted back, strong and clear. Not ill. "Stop where you are."

Bishop and Firecrow did so, just a hundred yards or so from the gate.

"Who is that with you?" Terry asked.

"I am with Constable Firecrow," Bishop yelled back.

Terry considered that. "Are you his prisoner? Have you come to surrender?"

"I have nothing to surrender *for.* We have come from the Cheyenne settlements where we just treated a pox. I am a doctor. I can help."

Terry said, "You are a felon. You will surrender or you will be shot where you are."

"I am nothing of the kind. Major, a question. What happened to Marshal Duffin?"

"Maybe you can tell me," Terry challenged.

"I don't understand. I left him with a Confederate. A prisoner, in handcuffs."

"He came back in a buckboard, sick and near death, his nose torn away. He was brought here by a man whose skull had been partly caved in."

"Is he alive?"

"Barely."

"Major, he knows of my innocence. Tell me, do you have illness there?"

Terry's silence was confirmation. And Bishop understood. The operational status of the fort was privileged military information that he would not share—if it were compromised.

Bishop went on. "If the disease—if there *is* a disease—did not come from water, it was airborne. You recognized that or you wouldn't have your men up there. Please. Let us in. If nothing else, we *must* figure out who is truly behind this."

Terry was silent.

"At least let me try to help Marshal Duffin. He may have essential information."

Terry was no longer silent. "You hitch off that cannon," he ordered.

Bishop obliged, removing the straps and taking the gun under his good arm, barrel pointed backward.

"I can help you," Firecrow offered.

"You are. With the torch."

"Open the gate," Terry said. "Rifle squad, assemble outside the mess."

"He does not trust," Firecrow observed.

"More than you know," Bishop replied, urging the horse forward. "He could have covered us from the wall. Those men in the compound? They will be stock-to-shoulder, aimed and ready to fire."

The gates opened, spilling orange torchlight on the open field. The entire fort was lit up like the Fourth of July. That was probably so that Terry or his second- and third-in-command could immediately see if anyone dropped. A quick headcount as they entered suggested that unless the off-duty troops were in the barracks, anywhere from ten to fifteen men were sick. That was the bed capacity of the average infirmary, and there was no one outside.

Major Terry came down the wooden steps to meet them beside the rifle squad. As Bishop had expected, each of the four men had a Springfield pointed in his direction. Like a firing squad. Hungry.

The officer came forward, his eyes on the gun first, then on the man.

"I'd like to go to the infirmary," Bishop said. No preamble.

"Where I'm taking you," Terry replied as he continued walking. He was well to the right of Bishop in case it was necessary for the rifle squad to shut the famed Shotgun down. The men on the wall looked down, even those who were supposed to be lookouts. It was not every day that a person of celebrity walked among them. Senators and even the Vice President of the United States had drawn less attention.

Bishop stepped onto the wooden walk and entered the open door, followed by Firecrow and Terry. The rifle squad, at a signal from the major, stood down but stayed where they were, just outside. The new arrivals all donned surgical masks that were hanging from a peg inside the door. They were not introduced to the medic, who was writing in a medical log at his desk. He looked over, not bothering to speak through his own mask, which had a damp oval where the mouth was. Exhalation. He was breathing in from his nose.

The infirmary had an antiseptic smell. Alcohol, mostly. The two hanging lanterns added their own touch of kerosene. But they did something more important than that. They illuminated a face that Bishop did not expect to see.

"Avery!" Bishop exclaimed.

Terry spun at the newcomer. "Who is he?"

Bishop's mind was trying to connect pieces that did not logically fit. "Joseph Daniel Avery, mayor and sheriff of Good Fortune," Bishop said. "Marshal Duffin would have known him—but how the hell they *got* together . . . ?"

Bishop took a quick look at the other men in the room. All of them were wearing masks, a sensible precaution by Dr. Gibson. The others were five in number. One was an exceptionally large man wearing sergeant's stripes. The other four were privates.

"Stretcher detail," Bishop said.

"That's right," Terry answered, with an edge of being impressed.

"They were the only ones who were close to Duffin and Avery, correct?"

"Yes."

"This is an experiment, Major," Bishop said. "Water-carried, then airborne. Someone is testing biological tools for war. Or extermination."

CHAPTER THIRTEEN

The Many Ways of Healing

"I must go to work here," Bishop announced.

Now he handed the gun-arm to Firecrow. Before anyone had answered or given permission, he was at Avery's side in the nearest of the cots.

"What medicines do you have here?" Bishop asked the doctor.

"Everything the same as the trading post," the medic replied. Without revealing too much, he added, "I am familiar with some of your experimental thinking. Very impressive."

"Thank you, Doctor—?"

"Gibson," he said. "Lester."

Gibson was a young man, not long in the military or out of medical school.

"You examined the bodies for marks—Avery and Duffin?"

Gibson nodded. "There was a puncture wound on the marshal," he said. "Right arm. Venous."

"Living disease," Bishop said.

"That was my conclusion. From the blood to the respiratory system, then exhaled."

"What have you given these men?"

"The quinine," he replied, "mixed with mustard seed and stramonium leaves. The yellow bottles."

"I want the blue," Bishop said.

Dr. Gibson went to the medicine cabinet beside the desk. "Poke and prickly ash in rye whiskey."

"Right." Carefully assuming the tone of a colleague, not master-to-student, he said, "It reduces inflammation, induces blood flow. Breathing is the best curative. Let the body heal itself." He cocked his head toward the back of the room. "And open the windows, Major. Ventilate."

Bishop took the bottle from which Dr. Gibson had thoughtfully removed the stopper. Bishop knelt beside Avery, who was wheezing thickly—more than his usual rale. Gibson used a finger to hook the mask back slightly. Bishop poured the same amount of medicine as he had given White Fox. The same way.

"I'd like my sergeant back, too," Terry said.

"You'll have him. We must know how this man got here. Doctor? I'd also like spirits. If anything will bring him back, even briefly, scotch or whiskey?"

"Rum?"

"Fine."

The doctor got a bottle from his desk. Having finished dosing the mayor-sheriff with the cure, and once again with Gibson's help, Bishop poured two capfuls of the rum over his tongue. He rose and looked down, listened to his breathing. Avery's big chest seemed to ease slightly, almost at once. That would be the rum. The medicine would take a little longer.

"Give this to the others, the rum, too, if you haven't already," Bishop told the doctor, handing him the bottle. Realizing he had no standing here, he added, "It was what we used in the war."

"The true medical school," Gibson said, understanding.

Bishop pulled over the wooden chair from the doctor's desk and sat beside Avery. The newest jagged crack in his skull was another assault. If someone had wanted information about Bishop, all they would have had to do was offer him money. Or threaten to hit him. This was something else, possibly the prelude to an abduction.

"What about the marshal?" Terry asked.

"He has been ill the longest," Bishop answered. "If he can be saved, it will not be before the others."

The major walked over. He took a cigar from his vest pocket, replaced it when he realized his mouth was covered. "Dr. Bishop," he said, for the first time showing empathy or respect. "Why would someone want to frame you for these crimes? Convince me that they would have to."

"I don't know the answer to that," Bishop said. "As for convincing you, pitting a man's word against suspicion against that man is a hollow exercise. Fact is needed, or corroboration. I am not guilty of the crimes here or against the Cheyenne. I can say no more."

"But you have killed."

"Those who sought to kill me, no one else." He turned to Gibson. "That is not the oath we took."

Gibson nodded, pleased, again, to be considered a colleague of this eminent and possibly infamous figure.

Sergeant Manat was the first to regain consciousness. The medicine plus an iron physique proved to be the perfect combination. The other four soldiers recovered more slowly, but they started to come around. Avery and Duffin were still stubbornly comatose.

"If you don't mind," Bishop said to Gibson, "I would like to remain here. Accommodations for the constable?"

"You've both been in the Cheyenne camps. You can stay in the jailhouse. I think that will be safer."

That wasn't the reason, but Firecrow did not protest. The only Indians who slept with the regulars were regulars themselves. Mostly scouts. It didn't matter to the brave. The others were not worthy of him.

"If you're going to stay, Doctor," Gibson said, "would you mind if I shut my eyes? Been at this problem since it first broke among the Cheyennes."

"Please rest," Bishop replied. He did not bother mentioning that he had been up since before dawn himself.

Major Terry went out with Firecrow, leaving behind a look that was not sympathetic but neutral. At least it wasn't hostile.

Bishop thumbed through the patient records in a book on Gibson's desk. There was no new information; it was the same he had seen with White Fox. A disease that caused high fever and blotches if left unchecked. A measles variant, caused by an infectious agent in a patient's blood. But more potent, virulent. If not occurring naturally, it would have to have been created, like Gregor Mendel's recent experiments with peapods in Austria, by someone with scientific skill. Most likely a doctor, if it was injected in Marshal Duffin.

And they call me a monster, he thought.

Bishop returned to the chair and sat just by Avery's head, thinking of all the cots he had been beside—and in. And the one critical time when a bed would have been welcome. It was one of the moments that made him and White Fox what they were.

It was about the rig. There had been shotgun fire outside Huckie's Saloon in the mountains and they had been forced to run, fast and hard. The gun-arm complained; loudly and painfully. Its obtuseness, its unfamiliarity, had caused it to start to bleed around the leather cup that was fitted to Bishop's left arm just below the elbow joint. It was a standard prosthetic that boys of both the North and the South wore as a kind of battle prize. There was not a one of them who would not have preferred the return of his limb. But for the ability to get compassion from the ladies and to scare rude little children into a running fit, it had merit. The benighted blacksmith had modified Bishop's prosthetic to allow the short stock of a Greener .12-gauge shotgun to fit where a metal hook would have replaced the amputee's hand. The stock was secured in the cup with small metal bands that joined the shotgun and prosthetic together as one.

In this instance, the leather cup had eaten his flesh raw. Bishop and White Fox had found themselves in a cave, a huge, yawning smile beneath a jagged slope of blue rock, sheeted by snow and protected by daggers of ice formed by the flowing water flowing from up-mountain. Sequestered there from trouble—from the trouble that had caused the arm its discomfort—White Fox had loosened the ties that held the cup tight to Bishop's arm, and pulled the entire rig away, revealing a bleeding stump. She had fed him what little mescal remained in the heel of the bottle they had, and Bishop's head lolled back as she checked the arm for fresh wounds. Nothing had opened up too badly, but he remembered her examining the corrupted skin and muscle that was a knot around the bone. He watched her check, check closely, without flinching, to make sure that none of the crude surgical scars lacing it together had ruptured. The blood was smeared from small wounds around the elbow, where the amputation point met the healthy rest of the arm. White Fox had swabbed away the streaks of wet red.

Bishop could still hear himself saying, in the mescal-rough voice, "*I'm the doc, but you're the surgeon.*"

And he could hear White Fox reply, as she dressed the wound with salve and wrapped, "*I still am, Bish-op.*"

It wasn't long ago, just—weeks? Yet it seemed as if it had been years the two had been a team. A unit.

A couple?

Bishop kept returning to the idea, angry that he denied it out of loyalty to his dead wife. As long as White Fox accepted that, and him, he did not try to fight it.

A blubbering sound from Avery's cheeks, beneath the mask, snapped Bishop to the present. He looked at the man's eyes, waited, hoping. He put the back of his hand on the man's forehead. There was fever but it was not as high as in the doctor's ledger.

"Avery." Bishop leaned nearer and said it again. "Avery."

There was no response as such. But the man sighed from deep in his throat. The airway had opened. Bishop got more rum, poured it through the mask so it would reach his tongue and nose. The man sighed again, then his head moved a little from side to side.

Bishop went to the open door. His "honor" guard was still there. "One of you get the major. I think one of our patients is waking."

The former lieutenant sat back down, watched as Avery's eyeballs moved a little beneath the lids. Major Terry charged in, pulling on his mask, and stood beside Bishop. Dr. Gibson followed. All saw the man coming to life and watched without speaking.

And then the beady eyes opened and teared from both sides and squinted in the light and tried to focus.

They saw Gibson without recognition. They saw Terry—the same. And then they saw John Bishop.

That was the greatest balm of all.

It was not an army.

At a total of thirty-two souls, plus one leader, it did not have the manpower, discipline, or boundaries to defend. It lacked artillery and ships. There was no flag. The clothing was more or less identical yet no one would call them the Muddy Linens uniforms. But this fighting force had something that few armies possess: just one target to defeat. The only soul in the territory with the mind and experience to stop him.

And, failing that, the leader of this army had a disaster scenario that would still achieve his goal. The goal of the megalomaniacal mind, as even he himself would admit.

The forced march of the makeshift cavalry began at dawn. Smith and his whip were in the lead, Cavanaugh beside but slightly behind him, everyone else in a column of two. The general, Weiber-Krauss, was in the rear. Each man was armed with a repeating rifle, two six-shooters, one hundred rounds of ammunition, and a bayonet. There were canteens in the trunk on the back of the black buggy Weiber-Krauss drove. He also had his Bible, his map, and duty roster of the fort, bought from a chicken farmer who had delivered eggs to the place until beak necrosis killed his livelihood . . . and his glass globes. The ones with toxins. Enough poison, in each, to make dozens sick directly and thousands or more by contact with the ill. Those were in a carpetbag at his feet.

The plan of action was simple. They were riding west to find one person. And, finding that person, they would use her to bring John Bishop to them. It did not have to be quickly, though he suspected it would be. Weiber-Krauss intended to leave White Fox with the Muddy Linens until John Bishop showed up and then died. Their only instructions would be to make sure she did not escape . . . and not to kill her. He needed her alive. Smith would be there to supervise. As the Muddy Linens knew, he could flick a bug from a sleeping man without waking the man.

"Imagine," Weiber-Krauss had reminded them, "what he could do to your private members if you do irreparable harm to the squaw."

The men rode with the rising sun, as if the solar orb were their guiding light and guardian spirit. They rode if not proudly, then at least with interest in their work and eyes on the multiple prizes.

Weiber-Krauss and his nearly two-score men did not try to conceal themselves or their journey. The only force capable of stopping them would be under quarantine by now, not permitted by regulation to ride out. And Major Burton Terry was a man of regulations. The chicken farmer had assured Weiber-Krauss of that too.

A march played in Weiber-Krauss's head as he watched the tail end of his militia. It was the Radetzky Opus 228, composed by Johann Strauss Sr. in honor of Field Marshal Joseph Radetzky von Radetz. Weiber-Krauss had heard the great work when he was a boy, at its debut in Vienna in August 1848. It was the first music he remembered, and Weiber-Krauss considered it his.

He was annoyed, still, at those who had failed him. But the beauty of Anton Weiber-Krauss III was that he refused to rely solely on any one person for anything. Therein lay disaster—with one exception.

Weiber-Krauss had never let himself down.

"Bi-Bishop?"

It was not a word John Bishop ever expected to enjoy being puffed from the mouth of Mayor-Sheriff Avery. But this was an exception. And it was the second time that day the moody avenger smiled. First for White Fox, now for this antagonist. Days did not come any stranger.

"It's John," Bishop said.

"We . . . we are both . . . dead?"

"Not dead," Bishop assured him.

Avery squinted up at the other man's mask, put thick fingers on his own face, felt the fabric there. "Wha-what?"

"You were infected with a highly contagious disease," Bishop said evenly. "You are mending. The rest of us do not wish to catch it."

The big bald head nodded. "That . . . creature."

Bishop's expression darkened slightly. "Tell us."

Avery's eyes looked away, took in the others. "Who . . . ?"

"Major Terry, the commander of Fort Collins—that's where you are—and his medical officer Dr. Gibson. Who saved you."

Avery was still disoriented. Bishop had to bring him into focus.

"Someone put you in a cart with Marshal Duffin. He is still unconscious and may not recover. Who did this? And where?"

Avery jabbed a fat index finger toward Bishop. "You . . . know."

"I know?" Bishop shook his head, not comprehending. Then, suddenly, he did understand. "I *know* him. Is that what you're saying?"

Avery's chins nodded; his head stayed deep in the pillow. "Bastard."

His eyes began to close. He turned, picked the rum up from the floor where he'd left it, right beside his gun-arm. He poured a long glug through the mask, intentionally making Avery gag. The man coughed, his head rising as his chest convulsed. It was uncultivated bedside manner but it kept Avery from drifting.

"Who is the bastard?" Bishop demanded.

Avery cleared his throat once, then again, then a third time. His eyes opened, a little livelier now.

"German. Name . . . Weiber-Krauss."

Little Hen was upset to have been moved from White Fox's tepee to a smaller one with another little girl. But Knob Pipe promised she would be allowed to return as soon as the woman was well.

The chubby little Gray Bird had also been sick and she breathed too loudly for Little Hen to be able to rest. So Knob Pipe allowed her to take a blanket and lie where the horses were kept, at least during the hours of sunlight.

Little Hen liked it out here. There was no smoke, nothing closing her in. Lying under the blue sky, the girl remembered the fire. She did not want to; she preferred to look at the eagles. But the fire came, like it came then, burning through everything in its way.

She remembered getting in the river with her mother, but falling trees, fire, forced them to go to the middle where the water was fast and deep. Her mother was lost in a raid. Little Hen floated. The fire still burned and she could not come ashore. There were places where trees hung over the water. A few had berries. Her mother had shown her how to pick the ones that would not make you ill.

And then, just before dark, she saw the Demon. It floated by her on its back. There was a large hole in its chest, a pair of black birds nesting inside, picking at strings of tissue. One side of the Demon was a little more under the water. In the glow of the fire she could see the orange-silver glint of a gun. The Demon was so stiff it just turned and turned as it passed by. And then she saw its eyes, open, staring at her. One of the birds cawed her off.

Fire and the dead, like the old woman without teeth, *xaaméné*, Smiling Face, was always talking about. Around the campfire, making shadows with her fingers, using words that painted horrible detail in those black images. Words that told of a place where bad children and frightened men and disobedient wives were sent to burn for all time and be eaten by buzzards. Where each new day their picked-off flesh would grow back so it could be bitten away all over.

"If the demons of this dark place, this *aahkévåhoeše*, should see you, you must hide!" the woman had exclaimed. "Hope that they pass you by and then make yourself a better child so that they may not come again."

As the Demon passed, its cold metal hand touched her leg under the water, and the birds roused, splashing her with its wet, red insides . . . the little girl had run. Run to the log bobbing at a place where the shore had eroded and a tree had fallen. Crawled inside, tearing shredded wood flakes from the pulpy interior. Bleeding as they scraped her, bleeding from her fingertips, putting her fingers into her mouth to send the scream back down her throat so the *hávêsévemâhta'sóoma* would not hear her. She held her legs together, tightly, so it would not smell her as dogs did one another. She pulled herself into a ball so tight inside this space so narrow that she felt like the wood grubs she used to watch as they coiled whitely in and out of trees.

Little Hen did not fear the fire, now. Or the Demon. She was safe again under happy skies. She was loved by White Fox, by the funny little Knob Pipe who walked and scowled like she imagined the *vo'estane-hesono* did. The race of little men that Smiling Face used to tell of. Angry dwarves who mined precious metals, lived in the mountains, and made war with the Cheyenne when the sky was dark and the moon was hidden. White Fox and Knob Pipe would care for Little Hen until her mother and father returned.

Thinking of her parents, of her home, caused her eyes to grow heavy. She slept with the first smile she had known since her mother swam away. She remembered something else, too, that Smiling Face had once said.

"*The Earth is the mother of us all. She will never leave us orphans.*"

Knob Pipe gave White Fox another few drops of blue medicine, poured water between her lips, and then left the tepee. He pulled his pipe from its pouch on his belt, scooped in tobacco leaves, pressed them down with his little finger, and walked to a campfire to light it. He had wanted to hit the one-armed man with a club when he spoke of the spirits of illness. The little man had been to a talk at Fort Collins about hygiene. The boy doctor, Gibson, had told them about treating diseases that marked the skin.

However, the Cheyenne was pleased that Bishop knew enough to stop this plague. White Fox was no longer shivering, and the few blotches that had appeared were not joined by others. It appeared that most in the camp would be well again.

As Bishop had also instructed, as many people as possible had been placed in the open air. The sun was low in the sky and there was a chill in the air. He went to check on Little Hen by the corral. For all the doctoring knowledge Bishop possessed, he did not think to allow nature to heal nature. The horses, immune to this sickness as White Fox's mounts had proven, had their own power and health to give. Any rider knew that, mounting, the spirit of the horse infused him with increased strength and courage. He felt that Little Hen would benefit there. Children did not yet possess the schooling that shielded them from real knowledge.

The settlement was unusually quiet because of all those who were not up and about, cooking dinner, tending to family, playing games, discussing tribal politics loudly and often angrily. There were few campfires, adding a shroud to the ordinarily proud array of tepees with their painted sides and the bold statements they made, the sagas they told.

Knob Pipe had lived for thirty summers or more. He had dwelt in many fields and foothills and in the lower mountains where the snows remained year-round. His bowlegs had straddled many a stallion. He knew a horse the instant he mounted; he knew a place the moment he arrived; he knew before entering his tepee when his wife Bright Fawn was less than glowing. That was one reason he so often smoked. It gave him something else to think about. The smooth smoke of the red leaves briefly obscured the world and its struggles large and small.

The Cheyenne walked from the corral to the field surrounded by chicken wire, the plot where the Indians grew their tobacco and vegetables. The tobacco was used for trade at the fort and trading post. It was the longest Knob Pipe had been anywhere, in his life. Moving here, moving there. Sometimes by famine or drought, sometimes by the cavalry, sometimes by the Arapaho, sometimes by the restless feet of a chief or medicine man who was searching for something. Searching and made everyone else go with him. That was one thing he admired about the white man. Alone or with a family, they went where they chose. Communities were built for their permanence—though that did not always work, as Good Fortune had proven. He had been there twice, once during the silver boom and once after. The first time was life. The second time—

A dead place is a grave. All those white corpses waiting to be buried—that was something a Cheyenne was too wise to do.

He rounded the field and was struck by the stillness out here as well. He looked back at the settlement, curiosity dipping his brow. It was as though a storm was coming but the skies were beginning to fleck with stars. Peering intently to the east he noticed a pale spot of yellow that was not, could not be, the sun—which clung to life in the foothills behind him.

He felt it. Someone was coming. Many someones. Many horses. A dog barked; he smelled it, heard it, saw it too. Knob Pipe did not believe that the white man was bringing more medicines. Overturning his pipe, the man stomped smoldering tobacco into the ground. Then he ran toward the tepee where the chief would be offering his thanks for the recovery of his people and praying for guidance.

Typically, a chief asked for the spirits to talk to him while he slept. Knob Pipe feared that they would not have so long. As he ran, the radiance of the false sun expanded, growing on the wings of many torches.

CHAPTER FOURTEEN
An Uncivil War

The name was a shock wave, like the recoil of his arm. It was as though, in that moment, cloud struck cloud, producing rain and thunder. Worlds collided, the past and present. The healthy and the unhealthy . . . and he was not thinking about the patients they jointly treated. It was the mind of a man who was willing to sacrifice the ill to learn more about cures.

Try this. Try that. Heat them. Freeze them. Transfuse them with the healthy until they were well. Transfuse those giving blood with others. Set up a line of bloody tubes, cot to cot to cot. Anton Weiber-Krauss had a mind as active as Santorini, which burned for four years. A mind with thoughts that were as dark as that volcano's clouds.

Bishop had stepped outside, pulled off his mask, leaned his hand against the guardrail for support. Major Terry followed him. He waved away the rifle squad, which was showing signs of fatigue.

"What is it?" the officer asked, hooking his own mask away with a finger. "Who is this Weiber-Krauss?"

"A brilliant madman," Bishop replied. "I should have recognized the signs. But I thought he was gone."

"Gone where? What signs—"

"Shut up," the doctor snapped. "This is not a bayonet charge, Major." He turned to the officer. "I'm sorry. You've been very patient. Trusting." He shook his head, looked back across the torch-lit compound. "He is a medical doctor who was, is, obsessed with disease. If sickness were a woman, he would be bringing it flowers after each epidemic."

"Your man in there said something about Lady Freemont."

"The mine," Bishop said.

"Right. That's where I heard it. Outside of Good Fortune."

Bishop nodded. "He must have set up a laboratory there. Experimented. Tested what he bred on—on human subjects. And when he was happy with the results, he floated some of them down the river to test them on the Cheyenne. I suspect the first test was to transmit disease by water. The second"—he cocked his head toward the infirmary—"airborne."

"Good Jesus Christ." The shock wave had finally hit Major Terry. "What the hell do we do?"

Bishop was thinking. "Those globes at the shack, the grenades. He tested those there too. Infected the blacksmith. Then killed him to implicate me."

"Your schematics," Terry said with understanding.

"I was the easy, obvious target. The penny dreadfuls had me killing indiscriminately. It stood to reason that I had lost my mind, continued my own research, turned what were supposed to be means of curing into methods of mass murder."

"Doctor, we had better ride to the old mine, and quickly."

Bishop regarded him. "With whom? Your men may be infected. You ride out, half of them may fall over. You'll have to peel off men to escort them back. Weiber-Krauss was a soldier. He saw how troops were deployed to conquer and defend, as I did. Only he was probably paying better attention to that, if he already had this scheme in mind."

"Your gun," Terry suggested.

Bishop snorted unhappily. "I'm thinking of all the things we had talked about packing into glass grenades," he said. "Toxins were not one of them, but poison gas? Acid? Angry wasps? We considered a great many applications. I am guessing that he is well stocked with several if not all of them. He has surely had the time."

"Well, we have to do *something*," Terry said.

"What would you do, armed like that and bent on conquest?" Bishop asked.

Terry shrugged. "I'd conquer."

"Exactly. He will ride out, especially if—as he likely knows by now—his attempts to blame me *and* murder me have failed."

"Sentry!" Terry shouted.

The ranking noncom on the wall turned. "Sir?"

"Watch for torches," he said. "Listen. You hear anything larger than a pack of coyotes in the brush, I want to know about it."

"Yessir!"

Bishop was thinking hard and fast, pulling together the new pieces. He ducked back into the infirmary to get his gun-arm and a pair of surgical masks, then started at a run toward the small, two-cell jail.

"What is it?" Terry asked.

"I have to wake Firecrow," Bishop called back. "I will need four horses," he said.

"Why?"

"Because we will be riding hard and I won't have time to rest the horses," he told Major Terry.

"Dr. Bishop, what is this all about?" the officer demanded.

"A damned loose end," Bishop said hotly as he reached the jail and roused the slumbering Cheyenne. "Come," was all he said, and Firecrow was immediately on his feet, walking beside him.

The brave did not understand, nor did Major Terry, why Bishop was cursing himself as they ran toward the stable. The horses were saddled quickly and the men left with what they carried, the weapons Firecrow had brought and the gun-arm, which Bishop attached in the minute it took to ready the horses. A trooper handed Firecrow a torch, and he held that and the reins of the two spare animals in one hand as they rode through the opening gate into the night.

Bishop was still cursing. Cursing the overconfident, underestimating fool he had been for having allowed Walter G. Dent to ride on.

The line of Muddy Linens made their deliberate way through the plain, through a sandstone canyon, across a river—a river Weiber-Krauss felt he owned, given the role it had played in this project. They approached the Cheyenne settlement without haste. And when they arrived there would be no deployment.

As Weiber-Krauss had seen or heard of in battle after battle, a single line of cavalry offered less of a target than an array of galloping soldiers who could not return fire coming from a trench or some natural formation that served as fortification. He remembered the white-haired, leather-cheeked advisor in a fresh new uniform telling Colonel Zebulon Francis how, as a young man, he had been part of George Washington's "crossfire detail" that set up roadside ambushes to pick off redcoats. The greatness of the military mind was its history of tactics; the limitation of the military mind was also its history of tactics. They were predictable. In that respect, the Cheyenne were more interesting. Riding into the sleeping settlement, Weiber-Krauss did not at all know what to expect. Braves might charge or women might attack from tepees. The books about these peoples were full of surprises.

So was he.

The night was still deep when they arrived. As they came closer, Cavanaugh spotted a few curious Indians and rode back along the line to inform Weiber-Krauss.

"I noticed them," the German said to the face in the wind-blown torch. "Three, yes?"

"Yes."

"Fine. Ride back and pick one. Inform him that I wish to see the squaw White Fox."

"If she doesn't come?"

"Shoot the one you asked and ask again," Weiber-Krauss said, as if he were asking the apothecary for his familiar tobacco.

"If they don't understand?"

"Keep shooting Cheyenne until someone does."

The Confederate threw off an informal salute and wheeled 'round. "Cavanaugh!"

The man halted and turned in his saddle. "Doctor?"

"If we are forced to move out, tell the men to follow my lead. Pass that back."

Cavanaugh nodded and continued on.

The German noted the direction of the wind. That was important. If he did not get what he wanted, they must be sure to ride into it. There was another settlement and there was a fort, all within a day's ride. This would not end here.

Laying the reins over the dash rail of the buggy, Weiber-Krauss bent and carefully opened his carpetbag. Carefully lowering his right hand through the masses of cotton, he selected a glass bulb. This one was filled with smallpox of his own creation, airborne and fatal within a day. There was no cure. The effective range was, he had calculated, at least a mile. He shut the bag with his left hand, cupped the sphere in his right, and lightly rested the back of his wrist on the velvet-covered arm rail. The globe reflected the distant torches, like fireflies buzzing to escape.

"Soon," he murmured.

Cavanaugh had reached the front of the line. He said something to the first of the Muddy Linens, who turned and told the next and so on down the line. Meanwhile, the Confederate stopped beside Smith who raised rifle to shoulder. The bullwhip was coiled around the other arm; Weiber-Krauss was not surprised to discover that the bloody man slept with it.

"Who speaks English?" the Confederate demanded.

"A little," answered a small man, thumping his chest.

"What is your name?"

"Knob Pipe," the man answered proudly.

"Listen carefully, Knob," the Confederate said. "We want to see the woman named White Fox. Go. Bring her here."

"She ill."

Cavanaugh hesitated. "Then carry her. My chief wants to see her." He jerked a thumb toward the dark buggy.

"Shc *too* ill," the man replied.

"I won't ask again," Cavanaugh said through his teeth.

"Good," Knob Pipe replied amiably.

Smith put a bullet through the man's heart. He flopped back, arms splayed, a pipe jumping from his pocket and landing at the feet of the brave beside him. Cavanaugh looked at that man. "You speak English?"

The man shook his head.

"White Fox," the Confederate said. "Squaw. Get. *Now!*"

The man understood that. Turning into the darkness, he motioned for the other Cheyenne to come with him.

Cavanaugh, Smith, and the Muddy Linens remained on alert, weapons raised, in the event that Cheyenne decided to attack. They did not. There might not be a sufficient number of healthy braves to do so. Or maybe they were being smart, for once. Contrary to the popular conception in the East, Indians did not ride stupidly to their destruction. Winning *that day* simply was not important enough. The wise brave knew that there would always be another opportunity, but only if he were alive.

The two men walked back carrying a bundle between them. They held it carefully, also looking away as they did. Weiber-Krauss grinned. This White Fox was ill. Someone had told them not to breathe near her. Damned Bishop. It could only have been he. The son of a devil meddled with everything.

Being diseased, we will have to keep her separate, he thought. The men can hold her. He looked to his left and right, saw a spot downwind by a large rock.

The two men reached the point where they had been standing before.

"Bring her out here," Cavanaugh said, underscoring that with a wave of his free hand.

"Cavanaugh!" Weiber-Krauss shouted.

"Sir?" the Confederate shouted back.

Careful not to move the hand with the globe, he reached across with his left arm, under the lantern hanging from the roof top nut. "The rock!"

"The rock!" Cavanaugh repeated and sent the men in that direction.

"*Áahtaotsé'tov!*" a voice cried out from the camp. "Stop and listen!"

Weiber-Krauss had no idea what had just been said, other than that it had been a sharp command probably telling the men to go nowhere. Because, a moment later, they stopped moving.

"Cavanaugh!" Weiber-Krauss shouted.

"Sir?"

"Shoot the men if they do not move."

The Confederate turned. He held the torch. He opened his hand beside it. "Five fingers." He lowered one. "Four fingers." He lowered another. "Three fingers. You die in"—he lowered another—"two fingers—"

"And you die before they do," a voice cracked from the dark.

Cavanaugh stopped counting. Smith turned, lowering his rifle, peering into the dark beyond the

Confederate. The voice had come from behind them. They looked there, seeing nothing.

Weiber-Krauss turned to his right, looked over the deadly globe toward the lethal shadow hovering in the dark. A shadow with a very distinctive three-quarter profile, most of which was facing the front of the line. But the speaker was only about twenty yards from the back of the line, near the buggy.

"Bishop," the German said, making it sound very much like an oath.

The man with the gun-arm rode toward the lantern. Though he came toward Weiber-Krauss, the gun-arm remained turned toward the line of Muddy Linens. He noted the formality of his homburg, his clean black duster with leather lapels and gold buttons. Custom-made, the arrogant European aristocrat. This was a near-religious moment for the man. Bishop also noted the globe in the German's hand. He noted the familiar, smug, Teutonic smile on the smooth face of the onetime medic.

"Thought of everything, didn't you?" Bishop said, inclining his forehead toward the globe.

"I believe so," Weiber-Krauss replied. "I don't suppose there is anything to be gained by my asking you to join me."

"Only that waste of breath," Bishop answered.

"Sad. You know you cannot shoot me. That you and everyone here will die. This is something I call Great Pox. There is nothing small about it."

"I saw the test infections," Bishop said.

"Nothing, compared to this," the German informed

him. "Your U.S. Army medical supplies have no cure for it."

"If for no other reason, that's your death sentence," Bishop said. "Unless you care to put it down."

"I know you would die to stop me, but what about them?" He threw his free hand toward the camp. "They are downwind. They will all die."

"You have to be stopped."

Weiber-Krauss shook his head. "You were the only one I admired here. And hated. And feared."

"That *is* a conflict," Bishop observed. "Maybe we can resolve it before you hang."

"That is one thing I will most certainly *not* do. Hang," Weiber-Krauss told him. "I will triumph here or we will all die here. But you dare not kill me." He raised the globe menacingly.

Bishop smirked dismissively. "I remember asking that scum Walter G. Dent if he was prepared to die on that wagon full of medical supplies. He wasn't. You are?"

Bishop noticed the man's left hand drift to the reins. There it was. The lunatic did not intend to die. He intended to drop the sphere and flee, and Bishop knew in which direction.

A blast broke the night and the head of the horse attached to the buggy vanished in a wave of red. Up and down the line, horses shied and reared. The dead animal dropped with a fleshy thump. Weiber-Krauss seemed genuinely surprised. He turned to Bishop.

"Well that . . . that was different," the German said, mild shock in his face.

"So now you're here to stay," the gun-armed man

went on as if nothing had happened. "Again. Are you here to die?"

The German drew himself up in the bucket seat of the buggy. "One way or another, if you try and take me, many will die. Great Pox, gunfire. Many."

"You're right," Bishop said. "But you will be the first."

He moved the gun-arm ominously back and forth, just a little, to remind the men in the line how vulnerable they were. His eyes remained on Weiber-Krauss as he listened carefully for the click of a hammer, for movement in the saddle, the whinny of a horse. Nothing.

And then the German had had enough.

"Kill him!" he shouted, swinging from the opposite side of the buggy and ducking behind the big rear wheel.

Now Bishop heard clicks but they were drowned in the perforating blasts of his shotgun. As Bishop turned to grab a little shelter behind the carriage and keep his eye on Weiber-Krauss, Muddy Linens fell left and right, back to forward along the line. They broke ranks, panicked, a few firing but no one firing straight in the predawn light.

The two men up front were not Muddy Linens, however. Unshouldering his bullwhip, Smith turned his horse toward the left side of the crumbling line, Cavanaugh to the right.

Both men had failed to think beyond Bishop, who stopped firing.

"Rebel soldier!" a voice cried from the settlement.

Cavanaugh spun the horse back around to face a brave in war paint and full headdress riding from the settlement, charging down on him with lance extended. The Confederate swept his rifle around, fired, but Firecrow ducked to the opposite side without losing his seat or breaking stride. The large, sharpened stone tip ran through the appendix of the rider, cut through his stomach, and emerged from the other side. He cried out and fell over, writhing on the ground as Firecrow released the weapon. Wheeling 'round, the brave pulled the knife from his belt and dismounted.

Riding down on the Indian, the snarling Smith switched the rifle to his left hand, uncoiled his bullwhip with his right. He did not get to snap it. A bowie knife went through his left thigh, causing him to scream out and drop the rifle. He listed hard to that side but did not fall. That gave White Fox a chance to pick up the rifle, squat, brace it on her knee, and shoot upward through his jaw and out the top of his skull. The dead man somersaulted backward from his horse.

Bishop was on the other side of the buggy, staring down at Weiber-Krauss. The German was squatting, one hand on the wheel, the other holding the globe. Bishop threw a leg over his horse and dismounted without taking his gun-arm off his quarry.

"You want to kill us both?" Bishop asked. "Now's the time."

"We could have owned this country," the German hissed.

"Don't want it," Bishop told him. "But I will bargain."

"How?"

"I'm still a doctor first and above all. You've a brilliant mind. We need cures. Put the globe down and we will talk."

"About my surrender? Life imprisonment? Test tubes and beakers and a microscope—do you think any prison will give me that?"

"I'm not the law. Not even a lawman."

"They won't," Weiber-Krauss said. "That is why I have done all this, because those who lead us are stupid. Shortsighted. They are not visionaries."

Bishop did not know what to say to that.

"Here is what I propose," the German told him. "Let me go. I will leave everything in the buggy with you. Destroy it, study it, do what you wish . . . other than give it to the army. My fortune is intact. I will—I will *go* someplace and we can work together on these cures, if you like. Together. Two great inventors. Isn't that better than *this*?" He thrust his unimposing chin at the shotgun.

"Put the globe down first. That's ragweed," he pointed at a patch with the toe of his boot. "I don't want you to sneeze yourself and me to death."

Weiber-Krauss looked over at the clump of flowers. The bastard was right. He tittered. Then he laughed. Carefully, the German set the globe on the ground.

"Now back away from me, from the buggy," Bishop said.

"I will not harm you, anyone," Weiber-Krauss reassured him but did as he was told. Bishop crouched slowly and recovered the fragile glass sphere. Then he rose. And shot Weiber-Krauss once through the throat with force that carried him away from the sphere. The man lived long enough to register shock and throw his hand toward the massive wound until he fell to his side pumping his life into the earth and watering the ragweed.

Bishop looked down on him. "I didn't want you to sneeze to death because I wanted to be the one to finish you."

CHAPTER FIFTEEN
The Beautiful and the Bad

Firecrow had already lifted White Fox from the ground when Bishop arrived. He was holding her in his powerful arms, a bold silhouette before the rising sun. Around him, braves from the camp—having stayed, as he had instructed when he rode in from the south—were coming out to check the Muddy Linens. All were dead. Fortunately for them. The women would have castrated any of them who were still alive and served the body parts to the dogs.

"Foolish to leave them in one line," a brave remarked who had witnessed the carnage.

White Fox was awake and smiling up at Bishop. He had replaced the globe in the carpetbag and motioned for no one to come near. Pulling on the surgical mask as he hurried forward, he caressed the woman's cheek with a gentle touch.

"You are a *Great* White Fox," he said to her.

She tried to smile, but the loss of Knob Pipe was too great. Bishop could also see the pain in the eyes of Firecrow, the red highlighted by the whiteness of the mask that he also wore. Already the man's sobbing widow, the sister of Firecrow, had come over to embrace her fallen husband.

"I'll take her," Bishop said to Firecrow, indicating that Firecrow should go to the widowed woman. The brave lay the slight figure across his arms, the human arm bearing most of the weight, the gun supporting her legs. The doctor carried her back to the tepee.

"You . . . you will get sick?"

Bishop shook his head. "This fabric is fine enough. And your body has been cleansing itself—you may not be a carrier any longer."

He ducked through the flap and lay her on her blankets. He gave her water and told her not to leave.

"I'm going to pin the flap open," he said. "Air will do you good."

"What will you do?"

"I have work to finish, at the fort and elsewhere. Then I will return. Yes?"

She nodded weakly, then grabbed his hand gently. "Before you go . . . find Little Hen. She has the necklace that is not Cheyenne. She was ill . . . see that she is all right."

Bishop pursed his lips and nodded. Kissing her hand through the mask, he rose and left.

It was easy to find the girl. She was asleep beside the corral. Had slept through it all. As he had discovered during the war, sickness, especially delirium, was the best insulation from reality, better than anything found in a bottle. Reality was not distorted; it was eliminated entirely.

Bishop knelt and felt her forehead and cheek. The precious little girl was barely feverish. She woke when he touched her. She looked at his unfamiliar face, then at the arm he held at right angles to his side. It was golden, shining, like bracelets on the arm of the proud and caring tribal chief had been.

She touched it, then suddenly threw her hands around a neck thick with sweat and grime from the hard two-horse ride.

"*Neisonoo,*" she said in a voice that was soft and lyrical. "*Neisonoo.*"

"Yes," he cooed back warmly.

Bishop did not know her language, could not have known the word she was saying.

"*Father.*"

Bishop left Little Hen in the care of a slender young boy by the name of Young Bear. He had been hovering near the growing fields, probably watching over the little lady. The doctor motioned for the boy to come over as he departed, leaving him with the surgical mask, which the young man donned promptly. He suddenly seemed very grown up, kneeling beside his charge.

The doctor walked wide of the encampment, since there was still active disease in the air, though when he reached the killing grounds he sought out Firecrow, who was outside his sister's tepee. He motioned the brave over.

"I'm going back to the fort," Bishop said, his eyes seeking the horse he had ridden. "I will send someone for the other animals—unless I find them along the way. And I will also send more medicine. The worst is past but we should be careful just the same." He clapped the man on a shoulder. "You did well, Fire-crow. You are a great constable."

"I had a great deputy." He smiled.

Bishop took the intentionally self-effacing compliment as it was intended—the highest praise.

Bishop smelled the fresh morning as he walked over to the big cavalry horse. It was grazing east of the settlement, covered with sweat from the run. It will have earned its pasture time this day. He gave it a grateful pat before leading it over to the buggy. He left the animal several paces back, tied to the stump of an old lightning-struck oak, since the presence of the dead horse would have spooked it. That was the only death Bishop regretted in all this.

Carefully unhitching the buggy, he pulled it around with his good arm and harnessed it to the big, black animal and set out in the direction of the fort.

There was no delay this time admitting John Bishop. Once he had identified himself the gate swung wide. He did not, however, enter, even though there was no rifle squad to meet him, no sentry to watch his moves. Only Major Terry, who stood in the opening. His bushy brow seemed confused by the buggy and just one horse.

Bishop braked the buggy and stepped out. Carefully, he removed the carpetbag. He set it down in front of the carriage. Terry stopped facing them both.

"I expect there is a story," Terry said.

"I did not see the two horses we cut loose, I'm

sorry," Bishop said. "The other is with the Cheyenne. They will need more medicine but they are mending."

"More medicine," Terry said crossly.

"The army will give it to you, happily," Bishop said.

"Why is that?"

"Because in this satchel is a disease created by Anton Weiber-Krauss, one that is presently fatal. They will want to study it and come up with an antidote. I suspect there are notes at the Lady Freemont. You might go look for them."

"And Weiber-Krauss?"

"Dead as Otto the Great," Bishop informed him. He said no more. He did not have to.

"There were others with him?" Terry asked. He looked as though he wanted a reason to summon his healthy troops.

"There were," Bishop answered. "More than thirty. They predeceased their leader. But the settlement is safe. There was one casualty, a good man, Knob Pipe. Please remember him if you go there. White Fox and Firecrow are well." He looked at the fort with something approaching sadness. "It was a day when all Americans, red and white, united to defeat a common foe. I have rarely been prouder than this day." He turned and stroked the horse. "Even they rose to new levels. It's as if they knew what was at stake."

Terry took a cigar from his pocket, struck a match on his heel. "Maybe they did. You won't convince me they are dumb."

"No," Bishop said. "Not like some people." He pointed his rig toward the carpetbag. "You will want to be very, very careful handling these. You saw samples of the glass grenades?"

"I did."

"Then you know what we're dealing with." Bishop stepped forward several paces. "How are Avery and Duffin?"

"Avery is recovering, Duffin is still out. But his fever is lower. The doctor says he will likely survive."

"That's good," Bishop said. He started forward. "If you'll excuse me, I want to talk to my acquaintance."

Avery was still lying on his back, but his eyes were open and there was food on his unfolded lap. Bishop held a mask over his mouth as he entered.

"You . . . you are all right," Avery said with what sounded like genuine satisfaction.

"Better than the man who sent you here," Bishop said.

Avery's flesh formed a smile. "Good. Good-bye. Adios."

"I want to ask you something," Bishop said, standing over the man.

"Anything. Old friend."

"The German abducted you, right?" Bishop pointed with his rig. "The injury on your scalp . . ."

Avery flinched under the barrel. "Yes. They hit me. I don't know what happened to the man who was with me, Homer."

"What did he look like?"

"Older. Heavy, sort of short."

Bishop frowned. "The other man in the shack," he said.

"Eh?"

"Murdered by Weiber-Krauss's men," he said. "I wondered who that was."

"I'm sorry to hear that," Avery said earnestly.

"Did the German pay you?" Bishop dropped.

Avery started. "Pay me?"

Bishop looked down at him over the mask.

The mayor-sheriff seemed as though he wanted to lie and did so anyway, but not overtly. "He . . . there was talk of expenses to cover my journey," Avery said.

"Through the plains."

"I needed . . . supplies."

Bishop continued to regard him like a specimen to be dissected. "I have somewhere to go," the doctor said. "When I come back, I will see you at the Hospitality House. We're going to finish this talk then."

"Your stay there will be complimentary," Avery said. "You know that. You saved my life."

"That's about the correct value for services rendered," Bishop noted.

The man with the gun-arm turned to the bed where Marshal Duffin lay. The young man wheezed through the bandages that covered his missing nose. His eyes were shut but his color wasn't bad. Gibson was right. He was a good candidate for recovery. And a leather patch for a new nose. Bishop walked away.

"Wait," Avery said. "Where are you going?"

"I have business elsewhere in the territory," he said.

"Is it something I will be reading about?" Avery asked.

Bishop left him with a grim smile. "It is a possibility."

Bishop stayed at the fort, happily nestled in the jail cell. He had a long and needed rest and then a pleasant breakfast with the young Gibson. Bishop commended the man for the work he had done with the Cheyenne. For his part, Gibson said that Terry had given him permission to go to the two settlements personally, with the medicines, and provide whatever care was needed. In a region with so much mistrust and hate, where lies brought reward and the truth none at all, this was refreshing to hear.

Major Terry gave Bishop the horse on loan. He promised to have the painted returned to White Fox.

"It's been a special honor getting to know you," the man said around his unlit cigar. "I hope you will forgive our early misunderstanding."

"It was engineered by a tragic genius," Bishop said. "No blame falls on you."

Provisioned and settled on the steed—whose name, he learned, was Smokey—Bishop rode into the late morning light. The air seemed fresher, his mood—it was also fresher, lighter than it had been since the day his world had fallen to ruin. But God in heaven had His way and, for the moment, Bishop had his.

Northeast.

Littleton was only a few years old, becoming more than just the home of the Littles in 1871 when the Denver and Rio Grande Railroad came through. The main street was still a dust trap, the buildings on either side were still low-lying, unappealing wood shacks built large, but there was a sense of activity in the street and children playing with hoops and sticks and balls and dogs chasing after them. The town was going to become something.

Bishop walked through the town, saw what he was looking for, then camped well outside the village until nightfall. He did not like to enter a place where his face or his rig could be seen. One of them would be, but that could not be helped. When the sun set and he finally did ride in, he kept a blanket over the gun-arm and held both across the back of the horse where it was not likely to be seen unless someone was looking for it.

He rode directly to the storefront he had seen earlier. The weather-beaten sign on the front read DENT'S DETONATIONS. He dismounted, looped the reins over the rail out front, and went around back. The store was dark but a light shone in the window of the second, topmost floor.

Walter Dent was playing the upright piano that dominated the small living room. His mother was in a thickly cushioned rocking chair, listening. The piano was how the man kept his fingers supple, sensitive, but also strong for the work that he did.

He was playing Chopin's Revolutionary Etude—fast and a little sloppy but his mother did not seem to mind. It was more challenging than the nocturnes, which were so dolorous. Bessie Dent had had a hard life, widowed young with a son to raise on a washwoman's salary. She liked the rest of her life to be gay.

There was no knock on the door. There was a snap around the knob as it was kicked in. Bishop entered and his rig came up and Bessie shrieked thinly, like a canary, while her son turned to the door and then to stone.

Bishop heel-kicked the door shut. The latch didn't quite hold but it declined to swing back. The man with the gun-arm did not bother to pull away the blanket. It would not hinder what he came here to do.

Bessie Dent's hand was in front of her mouth. Bishop suspected that if she lowered it she would scream and never stop, until she was shot. Cautiously, without looking in her direction, her son raised a hand, palm out, encouraging her to stay both calm and silent. His eyes never left Bishop.

"We have open business," the new arrival said.

"Wh-what business? I–I killed no one, hurt no one. I did nothing to you."

"That's right," Bishop said agreeably. "You did nothing to me. But when you went to Weiber-Krauss—who is dead, by the way, along with his demented lieutenants and every last one of his ridiculous men—when you went to that misery, you gave him White Fox. You did not have to say *anything* about her, but you did."

Bishop's voice had been rising all the while. Dent's posture had been shrinking.

"I did—did *not* go to him willingly," Dent said, managing somehow to get the sentence out. His throat was clogged with fear. "I left the woods . . . rode . . . intending to come here. Men came to get me."

Bishop walked toward him. "You had to go. You did *not* have to mention her." His tone was unforgiving.

"Dr. Bishop, sir, hear me out," Dent said. "Two things. First, he has written a letter. I do not have it yet. It is a . . . a testament of some kind. Written in case he did not survive."

"He told you this?"

"I saw him writing," Dent said. "If you need it, if there is anything I can do . . ."

"P-please do not hurt my boy," Bessie Dent chirped.

Bishop looked from her back to her son. He put the muzzle of the gun to the man's forehead. "You turned a brave, innocent girl over to a monster. The *only* reason we are still speaking is because she survived."

"I–I am deeply thankful for that. Apart . . . apart from my own . . . situation."

Bishop took a step back and studied the man.

"This is what you will do," he said, "or I will come back."

"Yes sir, Dr. Bishop. Anything."

"You will sell that letter to one of the publishers of the penny dreadfuls. You know the magazines?"

"Of course. Certainly."

"You will make sure the money you are paid, every cent of it, goes to White Fox for the purchase of medicine for her people. Do you understand?"

Dent shook his head so vigorously that the doctor half-expected his neck to snap. For her part, Bessie's expression had shaded from fear to disappointment.

"There are only two reasons I leave without your blood on the keyboard. First, the promise you just made. Second . . . I want no one, ever, to hurt the way I hurt losing a son." He leaned in. "But Dent, I swear, you lie to me and there will be nowhere you can hide. Do you understand?"

"All in its entirety," he said.

Bishop raised the rig, the blanket sliding to his elbow. He drew it off, turned, tossed it to Bessie. "A gift, madam, and the reminder of a promise."

She nodded her white-bunned head. "Your compassion will not be forgotten."

John Bishop, the man called Shotgun, backed toward the door. He used a toe to open it and stepped halfway out.

"My compassion," he said thickly, "can change like the Denver weather. Do not disappoint me."

With that he eased into the black night, finding solace in the humanity that, for the moment, had trumped his own darkness.

Keep reading for an excerpt of the first book in the Dr. John Bishop saga.

***Before there was* SHOTGUN: THE BLEEDING GROUND *and* THESE VIOLENT TIMES, *there was the first story of Dr. John Bishop* . . .**

A DOUBLE-BARRELED AVENGER IS BORN

Dr. John Bishop thought he'd seen his share of death on the battlefields of America's great Civil War. Then his quiet life was shattered when a gang of outlaws invaded his home, killed his family, and tortured him within an inch of his life. John Bishop's soul may have died that day, but his mangled body lived on. A beautiful Cheyenne named White Fox nursed him back to health—and a gunsmith outfitted him with a special shotgun rig where his left arm *used* to be. A strap across one shoulder fires it, while the chip on the other fuels his quest for vengeance. Now the man called Shotgun rides deep into the Colorado winter to find and kill the men who murdered everything he once held dear. The hunt will lead him straight to the heart of a fiendish criminal conspiracy—and force him to confront the violent legacy of his own outlaw brother.

"You damn well know I'll do it."

"Major" Beaudine's spit-shined boot was flush against John Bishop's right arm, pinning it down, while he turned the blade in the moonlight to heighten the threat.

Beaudine said, "So, your choice?"

Bishop managed, "You're thinking I know something I don't. I swear, I've told you everything. You got no reason to touch my family."

Beaudine gripped the handle of the long cleaver, saying, "A liar always boils my blood."

Bishop was on the edge of consciousness, trying to take in the faces of the other men holding him to the frozen ground. They were dirty fragments: moustaches dropping into beards, fresh burns, and one curtained eye. Their names were nothing but jumbled noise, while the screams of Bishop's wife and son cut through everything to reach him. Their voices didn't even sound like them anymore, though they were just a few feet away. Bishop cried out, twisting his head to see, as Deadeye and another man gripped him by his ears and jaw.

"Them ears'll come right off!"

Deadeye asked, "Why are you tryin' to look, anyways?"

Beaudine let Bishop know, "They're breathing. I see her little bosom moving in and out, but it's not honorable for you to make your wife and boy pay for your being contrary. Do you understand the penalties, what it means to incur my wrath?"

Exactly fifteen minutes before, Amaryllis Bishop had joined hands with her husband and son for a Methodist grace. John always gently rubbed her fingers with his thumb while his wife asked for blessing, and she flashed her blue eyes in a way that was supposed to be annoyance, but was something else.

Their son giggled as he reached for a piece of chicken before the plate was offered. Mama issued a smiling warning. "I know somebody's birthday is in three days, but it may not come at all, if—"

Amaryllis's voice was cut off when the front door was kicked off its hinges.

"Major" Beaudine and his men exploded into the house, tossing the dinner table, splintering a bookshelf, and slapping the youngest to the floor. Bishop sprang at the "Major," but heavy fists from behind pounded him down, and Beaudine's heel cracked his ribs with little effort.

Beaudine warned one of the others not to do more. "Show restraint, gentlemen. Our friend is essential to our mission."

He knelt next to Bishop, measuring his words. "I am aware of the gold you and your brother liberated, one half of a million dollars. Don't deny it. The letters he wrote you from prison, finalizing your confidential plans? I wrote them. You know your brother could neither read nor write, and so he trusted me to set down his thoughts. Devlin and I were cellmates, until the morning he was hung. He took me into his deep confidence, which I honor. You have all that money, John, and you need to share. Your brother is departed, but I am here. Death's arrived, and I want paying."

"I'm swearing, I don't know a damn thing about any gold. There's nothing between me and my brother. Never was."

"No, that's not the answer."

"Where's my wife?"

"You must think clearly now, about the gold. Nothing else matters at this moment, I promise you."

The man with the trimmed moustache and salvaged grey Confederate tunic, who spoke as if he were reading holy scripture, pressed his knee deep into Bishop's back. Bones cracked. Beaudine asked again about the stolen gold.

"If anything happens to my son . . ."

Beaudine pressed his knee again and Bishop couldn't move, his thoughts slipping away with his bleeding.

Beaudine said, "There's a Foster Brothers cleaver with a polished blade on a thirty-one-inch handle resting across my saddle. It's a thing of beauty, but you do not want me to fetch it."

Beaudine put the last of his weight on Bishop's spine, dropping his voice. "You need to concern yourself with gold. Try again."

The outlaws waited for the answer, and Amaryllis swung a pork-fry pan from the Crawford stove, spattering hot grease across the face of one of them, sending him screaming into the cold. Time stopped for a few heartbeats as Amaryllis Bishop scooped up her son, his arms around her neck and their tears mixing on their cheeks, as she whispered a kiss to him.

That's when the first shot was fired.

CHAPTER ONE
Nothing Dies Like a Man

Huckie's Saloon, with its caving roof and sides, was a whipped dog cringing in front of the Colorado Mountains, ready to snap. It was the only place John Bishop saw with any signs of life, and he angled his horse toward it.

He was navigating a tough trail winding out of the steeper foothills that led to what was passing for some kind of a town. Bishop's bay horse was cautious with her footing. The snow on the trail wasn't deep, but a layer of ice beneath the white cracked under each footfall, throwing off her steps. Bishop patted her neck to tell her she was doing well as she managed a narrow cut between some tall pines.

There was another rider following, about half a mile back, but Bishop didn't even turn to see, his mind and eyes locked straight ahead, the reins steady in his left hand to keep the bay sure. She responded.

The frozen white was blowing just enough that he had to squint to read the battered sign that declared Huckie's. A pack mule snorted out front, and a mutt scratched at the front door, until someone let it in. There was loud, drunken talk followed by laughter. Bishop figured there had to be at least five in the place, including a cackling woman.

Bishop clenched the reins. His memories from months ago, the ones that beat hell out of him every other minute, had brought him to this place, but now he had to put feelings away. He was going to do this, and had to be clear about it. No backing down.

Chester Pardee liked Huckie's. The drinks and the one woman were so watered and worn that even he seemed like a big shot in the place. He took another swallow of no-name whiskey and tried to fan his cards, but they were too ear-bent to separate. Pardee then studied each of them, pausing for a sip, making a show of what a fine hand he was holding.

Chaney, who had killed someone someplace, was getting tired of the put-on. "You ain't droppin' anything on the table, Chester."

"I like to think my bets through."

"Nobody's got that much time. Play or fold."

Pardee adjusted his fingerless gloves, and reached into his pocket for the last bit of paper he had. He'd gotten the coat from a dead man, and it was stained with his fortune, but the money was his own, and he placed an old Union twenty on the torn felt like he was presenting a king's crown.

Chaney said, "The bill's got blood on it."

"What doesn't? I know'd every one of ya and your dirty habits. I say can't none of ya match it."

Chaney nodded. "Things are temporarily lean, but I have twenty-three in silver, and this banker's watch you've always admired. You're being raised, Chester."

Pardee reached into his jacket, and took out a letter that had been roughly folded into five sections, the words smudged by whiskey rings. Too many reads had frayed the paper, but Chester Pardee waved it at Chaney like a red veronica in front of a Brahma bull.

Pardee said, "You know what this is?"

Chaney didn't change his expression. "You jaw about it enough."

"Right, it's a goddamn treasure map. I'll throw ten percent—no, one percent—into the pot. One percent. One."

Chaney said, "You might as well say you wipe yourself with it."

"You won't take that much of a chance, Chaney? You ain't a gambler at all."

Chaney looked up from his cards.

The Colorado snow eased as Bishop rode to the hitch rail. He threw his weight to one side, angling his right arm from its special sling on the saddle, almost turning in the stirrup, before dropping to the ground. Here, the snow was slush under his boots, as he listened again to the voices escaping from Huckie's. Bishop rolled his shoulders and said something like a prayer before walking the last steps to the batwings that were banging against the front door.

The glass in the front door had a little split, and for some reason, Bishop almost knocked. Instead, he opened it with his left hand and let the door swing free inside, the glass breaking in half to announce him.

Pardee turned in his chair to see Bishop standing in the doorway. One of the others at the table belched, "You're gonna have to pay for that."

Bishop kept his head down with his arms straight at his side, his black duster a size and some too big, hanging scarecrow loose, but it gave him the freedom of movement he needed. The first time he saw himself, he thought he looked like a specter from Poe. Bishop cleared his throat, but didn't speak.

Huckie's was all whispers and mutterings; guesses about Bishop passed from the drinkers who sat at the old silver exchange counter that now served as the bar, to the laughing whore on the straw bed tucked away in a corner, with the pull curtain above it. Bishop had their attention, until he raised his eyes. The whispering stopped, and then started again, punctuated with loud snickering.

Bishop's face was softly round, and not protected at all by his blond beard—the kind of face that made men like these laugh among themselves before trying something.

"Chester Pardee."

Pardee paid no mind. He slipped the letter back into his jacket and said to Chaney, "You can't kill me for tryin'."

Chaney said, "Find somebody to stake you, or fold."

Bishop hadn't moved; he tried again. "Chester Pardee."

Pardee said, "It's freezin' in here."

"That's all you have to say?"

"We've got a game, jackass."

Bishop took a single step closer to the table. "Then you don't know me?"

Chaney said, "You lost, Chester."

Pardee said, "Hold up! You say you know me? Stake me to this pot. I got the cards, amigo."

"You really don't remember?"

Chaney said to Pardee, "I called, that's it."

Chaney laid out two pairs of faces, while Pardee tossed a weak five-high straight on the table. Chaney gave Pardee a smirk with some pity.

Pardee faced Bishop with, "Whatever the hell you're on about, it didn't mean nothin'! You just cost me!"

"Slaughtering a man's family doesn't mean anything?"

"What man?"

The first blast ripped through Pardee's shoulder and sent him spinning out of his chair, spurs catching the edge of the table, sending the whiskey, cash, and five-high flying. Pardee twisted on the bowed floor, screaming out for Jesus, but Jesus didn't make a move. Nobody did.

The whore burst into tears because she'd never seen a shooting up close before; everyone else rubbernecked for a look, not exactly sure what had just happened.

Bishop stood over Pardee, gun smoke drifting from the end of his sleeve where his right hand should have been, but wasn't. Instead, the two barrels of a Greener shotgun poked from the ragged cuff, which had been singed by the blast. Burning threads danced from the cuff to the floor.

The double barrels were in place of Bishop's right arm, attached somehow at the elbow, and held waist-high steady. He shifted his weight from one leg to the other, keeping the weapon dead-centered on Pardee's chest.

Pardee was still crying out for Jesus as he struggled to stand, red spreading across his jacket. He tried drawing his Colt with fingers that wouldn't work. "You ain't given me a sloppy Chinaman's chance!"

"What kind of chance did you give my wife and son?"

"Jesus Lord."

"I've still got the second barrel."

"Can't you just let me out, Bishop?"

"So you know me now."

"What happened wasn't my doin', I swear. That's not why I was there."

"I can barely see where my wife threw the grease from that hot skillet."

"Please, let me ride out and you'll never hear my name again."

"Beaudine."

Pardee said, "If I live another twenty years, it won't matter. I'm already dead."

Bishop had to shift his weight again, but, with effort, he kept his voice calm and the shotgun aimed at Pardee's chest, "You wanted to know about gold I didn't have. Well, now I want to know something. I'm counting."

"Beaudine's crazy, and I fell in with his gang. That's all it was: us tryin' to eat. Nothin' personal."

"I'm only going to five."

Pardee stammered through tears, giving up a crossroads where Bishop could look for Beaudine, and kill him, if that's what he intended. Pardee even gave his permission.

Bishop said, "You know what retribution is?"

"It means I'm done."

"If you can get off the floor, I'll let you try."

Pardee didn't move. Bishop said, "I'm not a murderer."

"You're a blessed man, Doc. Better than I'll ever be."

Pardee dropped his words as he grabbed Bishop's left hand, and yanked him forward, slashing him with a rifleman's knife he had strapped to his boot. The blade sliced deep, from earlobe to the corner of Bishop's mouth.

Pardee whooped, "How you like that—?!"

Bishop heaved backwards and brought up his right arm in a single motion. Buckshot 'n' fire erupted from the sleeve a second time, rag-dolling Pardee into a stack of empty beer kegs. Wood and bone shattered together, then settled into silence. Pardee's eyes stayed wide and his grip on his pistol never relaxed.

Everybody froze for a moment, and then the talk started, along with nervous laughter. One old boy said something about a "nice killin'" and spit a stream of tobacco juice that spattered a brown halo around Pardee's head.

Bishop waited for someone to try something, but no one bothered. The mutt in the corner wagged his tail and barked his approval. Chaney, the card player, scooped the poker pot into his hat as Bishop took careful steps to the shattered door.

Chaney said, "You blew both barrels."

Bishop jerked his arm, and the shotgun breached inside the duster, the sleeve tenting the open barrel. Bishop reached inside the sleeve, coming out with two spent shells, and dropped them on the floor. He grabbed two fresh from his jacket and reloaded before bringing his arm upward in a motion that snapped the barrel shut.

This took moments, with everyone watching, their eyes wide and "goddamns" whispered. Bishop aimed the rig directly at Chaney's gut. Chaney showed his palms. "Hey, nobody gave a shit about Chester, except you."

"You going to bury him?"

Chaney shrugged while winding his watch.

"The railroad's probably put up a price."

Chaney said, "Knowing Chester, they're offering the lowest bounty in history."

Outside, the midnight wind stung Bishop as he checked the cinch on his bay, but his one hand was shaking, and his chest pounded. A lot had led up to this, and in a few moments it was over. Well, Pardee was over, but there were still the others. At least now Bishop knew he could go through with it; he had to keep that in his mind, the knowing, no doubts at all. He had to.

His face was sticky with the wash of blood from his sliced cheek, and as Bishop calmed, he started to feel the pain. The batwings creaked, and a few drinkers poked their heads over the doors. The whore moved to Bishop, holding out a lace handkerchief. "It's clean."

Bishop wrapped the handkerchief around his face to soak the bleeding. He felt the girl behind him tying it off and caught her heavy perfume. Bishop thanked her and she nodded before wiping her wet eyes on her sleeve.

The others hung back on Huckie's porch, watching as Bishop hefted himself onto his saddle, again throwing himself wide and keeping the shotgun clear of any tangle. He played it slow for them, settling against the leather, and sliding his double-barreled right arm into the canvas sling.

The bay was ready to run, but Bishop kept the reins tight around his only knuckles, holding her back.

Old Spitter hollered, "Hey! You busted some good bottles killin' that piece of sheep dip! Plus the door, and a couple of chairs!"

Bishop took fifty from his vest and tossed it. "You're going to tell folks about this, right, friend?"

Spitter gum-grinned. "I'll be talkin' about tonight for the next five years, five months, or five days. Dependin' on how much time I got left."

"God only knows, and I'm obliged to you both."

Bishop brought his horse around slow for that last look, and then heeled her. The bay took off toward the blue-black silhouettes of the rising hills, and the high Colorados beyond.

Spitter whistled with gums and two fingers, but Dr. John Bishop didn't hear it. His horse was running strong into the winter night, knowing where to go, even if his mind was taking him someplace else beyond the hurt—maybe back to his wedding day, or the birth of his son.

Behind him, a rider was charging hard to catch up, a Cheyenne war club in their hand.

CHAPTER TWO
The Fox

White Fox kept her body low and tight against the painted stallion. They moved as one, racing down the trail, the snow kicking up around them like bursts of brake steam. She grabbed the horse's mane, fingers tangled in wiry brown, and gently pulled. The painted slowed as the path through the trees widened into an easier slope that led to the "town" just below. It was a mule squat for drifters who still had hopes for the played-out silver strike at Cherry Creek—stop for a drink or an ash hauling, and ride on.

But this was where Bishop had to go, so White Fox had to follow.

She pulled up to watch Bishop's silhouette pause outside Huckie's, say something with a roll of his shoulders, and then go in. White Fox dropped from the painted, and walked him around the burned skeleton of an old barn to a water trough thick with ice. She broke the icy surface with a kick and tossed away the pieces.

The painted inspected the trough with his nose, then drank.

While he watered, she scraped packed snow from his hooves with a six-inch blade. She had the feeling everything in this place was dying or dead. Two loud voices from Huckie's stopped her.

White Fox stepped into the moonlight, craning her neck toward Huckie's to hear. A voice she didn't know was yelling about Jesus. Two shotgun blasts followed; that low rumble mixed with those louder cracks that ring in the air and ears.

The painted lurched as the blasts smashed against the hills. White Fox said, "*Nâhtötse,*" close to the stallion's ear, calming him, before swinging herself on his back, and circling around the far side of the barn. She saw Bishop on his bay, talking to the Spitter on the porch. White Fox dug in, and the painted broke into a run, while Bishop rode off without looking back.

The Spitter whistled loud after Bishop, before looking up to see White Fox charging toward him. It was either an image from some kind of holy book or his best damn whiskey dream ever: the beautiful Cheyenne woman, onyx hair spreading behind her, riding out of the night just to take the old man away. White Fox pulled a war club she'd tethered to her belt and held it high.

Spitter closed his eyes and smiled, thinking, *This is a hell of a way to go, and why not?*

White Fox rode close, swinging the club into the skull of the drunk standing next to the Spitter, creasing his head. The drunk fell forward, the revolver in his hand hot-blasting the muddy snow instead of John Bishop's back, where he had been aiming.

Spitter grabbed the pistol for a trophy, and White Fox threw him a stony nod while the painted galloped toward Bishop. Bishop turned at the sound of the shot, just as White Fox rode up next to him, still holding the war club. They rode side by side for a moment, the legs of the painted and the bay falling into sync.

White Fox said, "*Hetómem.*"

Bishop spoke through the bloody handkerchief, "He remembered me."

White Fox pointed to the nearest mountains with the club, and broke ahead. Bishop heeled the bay.

The cave was a huge, yawning smile beneath a jagged slope of blue rock, sheeted by snow and protected by daggers of ice formed by the water flowing from up-mountain. Bishop followed the barely-there trail for more than a mile, guided by a small fire White Fox had left burning inside the cave's mouth, its drifting heat melting hanging icicles. Bishop felt comforted by the distant, flickering orange, even as a raw burning raced across his face and down his right half-arm.

The painted was tied to a Rocky Mountain birch, eating fresh snow, when Bishop reached the cave. White Fox stood just inside, waiting to see if he could get down from the bay by himself. He did, a scream jamming the back of his throat. Fresh blood specked Bishop's sleeve and the shotgun barrels. She took a step toward him that he stopped with a raised hand. He nodded that he could beat it, allowing himself a moment to let the throbbing from his arm and face ease with deep, cold breathing. It didn't.

White Fox slipped herself under his shoulder and helped him to the fire. "Bi-shop."

Bishop smiled at the way she said his name, breaking it gently in two, as if each syllable had a spiritual meaning. She eased him onto a blanket on the cave floor, where he stretched out, propping himself on his right elbow, the shotgun rig resting on his knees.

White Fox pulled off the blood-flecked duster and folded it carefully, before putting more wood on the fire, sparking the flames. She then opened one of the redware jars she'd arranged around the cave, along with bedrolls, a cook pan, a coffeepot, a lot of ammunition, and a small leather satchel that had Bishop's initials stamped on it in gold.

Bishop said, "You're nesting—Jesus!"

He cried out raw as she peeled the pink handkerchief from the drying blood caking his cheek. White Fox tossed the rag, and dabbed the wound with a soft cloth she'd wetted with melted snow. It was cool, and felt good against the damage.

Bishop said, "Stitches. You know how."

White Fox ran her fingers along the inside of the jar, gathering yellow salve. She smeared the mixture on the wound, then cut a piece of yucca in half, opened it flat, and pressed it against Bishop's face.

She took Bishop's left hand to hold the plant in place and he said, "This won't be enough. *Ma'heo'o Ôhvó'komaestse.*"

Bishop got the words out, but White Fox didn't hear them. Her jaw was set, which meant that she would take care of him in her own way; she didn't need white medicine.

She unbuttoned his shirt, and he automatically

leaned forward so she could pull the right sleeve free, gathering the rest around the shotgun rig, then slipping it off. The shirt caught on the hammers, and White Fox yanked it.

Bishop swore in Cheyenne, and White Fox gave the back of his head a gentle slap before allowing him a swallow of mescal.

Bare-chested, he leaned to one side, his back toward her, so she could unhook the canvas strap that was tight across his shoulders and connected to the two triggers of the Greener twelve gauge. The strap dug into him, leaving marks like the bite of a whip, and was connected to a looped piece of fabric that ran down his right arm and anchored to the triggers, so that the action of bringing the shotgun up to waist level would pull on the strap, firing either or both barrels.

The bleeding started around the leather cup that was fit to Bishop's right arm just below the elbow joint. It was a standard prosthetic that rebel and union boys now wore as a battle prize, but had been modified to allow the short stock of the Greener to fit where a metal hook would replace the patient's hand. The stock was secured in the cup with small metal bands that joined the shotgun and prosthetic together as one.

White Fox loosened the ties that held the cup tight to Bishop's arm, and pulled the entire rig away, revealing a bleeding stump. More mescal from the heel of the bottle, and Bishop's head lolled back, his hand still holding the yucca against his cheek as she checked the arm for fresh wounds.

He said, "Nothing's opened up?"

She examined the corrupted skin and muscle that was a knot around the bone, and saw that none of the crude surgical scars lacing it together had ruptured. The blood was smeared from small wounds around the elbow, where the amputation point met the healthy rest of the arm. White Fox swabbed away the streaks of wet red.

Bishop said, "It's not setting right, rubbing raw. I know you don't understand everything, but you did a fine job. I'm the doc, but you're the surgeon."

White Fox dressed the wound with salve and wrapped it, saying, "I still am, Bi-shop."

"Not always, not always."

White Fox allowed the corners of her mouth to turn up, as she settled Bishop down on the blanket. A last bit of mescal and he closed his eyes at her touch treating his wounds.

"Where's my medical bag?"

"Close."

Bishop barely opened his eyes to see the small, black leather bag, age-cracked, with LT. BISHOP embossed in flaked gold on one side. It was Bishop's field kit, bloodstained and heavy with instruments. White Fox had arranged it among the other supplies, but knowing that piece of himself hadn't been lost eased Bishop, and he closed his eyes again.

Bishop said, "You take care of me."

White Fox rested the shotgun rig between the medical bag and the stacks of ammunition, all the time watching Bishop as he drifted, his words folding into each other.

"When your husband stabbed you, I sewed you up. And when he broke your arm? You were a good patient."

White Fox treated the slice on Bishop's face with the

last of the yucca pulp. His eyes were heavy with sleep coming, but his thoughts were fighting the peace.

"Pardee had never seen anything like me. Nobody had."

Bishop lifted what remained of his right arm to reach out to White Fox, but he couldn't. She touched the side of his face, lightly tapping the pulp onto the wound so it would dry in place.

Bishop said, "I've watched a lot of men die, but I never killed one. Not even in the conflict."

White Fox lay next to Bishop, pulling a blanket over them both, keeping one hand on his chest.

Bishop said, "It felt different than I thought it would."

White Fox understood but didn't react; she just lay next to Bishop, feeling the still-excited, rapid beat of his heart and quietly murmuring his name until his body eased, and he fell, peacefully, asleep.